LOVE, TINK

THE COMPLETE SERIES

LEE STRAUSS

ISBN: 978-1-77409-112-8

CONTENTS

LOVE, TINK

THE COMPLETE SERIES

LOVE, TINK

Episode One

by
Lee Strauss

1

Things changed in Neverland when the Lost Boys arrived. At least they changed for me, and all because of the dark-haired boy with sun-bronzed skin and a lousy shot.

Peter lets an arrow fly into the sky, and I pray he will miss the little red bird like he usually does. We hear a squawk, but nothing falls to the ground.

"Is your *boyfriend* blind?"

"*Shh*," I say to Jangle as we sneak through the forest of shimmering silk trees to spy on the boys.

"It's not like they can see me," Jangle says, turning up her pointed nose in that superior way that drives me crazy. She flaps her wings just to annoy me.

"Well, they can see me," I snap under my breath.

"Oh, yeah, how could I forget about your unfortunate situation when you constantly remind me? *Poor me*," she mimics. "I'm visible to humans. Poor me, I'm Captain Hook's little pet."

"Shut up, Jangle!"

Now *I* am too loud. The four boys we are so carefully stalking spin around in our direction.

"What's that?" The chubby one says, his round baby face widening with fright.

Then Peter, my perfect Peter, says, "Oh, Tubs, it's just Tinkerbell."

How does he know? How can he possibly know? Jangle breaks out in a giggle, and I throw her a look that almost shuts her up.

"Tinkerbell?" Peter calls. I can't resist his voice. I step out from behind the wide trunk of the silk tree. I feel my face grow hot and a rosy color spreads into my wings which flap erratically with nerves.

"Hi, Peter." My heart swells with affection, so much so, my chest weighs heavy and my knees tremble. I self-consciously push a wayward strand of yellow hair behind my ear. It tangles in the golden hoop that hangs there, and I wince a little to free it.

Peter flashes an impish grin, the kind that turns up slightly on one side as he tilts his head. The action that produces dimples and makes me swoon.

"Hey, Tink. Why are you always sneaking up on us like that?"

"Yeah, why, Tink?" Jangle mutters.

Peter's eyes dart about. "What was that?"

I shoot Jangle a look of warning. I will wring her fairy neck, no joking.

"Nothing. Just the wind." I step away from my so-called friend. I am surprised that actual words have flown from my mouth. I find it hard to think in Peter's presence much less speak.

Peter steps closer and my wings freeze straight up in the air along with the wide-eyed expression on my face.

"I'm not going to hurt you, Tinkerbell," he says, looking deep into my eyes. "In fact, I'm presenting you with an invitation. The boys and I were just on our way to the Mermaid Lagoon to swim with the dolphins. Would you like to come?"

Oh, fairy dust, would I! But my heart takes off like a stone hailing down Blue Mountain and I feel my head shaking in the negative. I scramble behind the massive silk tree trunk, disappearing from Peter's sight.

I hear him call out. "Maybe next time then, Tink." The other boys laugh and I wait until their chatter fades in the distance.

I glance up and gasp. Jangle's spiky blue head appears out of thin air. She stands right in front of my face, arms folded over her chest.

"Blink, Jangle, you scared the fairy dust out of me."

"Why don't you go with him?" she says, her right foot tapping. "Chicken?"

I stomp away. "I'm no chicken. I work for *Captain Hook* for king's sake." I'm shy. That's different from fear. I'm no chicken.

Jangle follows me. "I don't know what you see in him anyway. He's just a dirty human boy."

I *hrumph*. I don't have to explain anything to her. Besides, I don't know the answer to that. A fairy's heart is a mysterious thing.

~

Captain Hook lives in a cave overlooking the south shore bay where he beaches his pirate ship when it isn't at sea. I always enter cautiously, in case he's is in one of his moods.

A little sigh of relief escapes my lips when I discover that he's gone. A glance through a hole in the rock wall at the empty beach tells me he is out scouting the high seas with his men. What he hopes to find I'm not sure.

Though the captain is out, I don't have the good fortune of being alone. My fellow fairies, Tootles, Knobs and Cue, are in the office, getting into the captain's things again.

"Get out!" I shout.

"Oh, settle your wings," Knobs says with the captain's pipe in his mouth. "We're not hurting anything."

I shoot over to him and grab the pipe from his mouth. "Don't touch the captain's things."

Tootles *tsk, tsks* me. "But he has such pretty things, Tinkerbell. Why should you be the only one to play with them?" She lifts a jewel to the light of the sun coming through the window and gasps happily as the light refracts in patterns across the stone floor.

"I don't play with his things, but I'm the one who gets in trouble. He might not be able to see you, but he can sense you. He knows when his things have moved."

"Oh, you're such a poor sport," Cue says, tugging on his purple tunic. It is cinched at the waist with a belt and worn over tights—typical fairy wear.

"We can tell when we're not wanted." He flaps his wings sharply and leaves with Tootles and Knobs giggling as they follow him.

I scan the room and shift items an inch or so this way or that. A quill pen and ink jar on the captain's desk, a husk horn hanging crookedly on the wall, the empty parrot cage large enough for a fairy to fit in.

When I'm satisfied the room is sorted back to the way the captain left it, I borrow his looking glass and stand on a rocky ledge outside. Mermaid Lagoon is to the east, and if I turn the lens just so, I can find what I'm looking for.

Peter.

Ah, there he is swimming in the emerald cove with his Lost Boys, just like he said he would be. The dolphins have answered his call and jump excitedly. One pauses in front of Peter and he climbs on, patting its sleek, gray skin. Oh, such fun! If only I had said yes. Maybe I *am* chicken? Maybe Jangle is right about me?

Peter lets go of his dolphin ride just as a head pops up beside him. She has long, glistening black hair, and a pretty face. A broad tail reflecting the colors of the rainbow splashes behind her.

Blink! A mermaid. She tosses her head back in laughter. I zero my looking glass on Peter's face. His white teeth gleam through a big, sappy smile.

"Ugh!" I close the looking glass and stomp my pointy-toed slipper, sending a quiver up my body all the way through my wings. I'd experienced a lot of differing emotions over the last few years. Fear, anger, frustration... love. But this one is new. *Jealousy*. I don't like how it feels at all.

I can't help myself; I have to know what Peter and the mermaid are doing. I open up the looking glass, stretching the brass tube out long and into focus. Peter is alone with the boys, no mermaids in sight and I feel a certain measure of satisfaction at that.

Peter is pointing at something on the horizon. I follow

the direction of his finger and almost drop the looking glass. It's Captain Hook's ship. The captain's shiny, bald head and all the gold chains around his neck reflect in the sunlight. He has beady, brown eyes and a huge, hook nose—where he gets his name, I suppose. His pantaloons end just below his knees and touch the top of his leather boots.

Polly the parrot sits on his shoulder like she doesn't have a care in the world. I almost envy her, except for the part where she sits on the captain's shoulder.

The captain points at Peter and the boys, the puffy, white sleeve of his unbuttoned shirt ruffling in the wind. His main henchman, One Eye Gus, stands beside him with a pistol at the ready.

"Oh no."

He points it at Peter who has just made it to shore. The other boys are farther inland having had a head start.

I hear the gunshot.

I have the looking glass steadied on Peter. He falls to the sand, a red ribbon flowing from his arm.

2

The Lost Boys appeared two years ago, all of a sudden, like a flock of large birds falling out of the sky and landing in the middle of the poppy meadow when it was in full bloom. I was alone that day, having slipped away from one of the many fairy celebrations for a moment's peace.

Their screams frightened me so much; I crumbled to the ground and took cover under the mass of red petals. Despite my fear, I couldn't help staring. I recognized them as humans. They were younger, shorter and cleaner versions of Captain Hook and his crew. I'd wondered if these boys were as nasty as the pirates were. I'd since come to the conclusion that they were mischievous but not mean, though they'd gotten a lot grimier since.

Peter was the first of the boys to get a glimpse of me in those early days. They had already built a fort and set up camp in the woods. I had yet to alert the other fairies of their arrival, enjoying the feeling of having a secret, which was a scarcity in the fairy kingdom. Fairies are busy bodies and everyone knows everybody's business.

I spent many days observing Peter. There was something about him that captured my attention in a way no fairy boy had ever managed to do. He was strong and fearless leading the Lost Boys against the pirates. He was smart, too, teaching the boys how to survive in the silk forest. And the way he smiled, two beautiful dimples forming on his cheeks, it was like he had a secret. I was allured by his mystery. I stared into his sky blue eyes, wishing I could see my reflection there, wishing he could see me.

Peter never spotted me; he'd just heard the whispers of my movement like a breeze. Fairies are known to be impulsive and true to form, one day I acted impulsively. I'd stepped out of the cover of the floral foliage and into view. His eyes widened in surprise. Mine mimicked his when I realized he could indeed see me. That meant I was visible to all humans, not just the pirates, and I'd just given this human boy a glimpse of the fairy world. I dashed back into hiding.

"I'm Peter," he'd called out to me. "What's your name?"

I'd debated if I should answer him. I knew his name, what could be the harm in him knowing mine?

"Tinkerbell."

"Tinkerbell? That's a sweet name."

My little heart sped up with joy. The human boy thought my name was *sweet*. Later that night when Peter and the boys sat around the fire to tell stories like they did every evening (I sometimes hid in the vines and listened in), Peter told them about me.

"She looks like a normal girl, except she's the size of a large doll and has wings."

The boys just thought it was another story until they eventually saw me for themselves.

The moment the gun goes off and I see Peter fall to the shore in a heap, I drop the looking glass and engage my wings to fly to him as quickly as I can. It takes a lot of energy for fairies to fly, so we normally use our feet to get us where we want to go, but this is urgent and I summon all my strength to get me to his side.

"Peter!"

He opens his eyes with a moan. "Tinkerbell?"

"Are you all right? You've been shot."

Peter glances at his bloodied arm, then lets his head flop back on the sand. "It's just a flesh wound."

I shake my head and release my fairy dust onto his arm. "That should help," I say. "But we need to get you off this beach before the captain sends someone to collect you."

It's a good thing that fairies are stronger than they look. I wrap Peter's good arm around my neck and flap my wings to lift myself high enough off the ground so that he can walk,

By the time we reach the edge of the silk tree forest, I'm feeling the weight of Peter leaning on me and my wings falter.

"It's okay," Peter says, releasing hold of my neck. "I can walk on my own now."

Though I don't mind the feel of Peter's arm around me, I sink lower until my feet touch the ground.

"I'll accompany you back to camp."

Peter grins a little. "I've never heard you talk so much before, Tink."

I feel a blush flush through my face and wings, and a little giggle escapes my lips.

The fort the boys built when they first arrived has long since been abandoned, a maneuver they made when they first laid eyes on the pirates and realized they had flesh and blood enemies. Now they live in the root system of a gigantic silk tree in the middle of the silk forest, with a secret entrance that Peter, the largest of the Lost Boys, can barely fit through.

Peter squeezes in with a little difficulty due to his arm. "Ouch," he says loudly so the boys inside can hear. I've never been inside their hideaway before and I'm more than a little curious. Besides, Peter's arm is still healing and he might need more fairy dust. I slip in behind him, but tuck myself in his shadow.

Peter stands tall with hands on hips, his pointy elbows sticking sharply out to the sides. "You guys left me to die?" His voice commands the room.

"We thought you were right behind us," the redheaded, freckled-face one says.

"And you didn't think to check?"

Peter scans the boys' faces. "Curly?" he says to the blond boy, who does in fact have a mound of curls.

"We were just about to come look for you. Honest."

Peter strikes a match and lights a candle.

Hey, wait a minute. I recognize that candle stand and the pinkish wax cylinder. The light from the candle makes it easier to see the root house, and the things in it. Several knives that lie on a flat stone in the middle of the room look familiar as do two swords leaning against the wall.

I step out from behind Peter. "You guys are stealing from the captain!" And here I had blamed the fairies when the captain had blamed me. Don't they know how much extra scrubbing and dusting I had to do in penance? On the ship, no less. My stomach lurches as I recall the seasickness.

A collective yelp echoes through the cavernous space, and the redheaded boy snatches one of the knives. "Spy!"

"Calm down, Nibs," Peter says. "It's just Tinkerbell."

"But she works for the enemy," Nibs insists.

Curly jumps up. "She'll tell Hook where we live!"

"How do we know fairies can be trusted?" This from Tubs, the hefty one who rarely speaks.

Their talk makes me shiver and I press up against the wall. They are all silent now, staring me down. My throat seizes up and I feel faint.

"Tink?" Peter says gently.

"I'm fine," I squeak.

He turns to the boys. "Tinkerbell saved my life. She could've turned me over to Hook or left me to die. Besides she's known about our hideout for months. If she were a spy, we would've been discovered eons ago."

Peter's speech must make sense to the boys because their shoulders relax and they return to their lounging positions, each having their own hammock or sleeping mat they'd woven from vines. Nibs even returns his knife to the table.

My own poor heart slows a little, and I sit on the dirt floor.

Peter doesn't recline. He has his finger to his chin and his eyes narrow in deep thought. He paces back and forth past the candle, causing the wick to flicker with each passing. The boys' heads move from side to side in unison until Peter finally speaks.

"We have to steal guns now."

"What?" I say.

Peter ignores me and keeps talking to the boys. "This is the first time Hook has opened fire. Before now, he was content to battle us with knives, swords and wit. With this wound," he points to the pinkish spot on his arm that is now almost totally healed, "the game has changed."

Maybe if they stop stealing from him the captain would stop his pursuit. Nah, this island bores the captain to tears. Hunting the boys is his only form of fun.

"Yeah," Curly says. "This means war!" The rest of the boys cheer, but I feel frightened for them. The captain doesn't like to play fair.

Peter rouses them up with battle strategy, and though I try to follow along, they talk too fast. Instead I just admire Peter from my spot on the floor. The way he takes charge and how the boys follow his every word makes happiness bubble within. A sigh escapes my lips and my wings joyfully twitter.

I will tell him, I decide then and there. I'm no chicken. I will tell Peter how I feel, I will!

When the excitement in the room subsides, Peter offers to see me out of the forest before it gets dark. This is my chance.

"Peter?"

"Uh-huh." His eyes glaze over like he's deep in thought, his mind probably still on his plans to rob the captain again, but I have to speak now before I lose my nerve.

Still the words get stuck in my throat. *Just say it, Tink, tell him how you feel!*

"Peter?"

"Yes, Tink, I'm listening."

"I...you...um."

"Yes?"

Oh, blink!

"I'm going on a picnic tomorrow do you want to come?" The words come out in a rush. I can't' say how I feel about Peter now, but I will tomorrow. For sure. If he agrees to come.

"All right. Where?"

Well, that was easy. I scold myself for having waited so long to ask. Hmm, where? The Mermaid Lagoon is too dangerous, and besides, I can't chance one of those mermaids showing up and ruining it.

"The poppy meadow," I say. It will be perfect. The place where Peter first entered my life. "At midday."

3

I sit on the captain's desk chair and study my reflection in the pocket mirror he keeps in the top drawer.

Before Peter, I never gave my appearance a second thought. All fairies resemble each other more or less, and who was there to impress anyway?

But now I want to look pretty for my picnic with Peter, or cute, or at least not plain. Fairies could have any color hair: blue, purple, green. I have boring old yellow, but I wear it up in a knot and a few curls fall along my face, which is round and wide like a melon. I barely have cheekbones, and my nose is so small I can hardly see it. My eyes are big for my face, but a nice shade of green. I don't have much to recommend me, certainly not height, but at least I have good eyes.

I hear the captain's rhythmic stomp in time to put the mirror away and get back to the task of cleaning Polly's cage.

"That should be an end to their thievery," One Eye Gus says. He is the only one of the captain's crew allowed in the cave. The rest of the men reside on the ship and lounge about on the shore.

"But you missed the boy, the leader of the pack," the captain says.

Polly repeats, "You missed the boy," then flies off the captain's shoulder and lands on the perch that swings in the corner. The captain flops into his chair with a groan and stuffs tobacco in his pipe.

One Eye Gus shifts and crosses his arms. "I didn't miss..."

The captain gives One Eye Gus a sharp look. He doesn't like to be contradicted. He speaks slowly, as if talking to an imbecile. "He's not dead, is he?"

The captain lights his pipe and then leans back, putting his foot on the top of his desk. He lets a long puff of smoke out through his nose, reminding me of a dragon.

"If only I knew where they lived," he says quietly.

"If only I knew where they lived," Polly echoes.

I let out a little gasp and refocus on my task.

It is a mistake. The captain sets his beady eyes on me. "Tinkerbell?"

I pretend not to hear him.

"Tinkerbell!"

I stand sharply, hitting my head on the cage door. Ow. "Yes, sir?"

"My dear little fairy helper, do you know where the Lost Boys live?"

I shake my head and squeak, "No."

The captain pushes his chair back and steps over to where I stand. My eyes grow wider than normal and my wings shiver.

The captain stares down at me, his bald head sweating, his beady eyes dark and menacing. "Are you sure?"

Polly quips, "Are you sure?"

The captain's head swivels to the bird. "Shut up, Polly!"

"Shut up, Polly."

I bite my lip. The captain closes his eyes, deciding unfortunately to focus on me and deal with Polly later.

"Where are the Lost Boys?"

My heart shivers. "I don't know."

"Are you lying?" He bends over to get his face into mine. I shuffle backward a few inches. "If you're lying..." he punches his hand into his fist.

I keep my mouth shut. No way am I going to give away my Peter.

"You're just a stupid dog," the captain says moving back to his desk. Then to One Eye Gus. "She's like an animal. You let her out to do her business and then she comes back for food."

Erg. I'm not the captain's stupid pet, and he doesn't even feed me. I go back to my village every night to sleep and I feed myself. I'm just the captain's stupid slave. Do this, Tinkerbell, do that. *Hrumph.* I mean nothing more to him than a pet. In fact, Polly is more important to him than I am.

Maybe I *will* help the boys steal the guns. Serve the stupid captain right.

I'm still fuming when I get to my village. It sparkles in the sunlight because the cobble streets are made of tiny gems of every color. The blues, reds and golds also dot the hillside where they occur naturally.

Jangle and Cue are lounging at the waterfall, preparing

to swim. Tootles and Knobs chase butterflies. Why am I the only one who has to *work?*

Jangle calls over, "Hey Tink, are you looking for someone to go spying with?" She laughs and jumps into the water, splashing Cue who jumps in afterward.

No way am I going to ask her to come again. My wings curl at the tips and I keep going down the cobbled road, passing other fairies who stop what they are doing to watch me until I reach my hut.

Dust covers the surfaces of my furniture, and a rather large spider has taken residence in one of the corners. I'm too busy waiting hand and foot on the captain to take care of my own place. I head straight to my favorite spot, a rocking chair in the corner by the fireplace and sit down. The rocking motion soothes me and I wait until all my anger and frustration slip away.

Light streams through the open windows, magnifying all the dust, but it also casts a warm, cozy glow. I love my little home, and wish Peter could see into the fairy kingdom to visit me. Though, he'd be too big and tall to get inside my hut anyway.

The next day moves slower than fairy bee honey, until it's finally time to prepare for the picnic with Peter. I gather food and drink items and put them in a basket. I grab a blanket and tuck it under my arm. I ignore the citizens of my village as they watch me leave. I am an oddity, the only one who can mix with the humans. I am different, not like them.

Peter is in the meadow as promised, sitting cross-legged in the middle of a bald patch. My heart flutters when I catch his eye. He is alone and his expression eager. He wants to spend time with me. I couldn't be happier.

"Hey, Tinkerbell," he calls, waving me over.

His shaggy, dark curls blow across his face and I find myself desperately wanting to reach over and move them from his eyes. Instead Peter flicks his head, and the loose strands fall to the side of his face.

I lay out the blanket I brought with me and settle the basket on it. Peter sits down and peeks inside as I open the lid.

"I brought goat cheese and flat bread," I say as I pull the items out, "cherry tomatoes and prawns." Fresh this morning from the captain's catch. And for dessert there are peaches and blueberries with cream."

"Yum, Tink. Do fairies always eat this well?"

I shrug and smile. Fairies and pirates. It suddenly occurs to me that the boys don't fare as well when it comes to the food department. I would rectify that.

We nibble in silence. Well, except for the racket the birds and crickets make, the whistling of the breeze as it rustles through the nearby forest, and the sound of the ocean echoing through the valley. I battle in my head on how to bring up the subject pounding in my heart. I must tell Peter how I feel about him.

"Why are you the only fairy we can see?" Peter asks.

With the back of my hand I wipe juice away from the tomato that has dribbled down my chin. "Well, it's kind of a long story."

"We're in Neverland, Tink. We have all the time in the world." He says this with a smirk, but his eyes grow sad.

If my story will cheer him up, I'll gladly tell it.

"For many, many years, Neverland was strictly a fairy kingdom. We had a king and a queen and an uneventful existence. Day by day, year by year, things never changed, thus the name Neverland.

"Then one day Captain Hook and his pirate ship arrived. The fairy kingdom was in an uproar. Nothing like this had ever happened before. No one knew a way to get in and out of Neverland. At least that's what we were led to believe at the time.

"We spent many weeks observing our uninvited guests, and eventually we realized they couldn't see us, though they seemed to be able to hear us. They went on and on about the island being 'haunted', whatever that means. It was a good thing for us fairies, though. It kept the pirates afraid and they pretty much stuck to the one spot on the beach."

"And then," Peter prompts.

"Oh, blink."

"Blink?" Peter chuckles. "You're cute."

He thinks I'm cute? Then I will muster on with my unfortunate tale. "One careless fairy accidentally spilled her fairy dust on Captain Hook and for a brief moment he was able to see the fairy kingdom in all its glory. From that day on the captain was determined to find a way to break in again, constantly on the hunt for fairies and especially their fairy dust. Fairies bicker amongst themselves all the time, but never in all of our history were we ever at odds with any other kind, and never were we ever hunted.

"The king was so distraught by this new threat; he sent the offending fairy to the captain as a peace offering. One fairy he could see and boss around in exchange for his word that he'd stop seeking out the others."

"I see," Peter says, nodding. "And you were that fairy."

I hang my head.

"Oh, Tink," Peter says, lifting my chin with his finger. His touch sends a thrill through me so intense; I think my wings might pop off. "We all make mistakes. Believe me, I've made plenty."

I shake my head. Peter is perfect. I can't imagine him making any mistakes as serious as mine.

"No it's true. In New York City..."

"New York City?" I've never heard of such a place.

"It's the city where I lived, on Earth, before I came here. My parents told me they were getting a divorce and my dad was moving to London. I was so angry; I told them I never wanted to see them again. I met up with my friends and we made this dumb pact to rebel against all authority. We were all mad at something. Too many rules, too many adults bossing us around, telling us what to do, how to live. Too much school. We all agreed that we'd run away if we could.

"Then something weird happened. A strange storm passed through, stirring up debris along the back alley where we had gathered. Suddenly a green, fluorescent glow filled the alley and a funnel cloud swept us up, like we were in the middle of Kansas instead of the middle of New York City. It tossed us through the air, sucking us up like we'd been caught in a huge vacuum cleaner."

I don't know what a vacuum cleaner is, or what Kansas is for that matter, but I don't want to interrupt. I nod my head, encouraging him to continue.

"Next thing I knew, we were spat out here."

"From what I can see, you seem to like it in Neverland."

"Oh, yeah, Neverland is great." He makes a strange face, like what he's saying doesn't line up with what he's thinking.

"No adults, no rules, just one big, magical adventure.

'Course, there's Hook and the whole need to watch out for our lives thing."

"Hook used to hunt fairies before you came, but now he's happy he has something to hunt that he can actually see."

His face goes sour. "Yeah, well, I'm not happy."

What? Peter isn't happy! My wings twitter with consternation.

"But, Peter..."

"No, really, Tink. I've been here two years. I've marked every day on a tree, and I haven't aged one day. At first I thought being a thirteen year-old boy forever would be the greatest thing. But now, well, I just want to go home. I miss my parents. Their names are Joe and Alice Panelli, and I'm afraid I'm starting to forget them. I want to grow up and do grown up things. I want to be fifteen. I don't want to be killed by a maniac pirate."

Oh no! This conversation is going all wrong!

Peter turns to me and looks hard into my eyes. "Is there a way to get off Neverland? Do you know a way?"

My bottom lip pushes out as it trembles. Tears well up behind my eyes. I do know a way that might work. It's something we never speak of in the fairy kingdom, because the king has forbidden it. The queen left Neverland, the only fairy who ever has, and the king has never recovered from her departure.

"Tink? Can you help me?"

I can and I should, but I can't stand the thought of losing Peter. I shake my head and whisper, "No."

4

Fairies don't usually lie, but I'm anything but a usual fairy, and I've done more than my fair share of fibbing lately.

And I feel awful. A heavy, wet sandbag type of awful. A black cloud, get struck by lightning and stuck in the mud type of awful.

Peter, my Peter, deserves better. He deserves someone brave enough to tell him the truth, someone brave enough to give him what he wants.

I'm not that someone.

My wings can't bear the weight of my wrongdoing—they hang limply down my back and all the sparkle and shine slips away.

"What in the king's name has gotten into you?" Jangle says when she sees me. My little feet drag over the gemstone path that leads to the fairy village.

"I did something awful, Jangle." Big, alligator tears drip

down my cheeks. (And I've seen alligators cry, so I'm not lying. This time.)

"What? Did you beat Captain Hook over the head with his pipe?" She runs thin fingers through her blue hair and flutters her wings. "I wouldn't shed one tear over that if I were you. He deserves it."

"No, it's not that." I wipe the wetness off my face with my limp wing. It isn't any good for flying at the moment, but it sure makes a great hanky. "I lied."

Jangle blows out a lungful of Neverland air.

"To the captain? Because, no one would really blame you for that."

I *did* lie to the Captain but that was for noble reasons, so I could protect Peter.

This time I lied to hurt him.

"To Peter," I whimper.

She walks with me toward my little hut, padding softly against the gemstones under our feet, her nose wrinkling up to her forehead. "I don't understand. Why would you lie to Peter?"

"He wants to leave Neverland. He asked me if I could help." I feel my lip quiver but I have to confess the rest.

"I told him *nooo*." The last word turns into a blathering sob.

Jangle scolds me. "Get a hold of yourself, Tink! That wasn't a lie. You *can't* help him to escape Neverland."

I raise an eyebrow and stare at her out of the corner of my eye. "Well, that's not exactly correct, is it?"

She gasps. "You can't mean..."

"I do. And I'm going to see the king right now."

Jangle grabs my arm. "Are you out of your blinkin' fairy mind?"

"I owe it to him to try," I insist, tugging my arm free.

"You don't owe that Peter boy anything."

I wipe my nose with my other wing. At this rate, I'll never get my sparkle and shine back.

"I have to do something."

"Then convince him to stay. Remind him of all the great reasons to live in Neverland."

"Like what?"

Jangle's hands lock onto her tiny hips. "I don't know. There must be something."

"He's bored."

"Then make him *un*bored. What does he want more than leaving?"

I shrug. "Guns?"

Jangle's face breaks into a huge smile. "Then get him guns."

What she means is steal him some guns. Lying is considered a taboo in our fairy world, but stealing from the captain, well, that is another matter.

I wave goodbye and welcome the warmth and charm of my hut. This is my peace and sanctuary. Nothing will trouble me here.

Except my own mind.

I make a glass of warm coconut milk, being extra generous with the honey, and sit in my rocking chair by the fireplace. I blow a little fairy dust toward it, and it bursts into a bright, blue flame. I put my feet up and sigh.

Maybe I can convince Peter to stay. If I help him fight the captain, help him steal the guns. If I remind him that he really does like the adventurous life he has in Neverland. Wasn't he laughing loudly when he swam with the dolphins?

And the mermaids, but I refuse to think about that. Instead I think about Peter and me, and our friendship. Maybe he'll want to stay if I tell him how I feel, and maybe then he'll see that he feels the same way about me.

Maybe he feels the same way....

Peter's hair glistens in the sunlight, his eyes as blue as the Neverland sky.

We're sitting on the grass in the meadow, each blade a vibrant green, the wildflowers exuberant with joyous color. Butterflies circle around us and small birds chirp overhead.

I reach out to stroke Peter's face, moving straggly hair off his forehead. He leans in close and I can feel his breath on my cheek. My wings zing with excitement.

He whispers in my ear. "Of course I feel the same way, Tink."

My little heart beats uncontrollably and I hold my breath. My eyes grow wide with surprise as Peter's lips line up with mine. They're red and full, like fresh melon.

I close my eyes in anticipation. At any moment his lips will meet mine...

"Tinkerbell?"

My eyes spring open to darkness. My mind reaches for an explanation. What just happened? Where is Peter?

"What are you doing in the dark?" Jangle's voice. She snaps her fingers and the room fills with a soft light.

My eyes pinch together resisting the sudden glow.

"I fell asleep," I say feeling foolish about my dream. I'm so glad fairies can't read minds. "What do you want?"

"Just making sure you're okay," Jangle says, staring at me

suspiciously, "and not doing anything stupid."

Like visiting the fairy king.

"I'm not, okay. I'm just tired. Some people have to *work*."

"I've heard that beds make more comfortable sleeping surfaces than wooden rocking chairs."

She's right. I have a kink in my neck that hurts like crazy.

"I'm going to bed now, if you don't mind."

"Not at all." Jangle turns on her heels and lets herself out the same way she let herself in. I move to my bedroom. There's a soft bed in the middle with a shimmering, purple canopy. I climb in and close my eyes, hoping I'll meet Peter again in my dreams.

THE NEXT DAY I head to Captain Hook's office like I normally do, except this time there's a little hop in my step and an extra flutter in my wings.

I woke up with an idea, even better than stealing guns, though I'll help Peter with that later if he wants me to.

No, this is a much better idea and one I can't tell anyone about, especially Jangle. I have to make sure everything still looks normal because I don't want to draw undue attention. Which means I have to do my work for the captain before I can go see Peter.

I'm so excited my chores hardly feel like labor. I clean Polly's cage, and give her fresh water and food. I dust the captain's desk and polish his canteens. I peek out the window to check on his whereabouts. Yes, the captain is still on his ship, bossing his men around. He and One Eye Gus look like they're having a serious discussion. I want to get my chores done before the captain returns; otherwise he's likely to saddle me with more tasks.

I clean the captain's reading glasses, straighten his papers and sweep the floor. I double-check everything, making certain it appears obvious that I had arrived on schedule and accomplished my duties.

I am free to leave once my work is done. I'm grateful to the king that he made it clear in our agreement. I work for the captain: he doesn't own me.

Before I leave, I borrow the captain's looking glass to scan the horizon, especially Mermaid Lagoon, searching for Peter. I don't see him or the Lost Boys anywhere from this vantage point.

I slip away and let out a long breath when I'm safely out of the Captain's reach. I head toward the tree fort, dodging tangled vines and fallen logs covered in moss. The deeper I get into the forest, the more I strain to hear their voices. Eventually I hear chatter and laughter, and my lips tug up into a smile.

I'm careful to keep concealed, which with my size is fairly easy. I stay tucked under broad leaves and behind stout tree trunks.

Peter is sitting alone on a stump carving a piece of wood with a knife. My heart patters as I stare longingly at his form. The dream from the evening before where Peter almost kisses me is still fresh in my mind, making me tingle like it really happened.

I clear my throat then whisper, "Peter?"

His hand pauses and his head swivels in my direction.

"Who's there?" He jumps to his feet, his knife at the ready.

"It's just me." I slip into view.

"Tink, you startled me."

"I'm sorry."

"It's okay." He sits back down on the stump.

"I wanted to tell you I can help you steal the captain's guns, if you still want to do that. I know where he keeps the keys."

"Ah, Tink, I can't ask you to do that. I don't want to get you into trouble." His eyes crinkle as he smiles. "But it was nice of you to offer."

I move in a little closer.

"Are you still very unhappy, Peter?"

He shrugs. "I suppose."

"I want to show you something. Something that might cheer you up."

Peter's brow furrows as he ponders what I said. I know Peter well enough to predict his curiosity would get to him.

"Show me what?"

"I can't tell you. I have to show you."

He stands and sticks his knife into his belt strap. "Well, it's not like I have anything else to do."

Peter follows me through the silk forest, toward the other side of Blue Mountain. When we get to the foot of the hill near the village, we start climbing.

"I hate to break it to you, Tink, but I've been to the top of Blue Mountain before. A million times."

I giggle and wave him on. "It'll be different this time, I promise." Blue Mountain's not really that high, and before too long we're at the peak.

I stand on the ridge looking over our village, knowing Peter can't see it. All he sees is endless forest, the waterfall pouring into the river that snakes out to the ocean, and the climbing sun, brightening the crystal blue sky.

"It's gorgeous, Tink, I know."

"Close your eyes," I say. Peter eyes me nervously.

"It's okay. I'm not going to hurt you, or anything." I add "or anything" just in case he thinks I'm going to kiss him. Which I want to do, but I won't.

Peter closes his eyes and I flap my wings. I rise above the ground until I'm eye level with him. Fairy dust escapes from my flapping wings and I blow.

Peter's expression softens. "What was that?"

"Open your eyes and see."

I'll never forget the look on Peter's face as he takes in the view of our fairy village for the first time. His eyes grow wide as saucers and his mouth forms a big *o*.

The village sparkles with all the jewel work and is busy with a multitude of fairies who look a lot like me. The sounds of fairy life are like crystal glasses being tapped by the most sensitive composer, the sweetest music rising to fill our ears.

Peter finally sputters, "Oh, my goodness. Tink! It's incredible!"

Yay! The words I so longed to hear. Peter liked it! He'll want to stay in Neverland for sure now.

"You can't tell anyone, Peter," I say. "No one must know I let you see this. I'll be in big trouble."

Peter's face falls. "Then why'd you show it to me?"

"Because, I want you to be happy, Peter. I want you to stay in Neverland."

His mouth tugs down into a frown and all the happiness he just expressed evaporates in a moment. A cool fear ripples through my wings. I'm sure I made a huge mistake. I'm just not sure what it is.

"Peter?"

"What are you saying? I thought you said I didn't have a choice?"

I feel my face blush red, but I don't say anything.

"Is it true?" Peter continues, "Or is there a way out of Neverland?"

I swallow hard but stay silent.

"Tinkerbell, did you show me the fairy kingdom as a bribe? So I would stay?"

"No!" I finally shout, but the lie is evident in the way my wings hang.

Peter shakes his head and starts back down Blue Mountain. "I don't believe you."

"Peter!"

He tosses me a withering look "Friends don't lie to friends."

He's right! I've been a terrible friend. I go after him because I need to apologize. I have to engage my wings to keep up, but they're so limp from yet another lie, they don't work properly and I stumble and fall. By the time I get myself together, Peter is around the bend and out of sight.

I let him go.

I sit on a big, slippery leaf and choke back tears. No sense crying again. As Jangle is known to say, *tears don't change anything*.

And if tears won't help me, I don't know what will.

I finally brush myself off, shake out my wings, and head down the mountain.

His words resound through my head, *Friends don't lie to friends.*

They repeat over and over, so loudly, stinging my eardrums and my heart. I don't pick up on the commotion at the bottom of Blue Mountain until it's almost too late.

Captain Hook's voice bellows through the valley. "Stop right there, you thief."

Then Peter's voice. "Get out of my way, Hook."

My little legs take me the rest of the way down and I skid to a stop at the sight unfolding before me. Hook and Peter are sparring each other, Hook with a sword and Peter with only his small, whittling knife.

"Captain, stop!"

His lip twitches when he sees me. "You stay out of it, you little pest."

In normal circumstances I wouldn't talk back to the captain, but these aren't normal circumstances.

"It's hardly a fair fight," I shout out.

He takes another swipe at Peter, and Peter just manages to duck behind a tree.

The captain growls, "I said, stay out of it."

I hold my heart as I watch them fight. The captain is larger and stronger with more battle experience and he has a bigger weapon.

Peter's advantage is his stamina and flexibility. He gets a couple jabs in, but mostly he's dodging and ducking. I suck wind a couple times when the captain's sword gets too close.

Then Peter trips and falls backward. In a moment, the captain is standing over top of him, with his sword to Peter's throat.

"Gotcha."

5

My wings flutter wildly as terror grips me. I have to help Peter, but how? I scan the forest, searching for an answer, and then I see it. I fly to a hanging vine, grip it tightly then fly to where the captain is standing, sneaking up from behind.

I wrap the vine around his neck, pulling him away from Peter. The captain twists and falls to the ground on his stomach with a thud. Peter springs to his feet, kicking the sword out of the captain's reach. He drops to his knee and wrenches one of the captain's arms up behind his back. With his other hand he presses his knife into the captain's neck.

"Who's got who now, Hook?" he says sharply.

I don't like the look on Peter's face and I'm afraid he's angry enough to do something terrible.

"Peter?" I call.

"He asked for it, Tink," he says through tight lips. "He tried to kill me first."

"But Peter, you're not like him."

He grows still and then his shoulders slump. After a very long moment he scoots away from the captain.

"You're right, Tink. I'm not."

Peter disappears into the forest and the captain picks himself up, brushing leaves and twigs off his pantaloons before bearing down on me with his beady eyes.

"You!"

I scamper back. I'm too fatigued to engage my wings again to save myself. I wince as the captain reaches for me. He drags me back like I'm nothing more to him than a rag doll.

I finally shake free when we come to his office. The captain closes the door. Hanging from a big nail on the wall is an ornate key. He whips it off and locks the door with dramatic flair.

"You can't keep me prisoner," I say. "It's not part of the agreement."

The captain rubs a hand over his sweaty, bald head. "Oh, really? Watch me."

I've never seen the captain this angry before, and my breath catches. I back up against the wall and try to make myself invisible.

Polly sits on her perch in her cage. The captain opens it and she hops out and onto his shoulder. The captain closes his eyes and strokes her feathers like his sanity depends upon it.

Maybe it does.

Once his breathing slows, he moves to the desk and prepares his pipe. I relax a little. It takes at least twenty minutes for him to smoke it through, so nothing too unpredictable should happen until then.

Right?

We don't hit the five minute mark before there's a rap on the door.

I get up to answer it, which is a normal duty for me but the captain calls me back.

"Oh no you don't," he says glaring at me. Then he shouts, "Come in, ya cretin!"

The door handle wobbles. The captain forgot he locked it.

"Oh, blast it," he mutters under his breath. He moves his feet back to the floor, his pipe hanging precariously between dry lips, and unlocks the door.

As I expected, it's One Eye Gus.

He breezes in with far more confidence than I've ever seen him do before, and struts directly to the window.

"Look thar," he says, pointing at something outside.

"What is it?" the captain huffs. He takes the looking glass and stares hard.

"Is it...?" he begins.

One Eye Gus nods. "I believe so."

The captain lets out a little "whoop!" and breaks into an awkward jig.

"This could be it, One Eye. Our ticket home!" He presses the looking glass to his eye and watches whatever is out there again.

Now my curiosity has gotten the best of me. I flap my wings and rise high enough off the floor to peer over their shoulders and out the window.

I blink a couple times. Are my eyes playing tricks? On the horizon is a strange green glow, swirling like a funnel with orange flickering streaks crossing through it.

I've never seen anything like it before in Neverland.

Though I'd heard stories. There was something strange about the sky the day the pirates arrived.

And wasn't Peter's alley in his New York filled with green, too?

I fix my gaze on the captain and One Eye.

"It's the Bermuda, Captain," One Eye gushes.

"I think you're right," the captain says, nodding eagerly. But how far away is it? Can we reach it in time? Before it disappears again?"

I float back to the floor and scuttle into the shadows. Is it possible the pirates are leaving Neverland?

A little flash of joy shoots through my wings. Yippee! That means freedom for me, and perhaps Peter will stop wanting to go back to that New York place.

My joy is short lived. The captain and One Eye leave, locking the door behind them.

I'm a prisoner.

I bang on the door. "Let me out! Let me out!"

The window. I'll just fly out. I hop onto the ledge and look down. The cave is on top of a bluff that drops sharply to the water below.

One of the captain's henchmen stands on the deck of his ship with a rifle propped on his shoulder pointed right at the window. Right at me.

If I flew out right now, I'd be a dead fairy. I scuttle back inside.

The captain doesn't return. The sun sets and the green glow brightens on the horizon. My eyelids grow heavy and I think of Peter as I drift asleep. I awake with a kink in my neck, still alone in the office. I can't believe the captain hasn't released me. I hurry to the window and frown at the sentry on the ship, rifle at the ready.

The green glow appears smaller, but it's still pulsing. Whatever it is, it has the captain thoroughly pre-occupied. He's forgotten that I'm an organic creature who needs to eat.

My stomach growls loudly and I search the room for food. All I can find is Polly's dish of seeds. I scoop a handful and eat begrudgingly. Reduced to eating bird food!

This is so unfair! I know I'd been careless with my fairy dust, but this punishment did not fit the crime. It's awful being held captive against your will!

It's awful being held captive against your will...

Peter.

He's being held captive on Neverland against his will. This feeling of being trapped, caged, suffocated... it's how Peter feels!

I slide down against Polly's cage until I'm seated and I cover my face with my hands. My heart feels swollen and tender, and a hiccup erupts from my lips.

I need to help Peter get back to that New York place, even though it's going to break my swollen, tender heart to do it.

If only I can get out of my own trap.

Fortune is on my side. Suddenly, I hear pounding and voices coming from the other side of the door.

"Tink, are you in there?"

Jangle!

I rush to the door and shout up toward the keyhole. "Yes, I'm here. The captain locked me in."

"Just wait a minute," she says, as if I can go anywhere. I

hear Cue and Knob's voices, too, and sounds of shuffling against the door.

"Boost me," Knob says. More shuffling.

"You're heavy."

"Don't be a wimp."

"Here's the nail," Jangle says.

The handle jiggles and I hop excitedly. This will work!

Then the thumping sound of bodies falling.

"Blink!"

"Ow!"

"Get off me!"

I bang on the door, "Just fly!"

Knobs voice seeps through the keyhole. "We all flew here. Our energy is zapped."

I worry that this is taking too long. I go to the window and gasp. The captain is disembarking his ship.

"Jangle! The captain's coming."

I hear them hustle again on the other side of the door. It's not like the captain will see them, but he can see me, and if I'm not free before he gets back, I'll miss this chance.

"Hurry!" I say.

There's a click and the door springs open. A stack of fairies tumbles inside.

I give Jangle a big hug. "Thank you for coming for me!"

"When you didn't return to the village last night, I was worried," she says.

I bubble with joy because of my friends. Yes, I have friends!

"The captain's on his way. I need to go." I run past them into the woods.

"Where are you going?" Jangle shouts after me.

"I need to find Peter!"

I race through the forest faster than I ever have before. I find Peter picking wild berries with the Lost Boys.

"Peter," I call.

His eyes dart to me then back to the berry bush. "What do you want?"

My heart sinks. He's still angry with me.

"To make sure you're okay."

"I can take care of myself," he snaps.

"Please don't be mad at me."

His shoulders soften and he breathes out long and slow. "I'm not mad at you. I'm mad at me. I'm mad that Hook beat me."

"He didn't beat you."

"Yes he did. If it weren't for you, I'd be dead." He reaches for a berry. "I'm sorry, I should've thanked you for saving my life. I'm just embarrassed."

He turns and his bright blue, beautiful eyes lock with mine, sending a twisty shiver down my spine and through my wings.

"Thank you," he says

"I'll help you leave," I whisper.

His expression freezes. "You will?"

I press my quivering lips together and nod.

"Oh, Tink!" A grin spreads across his face, producing the dimples I love so much, and his bag of berries falls to the ground. Next thing I know, he has me wrapped in his arms. My heart beats wildly against his chest and I inhale his scent, a mix of sunshine, earth and raspberries, and I'm suddenly deliriously happy.

"Boys," he shouts, letting me go. "Come here. I have big news."

They each lumber out of hiding, Curly, Nibs, and Tubs.

"Where's the fire?" Curly says.

"No fire." Peter's face flushes with excitement. "Tink knows how to get us home!"

I wait for a burst of enthusiasm, but the boys remain stoic.

"How?" says Curly. All the boys turn their gazes on me.

I whimper a little. "I can't tell you."

There are certain fairy kingdom secrets I'm bound by oath to keep, even from Peter.

Nibs scratches his red head. "How do we know she's telling the truth?"

Peter's eyebrows pinch together and he settles his sights on me. "You are aren't you?"

I'm offended. Even if I have been guilty of lying, I'm not now. "Yes!"

Peter opens his hands like he's presenting a gift. "We've got nothing to lose by letting her try."

"What if we don't wanna leave Neverland?" Tubs whines.

Peter's face crumples into a deep frown. "What do you mean? Don't you think we've been here long enough?"

The boys break out into chorus:

"I like it here."

"There are no rules."

"It's fun."

"What about the Pirates?" Peter almost shouts. "What about growing up?"

"The pirates don't scare me, and I don't want to grow

up," Curly says. "I never met one grown up who was truly happy." The other boys nod enthusiastically.

"Fine," Peter says, with tight lips. "I'll go myself."

The silk forest grows very quiet.

"You'd leave us, Peter?" Tubs says in a near whisper.

"You don't need me. Look how well you do on your own."

"He's right," Curly spits out. "We don't need him. He's just a grump anyway, always spoiling our fun. We'll be better off without him. Let's go."

Curly leads the charge back into the forest and I'm left alone with a disappointed Peter.

I look up at him from under my damp eyelashes. "Are you sure you want to do this?" I hope he changes his mind, now that he sees how the boys feel.

His shoulders straighten with determination. "I'm sure. What do I have to do?"

He doesn't have to do anything. It's me who has to do it.

"I need some time," I say, mustering up as much courage as I can. "I'll be back soon, and then you can return to your New York."

6

I promised Peter I'd help him and I will, but it means I have to do something quite heinous. I have to steal from the king.

My heart stops at the thought of it. There's no way I can tell anyone, especially not Jangle. She'd wring my neck for sure.

The king is in possession of the queen's fairy dust, and, it turns out, royal fairy dust is the only way out of Neverland. It's how the queen got away.

Fortunately, I have a built-in excuse to see the king. Every few weeks I'm suppose to report back to the king about the captain. The king wants to make sure that he's obeying the terms of their agreement. The king uses me to be his eyes to keep track of the enemy, and I have a couple of important things to report this time.

The king's castle is perched on the southeast side of Blue Mountain, about half way up, overlooking the village. It's built with the best jewels, and in the mornings it sparkles like a second sun. There is a balcony facing the ocean where the queen used to take her tea with the king. The king hasn't been spotted sitting there since she left.

I reach the tall (for a fairy) door and bang on it with the knocker. A castle keeper opens it and I declare myself.

"Tinkerbell here to report to his majesty."

The keeper knows who I am—the fairy kingdom isn't very big—and nods to acknowledge me. I follow him inside and he closes the tall, heavy doors behind me.

The castle feels big to me, being a fairy, but I think Peter would have to watch his head. I follow the castle keeper to the reception room. The hall is spacious with rich, red carpeting, and bright light shines through the sunroof in the ceiling. The queen loved flowers and birds and had turned the castle into a haven for her exotic feather friends. Green and blue parrots, snow white cockatoos, and striped beaked toucans fly freely through the tropical trees that line the way.

I think the king keeps them around because they remind him of the queen, and his heart still longs for her. No one has seen him smile since she left.

The castle keeper leaves me in the reception room and I wait as he announces my arrival. There's a fountain in the corner by massive windows and I draw my fingers through the cool water. The trickling sound soothes me, and I breathe deeply to steady my nerves. I have to be strong. I have to succeed in my mission.

"My dear, Tinkerbell." The king's deep baritone voice resounds through the reception room. He wears his royal gown as usual, red with gold stitching and a gold belt cinched around a thickening waist. He has a full, dark beard and a kind face, one that smiled incessantly before the queen left. Now there is a constant sadness in his brown eyes, and his mouth rarely pulls up in the corners. A bejeweled crown sits on his head.

"Is it check-in time already?" he continues. "Time is speeding up."

I bow, and keep my eyes lowered. Not because I feel endangered in anyway, but because I know I am soon to deceive him and I feel ashamed.

"It's true, your majesty, I'm here earlier than scheduled, but I come with news."

"Please, relay it."

My mouth opens and my grievance pours out. "The captain locked me in his office over night! All because I stopped him from killing Peter!"

The king frowns. "Who's Peter?"

"He's one of the Lost Boys, and the captain doesn't like them at all."

"I see, so *you*, Tinkerbell, saved the boy? How?"

I hesitate. Even though I saved Peter, what I did wasn't very fairy-like. "The captain had Peter pinned to the ground with a sword. I wrapped a vine around his neck and pulled him away."

The king's frown deepens and I fear I've put myself in trouble. Then his face softens and his eyes lighten, like he's holding in a chuckle.

"You've got some gumption, Tinkerbell. A strong spirit. You remind me of the queen."

My wings quiver in shock. The king has never spoken of the queen in my presence before. And to compare me to her, I'm stunned. Words escape me.

The king clasps his hands behind his back. "Is there anything else to report?"

"Ah, yes, your majesty. There's a green glow on the horizon, unlike anything I've ever seen before in Neverland, and it seems to be of some interest to the captain."

The king moves to the balcony off the reception room and I follow. The castle is situated at such an angle that you can only catch the edge of the glow from this position. The king strokes his beard. "Yes, I see. And what do you think it is?"

"I'm not certain. The captain said something about Bermuda."

He nods. "I'm sure it's nothing to worry about." He turns to me with sleepy eyes. "Is there anything else?"

I'm a little surprised the king doesn't find this more fascinating, but there hasn't been much to pique his interest since....

Blink, I'm tired of thinking about the queen. Why did she have to go and leave anyway?

"No, that's all," I say.

"I'll summon the keeper to show you out."

"No," I add quickly. "No need to trouble him. I know the way."

The king studies me and I feel my nerve slipping.

"Suit yourself," he finally says. "Until next time, Tinkerbell."

"Yes, your majesty. Good day."

I focus on Peter and the promise I made. I have to do this next unpleasant thing so I can help him. I step stealthily down the hall that leads to the queen's chambers. I have a good idea where she slept because her balcony is filled with plants and bird feeders. We could see her from the village. She spent a lot of time there.

At the end of the hallway is an ornate door and I'm certain it's her room. I try the handle, half expecting it to be locked, but it opens easily. I suppose the king didn't think he had a reason to lock the queen's chambers.

I gasp when I'm inside. Her room is spectacular. It's filled with beautifully crafted wood furniture, including a lacy canopy bed that twinkles in the light; the floors are lined with thick carpeting and artisan wall hangings adorn all four of the brightly painted walls. I close my gaping mouth and head straight to the dresser with all her perfumes and creams on display in fancy bottles and containers. I can't help but stroke and admire them.

I feel awful about violating the queen's privacy, but she obviously doesn't care about that anymore. I find what I'm looking for at the back. Several small jars of the queen's fairy dust. I slip one into my sash and then on impulse, grab a second one. Though I'm the alone in the room, I tiptoe back to the door.

I'm near the castle entrance when a parrot squawks, "God save the queen," scaring me half to death.

Then another voice, "Stop!"

Not a bird, but the keeper. Oh no.

"Why do you trespass his majesty's castle?" he demands. His hand is on the sword handle at his belt, and I don't doubt that he will use the weapon on me. My blood drains to my toes, and my mouth is so dry I can barely speak.

"I'm merely lost. I mean no harm."

"Lost? Why has not the king summoned me to escort you out?"

"I thought I knew my way. I didn't want to disturb you."

"It is my duty to be disturbed."

His hand relaxes on his sword and he moves resolutely to the door, opening it wide. I get the message and scurry out, heading directly to the silk forest and the old tree fort.

My mind races along with my body. I can't believe I just stole from the king! What would happen to me if anyone found out? We don't have a prison in the fairy kingdom because fairies never do really bad things.

Oh my goodness, I'm such a terrible fairy! If I'm caught, I'd probably be given to the captain on a permanent basis, and exiled from the village forever.

The remorse I feel over my actions is overwhelming and I stop to hide under a silk tree leaf. My wings quiver with anxiety and I take several quick breaths to calm myself.

I remind myself of the greater good. I'm doing this for Peter. *Because he is so unhappy here and I want to make him happy.*

The queen is gone and no one will miss her fairy dust, anyway. Peter will be *happy.*

He will be happy, but *I* will be miserable. Neverland will never be the same without Peter.

Maybe I will go with him to his New York place? Yes, that's what I'll do. And we can be happy in New York together!

Except.

The queen's fairy dust only works to send someone away from Neverland if another important ingredient is added: self-sacrifice.

Peter can't leave unless I send him. Because I so desperately don't want to let him go, it's the exact sacrifice needed to release him.

Oh my bleeding heart!

A sob escapes my throat as I wallow in the unfairness of it all. I won't do it. I can't live without Peter. I'll just tell him I failed at my mission. Hopefully, he'll forgive me one day.

Then I remember the king and his sad countenance, and my breath catches. The truth hits me hard: The queen couldn't have left Neverland unless the king sent her off. He made this same sacrifice for the person he loved.

If the king wouldn't keep the queen against her will, then I won't keep Peter against his.

I wipe my face and tighten my ponytail. I'm strong. I can do this.

When I arrive at the tree fort, Peter is pacing outside.

"There you are," he says. "I was afraid you wouldn't come."

I lock onto his beautiful blue eyes, memorizing his face. The way his eyes crinkle at the corners when he laughs, the way they flash blue when he's happy and grow dark when he's sad. I'll miss his flop of dark hair and his dimples when he smiles. My wings droop as I realize I will never see Peter again after this moment. My chest feels heavy with sorrow.

"Are you sure you want to go?' I choke out.

Peter jumps, full of energy and anticipation. He has no idea how hard this is for me. "Yes! I do."

He looks so happy, and that's what I want for him. To be happy.

"Okay." I fly over to him, and remove a jar of the queen's fairy dust from my sash.

"Goodbye, Peter," I whisper. To his surprise (and mine!)

I kiss him softly on the cheek. I pour the fairy dust on his head. "I send you to your New York City," I say.

And then he's gone.

I float to the ground in shock. *Peter is gone.*

Blink! What have I done?

I pace around in circles like a crazy fairy. I can't believe I let him go. What was I thinking! I don't know what to do with myself.

And then I do.

My hand clasps the second jar of the queen's fairy dust.

I will go to New York City, too. I'll find a way.

NEW YORK, NEW YORK

LOVE, TINK - EPISODE 2

NEW YORK, NEW YORK

Episode 2 in the Love, Tink Series

by
Lee Strauss

SUMMARY

Tink makes it to Peter's New York and is more than a little daunted by what she discovers. Under the guise of Belle Fehr, Tink registers at the school Peter attends. Her dreamy reunion is crushed when she finds that not only does he not recognize her, he has a girlfriend named Wendy!

1

Time on Neverland is categorized for me now as life BP and life AP—Before Peter and After Peter. It has been many days since he left to his New York, and each day my thread of hope that he'll somehow return grows thinner and weaker.

The worst part, the agonizingly terrible part, is I can't tell anyone what I've done. I broke a major fairy kingdom law; I stole from the king! Who knows what he would do to me if he found out. Something far worse than being required to work every day for the insidious Captain Hook, that's for sure.

I'm so sorrowful these days, the beauty of the gems that sparkle under my feet, or the crimson hue of the sunrise shimmering on the ocean's horizon don't bring a smile. I can't even gaze upon the king's castle on the hill without being squashed by guilt.

Jangle falls into step with me as I head out of the village. "We should change your name from Tinkerbell to

Sourpuss."

"What do you want, Jangle?" I say wearily.

She tugs on a strand of her spiky, blue hair. "I want you to snap out of this funk you're in. What's the matter? Did Peter break up with you?"

I know she's just trying to be funny, but her words crush my soul.

"Just leave me alone!" I speed up to get away from her, and even though ditching her is exactly what I want to do, I'm still a little hurt that she doesn't chase after me.

I wish to go faster than my pointy-toed slippers can take me and I'm tempted to engage my wings and fly.

Except my wings are like withered plants drying out in the sun. I haven't flown since Peter left.

A familiar lump forms, thick and gooey, in my throat.

I know I'm in a bad way when I'm eager to be distracted by Captain Hook and the work I'm required to do for him. I get right to scrubbing the stone floor of the cave where the captain set up his office. A hole in the wall that acts as a window faces the bay below. A quick glance confirms that the captain is with his crew on the pirate ship. The morning sun reflects off his bald head and enormous hook nose.

Scrubbing floors is the thing I hate to do the most, which is why I tackle it with a vengeance. A type of penance. I'm the worse kind of fairy. A liar and a thief. And hopelessly in love with a human boy I will never see again.

A deep-rooted moan vibrates through my lips.

My situation is hopeless.

Unless...

No, I mustn't think about it. It's a crazy idea, and one I

foolishly allowed myself to dwell on for a short while in a moment of weakness and under extreme duress.

Yes, very extreme duress.

I can't leave Neverland. I'm a fairy. I belong in the fairy kingdom with other fairies.

How would I manage in a world full of humans? The ones that live on Neverland aren't exactly stellar examples of humanity. What if Peter is the only good one? What if his New York is full of people like Captain Hook?

Or the Lost Boys? I'm careful to stay out of their way now. They're not happy I sent their leader away. Last time they spotted me, they shot at me with their arrows.

Oh, blink. What a mess I've made.

I finish the floor by the door just as it swings open and the captain marches in. He steps in a slippery, wet spot and before I can say God save the king, his legs spring out from under him and he's flat on his back on the floor.

"Tinkerbell!"

Polly squawks, "Tinkerbell," and flies to her perch.

I scamper away into the corner. "Uh, I just scrubbed the floor, Captain."

"I noticed that." He pulls himself up and shakes out his puffy shirt and pantaloons. "A little warning next time?"

I nod just as One Eye Gus struts in and falls on his butt in the exact same spot. He cusses and I hide behind Polly's cage.

"Oh, get up off the floor, One Eye!" the captain sputters. "We have work to do!"

The captain and One Eye huddle around his desk while I quietly continue with my chores. It's best if I stay low and out of sight when the captain's in the room, so I clean the bottom of Polly's cage while they mutter to each other.

Fairies have good hearing, so I can make out everything they say.

"Those little rotters robbed us again!" the captain says. "How did they get onto the ship without notice?"

I pause. The Lost Boys are still after the guns. I for one hope they never succeed. Not if they're going to shoot at me.

One Eye shakes his head. "Dunno. All they got was some blankets and a pilla."

"That's fewer blankets and one less pillow for us, idiot. They're taunting us. It's that Peter kid. He's a smart one..."

My wings perk up at the mention of Peter's name.

"If we could just get him..." One Eye says.

The captain paces around his desk and stops to stare out the window and then he slowly turns to stare at me. I wonder if he's remembering how he would've accomplished his goal of killing Peter if I hadn't stopped him.

His dark, beady eyes pierce my being like swords and my veins freeze with fear.

"I haven't seen the Peter kid around lately, have you?" he says to me.

I shake my head.

He laughs. "And here I thought fairies didn't lie."

"I'm not lying."

"Really? Then you'll soon have the privilege of witnessing the boy's execution."

My blood turns from cold to hot faster than I can snap my fingers. "You will never kill Peter!"

The captain smirks with evil joy. "Ha. Watch me."

I stamp my feet, enraged that the captain could even

think to do harm to my Peter. "You will not kill Peter. He's not even on Neverland anymore!"

I clasp a hand over my mouth. My tongue is such a traitor!

The captain's grin flips upside down. "What do you mean?"

"Nothing," I squeak.

The captain takes two, long strides and clutches me in his large, bony hands. He hisses, blowing me with foul breath. "Where is he?"

"He's gone."

"Gone? Gone where?"

"To his New York," I say smugly. "And *I* sent him there."

The captain's beady eyes squint and his dark, bushy eyebrow raises like a caterpillar on the run.

"How did you, a mere fairy, send Peter back to New York?"

My eyes pop wide but I seal my lips. There's no way I can tell the captain about the queen's fairy dust.

He squishes his lips together, then says, "Can you send me?"

I shake my head. "It was a one-time only deal. All the other boys are still here."

The captain's face turns a nasty, tomato red. Then he tosses me into Polly's cage and locks it, hanging the key back on the nail in the wall.

He storms out of the office with One Eye on his heels. Polly stares at me from her perch and squawks. "Silly Tinkerbell."

2

I rattle the cage, and squeal out in anger. "Captain!"

I shout, but I know he can't hear me. Even if he could, he wouldn't release me. The captain seems to get satisfaction from locking me up. Jangle came for me last time when the captain locked me in the office over night, but she won't think to look for me until this time tomorrow. I can't wait until then.

"I need to get out of here," I say to no one but my own crazy mind.

"I need to get out of here," Polly repeats.

"Oh, stop making fun of me," I say. "You probably love that our roles are reversed." Usually I'm the one on the other side of the cage and she's in here.

"I need to get out of here," Polly says again.

Polly. Maybe Polly can get me out.

"Polly, you're a good bird," I say soothingly. "Get me the keys." I point at the ring hanging on the nail.

Polly looks at them and then me.

"Come on Polly," I plea. "Get the keys."

"Come on Polly, get the keys."

"Stop saying what I'm saying. Just get the keys!"

"Get the keys."

Oh, she's useless. I slump to the floor of the cage, glad I'd cleaned it.

I cup my hands over my face and weep. Why do bad things always have to happen to me? I hate being locked up and bossed around and controlled. I hate being a fairy. I wish I were a human like Peter. If I go to his New York City, we could be together and live happily ever after.

Oh, if only I could get out of this cage, that's exactly what I'll do. Find a way to find Peter. I would!

I'm startled by a clanking sound and something landing in the cage at my feet. My eyes zero in at the object.

The keys. Polly stands outside the cage, her yellow claws spread wide. She ruffles her blue and green feathers and stares at me with her tiny bird eyes She squawks, "Get the keys."

"Polly! You are a very good bird!"

I pick up the keys and open the lock.

I give Polly a big hug which results in more squawking and a peck on the shoulder that barely even hurts. I race back to my hut.

I STOP by Jangle's hut on the way, and shout through the doorway.

"Jangle, can you come over? I have something to tell you."

"Tell me now."

"No, it has to be my place."

"Why?"

Blink. Can't she be agreeable sometimes?

"It just does. Come right away." I leave before she can question me further, knowing full well her curiosity will drive her nuts and she'll be at my place within five minutes.

What I need is hidden in my bedroom, in a box under my bed. I pull it out, coughing at the dust bunnies that float into my face, and remove the lid. Inside is the final jar of the queen's fairy dust, and a small satchel of jewels.

I pick both items up and head back to my living room. Jangle is sitting in my rocking chair. She snaps her fingers and the logs in the fireplace burst into flame.

The chair creaks as she rocks. Her arms are folded, and she gives me a bored look. "So what's the big news?"

"Okay, I have something to tell you, but you have to promise me not to freak out."

"Why would I freak out?"

"Just promise me."

"Is this about Peter?"

My face gives it away.

Her arms fall to her lap and her jaw goes slack. "Oh blink, Tink. Tell me you didn't."

"I did."

"Oh my goodness, you..." she lowers her voice, "*stole* the queen's fairy dust?"

She's heard the rumors, too. Only the queen's fairy dust has the power to send someone away from Neverland.

I nod once.

"Are you insane?"

"Maybe," I admit. "But it's too late now. The damage is done. Peter is gone to his New York."

"So, why are you telling me this? I could turn you in, you know?" She springs out of the chair and paces in a small circle, practically wearing a hole in my green, hand-woven throw rug. "I don't really want to know this. What am I supposed to do with this information, Tinkerbell?"

"I have one more jar." I open my palm and Jangles hands fly to her face.

"I want you to send me."

"No!"

"Please, Jangle. It's what I want. I'm not happy here anymore."

Her eyes narrow into ugly slits. "That Peter boy has ruined you."

"I'm not ruined. Just changed."

Jangle sits back down on my rocking chair and rocks back and forth manically. I really can't chance her losing her marbles on me right now.

"I'll make us some tea," I say.

I fill the stone oven with dry twigs and snap my fingers to start the fire. I'm too impatient to wait for the water in the kettle to come to a boil on its own, so I blow a little fairy dust on it to speed up the process. I add a spoonful of dried and crushed raspberries to the teapot and pour in the steaming water.

When I return with the cups of tea, Jangle is calmer. I'm hopeful I can convince her to my way of thinking.

"I'm in love, Jangle. I need to be with Peter, wherever he is. Don't you see? True love must have its way."

She carefully sips her tea. "You take me for a romantic?"

"Aren't you? Surely you believe in love."

"I don't know. I've never been in love. I've only witnessed the love the king has for the queen, and look where that got him."

"But this is different."

"How?"

I'm anxious about how wrong this is going. I should be in New York by now, not having a tea party with an obstinate fairy.

"I just know it in my heart. You have to send me, Jangle. Otherwise, I'll spend the rest of my days slaving away for Captain Hook and die of a broken heart."

"You do paint a dismal picture." Jangle sets down her empty cup. "Okay, I'll do it."

I bounce with joy and almost spill what's left of my tea.

"Thank you, Jangle. You're the best friend a fairy can have."

I carefully hand her the jar. "All you have to do is pour the queen's fairy dust on my head and then say, 'I send you to New York City.'"

Jangles sacrifice would be for her to send me to New York even though she would miss me terribly, much in the same way I sacrificed to send Peter.

A worm of anxiety squirms in my belly. I'm not certain she feels strong enough about losing me.

Jangle nods. "Give me a hug first, okay?"

A huge smile spreads across my face. Maybe I'm wrong about her. Maybe it is hard for her to let me go. "Of course."

She grabs me into a tight, uncomfortable squeeze, pinching my ribs. She doesn't let go when she reaches up with one hand and throws the fairy dust on both of us. She speaks the words and my world goes black.

Two minutes later, I'm in a green park space, but I'm too dazed to take in the details.

Except for this one: a tall, human girl with spiky, blue hair is clinging to me.

I scream.

3

The blue-haired girl screams back at me.

My eyes pop wide and I make fish movements with my mouth as I take her in. "Jangle?"

She hardly resembles her fairy self, and if it weren't for her blue hair and turned up nose, I might not have recognized her.

"Tinkerbell?" she gasps.

Jangle steps way back and scans me with bulging eyes. Her mouth moves like a fish looking for food.

"You look so different," she finally sputters.

"You, too." I blink hard. "Is it really you?"

Jangle pinches herself. "Ow. Yeah, it's me."

Yes! We succeeded at coming to Peter's New York!

My new human brain slowly registers the "we."

"Jangle, what are you doing here? Why didn't you let go of me?"

She's spinning in circles looking at the tall, tall trees. A human on a contraption with two wheels whizzes by, barely missing Jangle's dancing form.

"Watch it, weirdo!" he says.

Jangle laughs out loud, hysterically. "We're out of Neverland, Tink!"

"I know that, but it was supposed to be just me."

Her laughter stops and she steadies her gaze on me. "Yeah, well you don't get to call all the shots, you know. I'm so bored of Neverland and I wanted to leave, too. So, I hitched along on your ride."

The queen's fairy dust only works if the person doing the sending does it as an act of self-sacrifice. It's true she didn't want me to leave, but it wasn't because she'd miss me. I frown as I consider Jangle's motive. She didn't want me to leave because she hated the idea I might have an adventure without her.

She punches me playfully in the arm. "Come on, Tink. Did you really want to do this alone?"

I scowl but stay silent. It's not like I have a choice anymore.

"We need to find a reflective surface," Jangle says, linking my arm. "You won't believe what you look like now."

Though not as beautiful as Neverland, Peter's New York City is a pretty nice place. Lots of green grass and trees unlike anything I've ever seen, many with pointy leaves that are several shades of yellow and red. There are a lot of humans like Peter mulling about. Some sitting on benches feeding birds, others pushing smaller humans in wheeled carriages, and even more with dogs on short leashes. Many adult humans seem to be in a hurry, running in tight fitting clothes, with bottles in their hands and cords hanging out of their ears.

"There," Jangle says, pointing. I see a cart made out of shiny metal. As we get closer, I notice a boy cooking something on it. He hands whatever he's made to the couple waiting there. They squeeze sauce on it, first red then yellow.

"An outdoor kitchen," I say.

We approach, and Jangle ducks to look in the reflective surface.

"*Oooo*," she coos, running her fingers through her hair and making strange faces. "I look...different."

No kidding.

I duck to see the new me.

My long, yellow hair is flying about in the wind and I untangle it from my gold hoop earrings with my hands. *Oh my goodness*. My face is thin, shaped more like a heart instead of a ball, and I actually have cheek bones! My eyes are still big and green, but they're altered. I don't look like the fairy me at all.

"I like it," I say. My wings zing and shimmer in the reflection. I check over my shoulder, and they're gone.

"I can't see our wings," I say, and then point to the shiny metal surface. "Except for here."

Jangle takes note, glancing over her shoulder and back to the distorted image. "Hmm. Interesting."

The boy clears his throat. "Can I help you?"

He's peering down on us with an amused grin. He wears a tight, black shirt and skinny trousers low on his hips, held on with a black, studded belt. He brushes his hair, the color of sand, across his forehead. A small, silver ring pierces through one eyebrow and there's another in his upper lip.

"You're not from here, are you?" he says.

I stand up slowly and shake my head. "How can you tell?"

He chuckles then straightens his look like he's afraid he just offended us.

"No one has checked themselves out at my grill before. Especially dressed like that."

Jangle and I examine our clothing. It's exactly the same as what we had on before, only bigger. Loose, long-sleeve shirts cinched with wide belts, and large, shiny buckles. Our trousers end just below our knees, and we have pointy-toed slippers on our feet.

"People in New York don't dress like this," I say. Of course they wouldn't. I look around New York, and there's not one person dressed like a fairy from Neverland.

"You see all kinds," he says. His eyes are on Jangle. "I like your hair."

She giggles and runs a finger behind her ear. A blush forms on her cheeks. "Thanks."

I toss her a sharp look. *Now* she likes human boys?

Suddenly, I just want to find Peter. He'll help us learn about this New York. We need to find a place to stay before it gets dark. Funny, I haven't seen one dwelling place or shop. Just signs that say "to the zoo" or "to the pond." Both lovely places, I am certain.

"Do you know Peter?" I ask.

The boy folds his arms. "Peter's a pretty common name and New York's a big place. Got a last name?"

Peter's last name? He mentioned it once, when he talked about missing his parents. What is it? I squeeze my eyes shut, and it comes to me.

"Panelli."

"Peter Panelli?" The boy says. "Seriously?"

I say with a straight face, "I'm perfectly serious."

"He's the boy who mysteriously showed up last month after being abducted for two years. It's been all over the news. Apparently, he won't talk about what happen to him, or where he's been. I don't know him personally, but he goes to my school."

My legs tingle with nervous excitement. "You know how to find him? You must take me."

The boy lifts a hand up. "Hold your horses."

I flash Jangle a confused look. I don't see any horses.

"I don't know where he lives," the boy continues, "but he'll probably be at school tomorrow. Do you guys live here now? Where do you go to school?"

I look at him from the corner of my eye. "Where do *you* go to school?"

"Central High."

I fake a laugh. "That's where we go!"

The boy eyes us carefully. "Cool. I'm Dylan, by the way."

"I'm Tinkerbell and this is Jangle."

His eyes brighten and his eyebrow ring dances. "I get it. You don't want to give your real names. That's smart, actually."

I glance at Jangle, not at all sure why Dylan didn't believe me.

"So, do you guys want a hot dog?" he says, after a beat.

My stomach growls at the mention of food. I nod eagerly. "Thank you, Dylan. That's so kind."

He hands us each something. Long and narrow in a long, soft bun.

"What is it?" Jangle says.

He scoffs. "You really aren't from here. They're hot dogs."

I know what a dog is, and though this is hot, it certainly isn't a dog.

It's good though. "Um," I say, appreciatively.

"Uh, that's three bucks each."

"Huh?"

"Three dollars each. That's what they cost." He points to a sign. "I'd just give them to you, but I'd get fired if I were caught."

Jangle's face twists with worry, and I feel it, too. We don't have any New York money.

I pull out my satchel and reach for a tiny jewel. "Will you take this?"

Dylan's jaw drops and he opens his hand.

"Where'd you get that?"

"From our kingdom," I say.

"I knew it," Dylan says. I'm comforted by the smile that crosses his face. "You're from some obscure European nation that still has monarchs, right?"

I don't know what he just said, but I feel that being agreeable is the wisest thing to do, so I nod again.

"Look, forget it." He hands the jewel back to me. "It's on me." He pulls six pieces of paper from his pocket and puts them with the other New York money.

"There's a place on 7th that will exchange that for cash. I bet a lot of cash, so be careful with it. Not every guy is as nice as me."

I think of Captain Hook. "I know. Thanks again."

"Can you point us in the direction of the dwelling places?" Jangle asks.

Dylan's eyes sparkle with amusement when he answers her. "There are hotels and hostels all over the city. You'll find them once you leave Central Park. Just stay on 7th." He points in the direction we're supposed to go.

"Okay, thanks again," I say. "We'll see you in school."

"I'll look for you." He shoves his hands into his pockets. "Hey, can I offer a piece of advice?"

"Sure."

"You'll have to get there early to register. And I'd get some different clothes before you come."

4

We get to where the forest ends and I nearly faint. My legs quiver and buckle, and Jangle and I hold onto each other. In front of us are impossibly tall buildings and roads filled with machines carrying humans. The noise is unbelievable and equally unpleasant. I release Jangle so I can cover my ears.

What is this place?

I turn back to the forest. "Quick, Jangle. Let's go back to New York!"

She runs with me and we don't stop until that awful scene disappears. My breath is short and quick. I'm confused and afraid.

"What was that?" Jangle says, puffing.

"I don't know. Peter didn't mention such a place when he spoke of New York."

"Let's ask Dylan," Jangle suggests.

We don't have a lot of options. I only know that I don't

want to spend the night sleeping on a bench. So, I agree. Dylan seems trustworthy. He did give me back my gem.

He's packing up his cart when we return.

Jangle smiles and bats her eyelashes. I bite the inside of my lip, not sure why her interest in this human boy bothers me.

"Hi again," she begins. "We've decided we want to stay in New York, and not that place, what did you call it? Seventh? We don't like Seventh. Can you help us find a place to stay here?"

Dylan's expression flattens. "Are you for real?"

Jangle glances at me and I look at her. We look real to me.

"We're right here, Dylan," I say. "Can't you see us?"

He bends over and laughs. "And I thought I'd seen it all."

"So, you can see us?" I press. "Please, will you help us? We don't have a place to sleep tonight, and we really don't like Seventh. Is there a place here in New York where we can stay?"

Dylan wrinkles his forehead and scratches his head. "Did you guys escape from an institution or something? Are you off your meds?"

Jangle and I glance at each other again, neither of us with a clue about what he just said, but my gut tells me that this is one of those times where agreeing isn't a good idea. I shake my head slowly.

"Okay, look. I'm almost done here. Just give me a minute to lock it up, then I'll take you where you need to go."

I feel an enormous sense of relief until he leads us back toward Seventh.

"Uh, Dylan?" I tap his arm. "Why are you taking us back to Seventh?"

"Because that's where the gem store is, so you can exchange your jewel for money. And there's a rooming house nearby."

"But, we told you we want to stay in New York."

Dylan stops and stares at us. "It's all New York City. The park, 7th, and every other street on this island."

Island? Of course. New York is an island like Neverland. But why would Peter want to come back here and live in a place as horrible as Seventh?

Dylan starts walking again. "Look, I've got to get home, so if you want my help, we need to get going."

We have no choice. I grip Jangle's hand and squeeze. For the first time since leaving Neverland, I'm really glad that Jangle is with me. We will survive Seventh together.

It's an entirely new and frightening world. Towering brick and glass buildings, a mass of bodies rushing in every direction, strange and unpleasant smells, and loud noises. The honking from the mechanical machines shuttling people around hurts my ears.

We wait at the street and when a little walking-man sign lights up, we cross. Humans rush in both directions, knocking into each other without using pleasantries like "excuse me," or "pardon me." I wince as perfect strangers nudge me as they pass by.

"Watch out for the Taxis," Dylan says, pointing to the yellow machines. "They don't always see you."

Somehow we make it to the other side without being killed.

The humans stare at us, and I'm nervous that we don't

look human enough. I try to ignore them and focus on the buildings that tower on either side of the street.

Eventually, we stop in front of one that has a big gemstone etched in the glass of the window.

Dylan opens the door and lets Jangle and me in. I feel relieved when he enters, too. There are many lighted, glass cabinets in the shop, all filled with pretty gems and sparkling jewelry. Jangle and I love shiny things so we are momentarily distracted as we ogle the pretty pieces.

Dylan approaches a man standing behind one of the counters and waves us over. "My friends here have something of value they'd like to sell."

I reach into my satchel and present one of the gems.

The man holds out a meaty, dry hand. He cradles the red gem in his palm and puts a thick pair of spectacles on his nose.

"Where did you get this?"

I glance at Dylan and he shakes his head slightly. He answers for me, "It's an inheritance. A family heirloom."

The man removes his spectacles and frowns. "I don't deal in stolen property."

"It's not stolen," I say quickly, taking offence. Then I remember that I am a true thief, even if I haven't stolen the gems. I drop my shoulders and glance away, feeling humbled.

He puts the spectacles back on his face and hums. Then he names a figure, and I look to Dylan for guidance. Is it an acceptable amount? Dylan nods and I smile.

Ten minutes later, we leave the store with pockets full of paper money.

Dylan grins. "You guys are all set for the next place."

He takes us through another set of glass doors and I stop short. Clothes! Enough clothes to dress every fairy in Neverland a dozen times over (assuming the clothes come in fairy sizes, which I know they do not.)

Jangle giggles and sifts through the racks. I'm overwhelmed by the choices; I don't know where to begin.

I look to Dylan.

"You want help?" he says.

"Please."

"Good thing I have sisters," he mutters, then rifles through the dresses.

"Try this, and this and this." He hands an armful of clothes to Jangle, before turning to me. "And this, and this and this."

He points to a row of large, narrow boxes each with its own door. "You can try them on there."

I find a skirt, a blouse and a sweater in my pile. I take off my slippers and fairy clothes and put the new items on. I come out at the same time as Jangle, who is dressed similarly.

Dylan whistles. "You guys look hot!"

"Hot?" I say, perplexed. "But you gave us the sweaters. Should we remove them?"

The corner of his mouth pulls up. "No, 'hot' means you look really good."

"Oh. Good."

Dylan outfits us with more skirts and blouses, several pairs of shoes and a number of trousers he calls jeans.

"You'll probably need one of these." Dylan points to a collection of large satchels. "All the girls here carry a purse."

"They're very big," I say. You could fit a young fairy

inside one, easily. I choose a purple one and Jangle picks blue, the same bright color as her hair.

We pay with our New York paper money and leave the store dressed in new clothes, with arms loaded with shopping bags.

"Thanks, Dylan," Jangle says. She leans in against his arm. "We couldn't have done it without your help."

He nods with his chin. "I'm happy to be of service. I don't know what it's like in your country, but good-looking girls in New York know how to shop. I'm sure you'll catch on quickly."

I find the heels a little awkward to walk in, but it's nice to not be stared at so much. I keep an eye out for Peter, but never see him. I still don't like the noise and the crowds, but I find I'm not as anxious anymore.

Until Dylan says this: "I'll leave you guys here."

"What?" I say.

He points at a sign that says, "Apartments for rent."

Jangle's posture sags and I feel mine do the same. He's leaving us?

"Not sure why you're here without parents or guardians, but it's none of my business. You'll have no problem getting a place if you pay for it with cash. I'd give them enough for two or three months, then you'll get one for sure."

My eyes lock on the sign and then the building. It's as tall as the king's castle and made of dirty-looking stone. This is a proper dwelling place?

I turn to ask Dylan if he's sure, but he's walking backward away from us. "See you tomorrow in school." He waves and turns a corner out of sight.

My heart seizes and I stiffen. Jangle and I are alone in Seventh.

5

"He's cute," Jangle says with a sigh.

I shoot her a withering look. She can think of a human boy at a time like this?

"What? You can like Peter, but I can't like Dylan?"

"You just met him."

"So? You fell hopelessly in love after seeing Peter for two minutes."

She's right, but I keep my mouth shut. This isn't the time to discuss matters of the heart. The light of day is growing dim, and we need to secure a place to sleep.

Inside the apartment building, there is a staircase that leads upward at right angles. A door to the left says "Manager. Ring for service."

I press the button and wait. A thin woman with wrinkling skin and curlers in her hair opens the door.

"We're here about an apartment for rent," I say.

The woman looks us up and down with glassy eyes. "Cash only."

"We have cash."

She studies us and for a moment I fear she'll turn us away. Then she says, "There's one furnished and one not."

"Furnished, please."

"Let me get the keys."

We wait at the door and I examine the hallway. Paint peels back from the corners and dust lines the baseboards. It's dark and unfriendly, and I shiver.

The woman returns with the keys and a paper and pen, and leads us upstairs to the second floor where she opens a door with a number 4 on it.

"It's got two bedrooms each with a single bed," she says sounding bored. "You have to get your own sheets and dishes."

Dust swirls in the low light shining in through a big window facing the street. There is a little kitchen in the corner of the living room. Two small bedrooms and a latrine for personal cleansing I'm not eager to use. It has gadgets I don't understand and smells funny.

"I don't know," I say, slowly.

Jangle jumps in. "We'll take it."

"You got references?"

I remember what Dylan said. "We can pay three months in cash."

The lady purses her lips, then says, "Okay, but no parties, or troubling the neighbors, otherwise you're out with no refund." She puts the papers on the counter. "What are your names?"

Jangle shakes her head subtly. Dylan thought we were joking when we told him our names. What will this lady think?

"Um, Belle?" I say. The lady writes it down, so it must be okay.

"And Jan," Jangle adds.

"Last names?"

Right. Like Peter's last name is Panelli.

"Uh, Fair..." I almost finish with Fairy, but the lady starts talking.

"That's spelled F-E-H-R?"

"Uh, yes."

She looks at Jangle. "And you?"

"The same."

"You don't look like sisters. Cousins?"

"Yes," I say again.

"I'm Mrs. Weeks, the landlady. Sign here."

We sign our fake names and she walks out with our cash, leaving us to wander about our new home with much lighter pockets.

"It's so dreary and unhappy. Nothing cozy, or homey about this place at all." I sigh. Nothing like our huts in Neverland.

"Jan," Jangle says. "We have to get used to our new names...Belle."

We walk down the short hall. Jangle chooses the room on the left and I walk into the one on the right. It's tiny, big enough for the narrow bed and one dresser. I drop my bags and hang up my new clothes in the closet and line up my new shoes in a row along the wall.

When I'm done I meet Jangle in her room. "We have to go shopping again," I say. "For sheets. And dishes."

Jangle fingers what's left of our money. "I hope we have

enough. We'll have to sell another gem soon. How many did you bring?"

I loosen the strings on my little satchel and count. "Four. We should be okay if we're careful."

Seventh doesn't close down at night. Nor does any street. In fact it seems to get busier with even more people in a hurry to get somewhere.

My whole being is exhausted. I can hardly believe I awoke this morning in my pretty purple canopy bed in Neverland. The swirl of Seventh makes me dizzy and I'm drenched with despair.

Oh what have I done! Why did I think that I could leave Neverland behind for a strange land! I'm the craziest fairy in the world.

Jangle looks as beat up as I feel. I'm wrong, though. I'm not the craziest fairy in the world—she is. I, at least, came for love.

"Tink...Belle," she begins. "I think that might be the kind of shop we're looking for."

She points to a brightly lit store, but I'm not paying attention to her. My eyes catch the back of a familiar head. It's a boy with dark, shaggy hair, and even though this version is taller and dressed differently, I'd know that swagger anywhere.

"Peter!"

My heart explodes. I've found him! "It's Peter." I run for him and Jangle follows.

I call his name again, but he doesn't seem to hear me. There's so much noise, I'm not surprised.

I can't wait to see his face again, pull him close. He's going to be *sooooo* surprised to see me!

My insides overflow with glee.

I have to dodge through the crowds, but I finally reach him. I tug his shirt and say his name again.

He turns and when he sees me he says, "Can I help you?"

My heart drops. This boy has brown eyes and his mouth is all wrong.

It's not my Peter.

6

I walk cautiously through the enormous store. It's super bright with high ceilings and slippery floors. I cup my eyes from the glare. Shops in Neverland are nothing like this. They're much smaller (of course), and warm, and colorful, and ... cozy. Plus you don't have to pay for the things you need. You just check them out. There's enough for everyone, all the time. Fairies are very efficient that way.

"Do you like this?" Jangle says, holding up a blanket for my bed.

I shrug. "Yes, it's fine. Let's just get what we need and go."

Normally, I'd be interested in how we decorated our home, but my heart is so discouraged and my new human body so tired, I just want to go back to our apartment and sleep.

We pay for our purchases and exit out onto the street.

I point. "Let's take one of those yellow machines."

"They're called Taxis," Jangle says. "And I agree."

She waves one down just like we watched other people do. It's my first time riding in a motorized machine, and I can't stop gripping the door rest like we'd die if I let go. I let out little gasps when we stop and start.

The Taxi driver yells out his window and honks the horn. "They're shooting a movie," he explains. "Always another movie or TV show. Who cares? I just want to drive through Times Square when I need to."

People here talk in riddles. I wish the driver would quit talking and just drive. My nerves are shooting off by the time we arrive at our apartment entrance. The driver points to the fee listed on his dashboard and I remove the bills from my big, new purse.

"That was fun," Jangle says, and I can't tell if she's kidding or not.

We put our dishes away in near silence. Neither of us can talk about just how topsy-turvy this day has been.

We say goodnight. I quickly make my bed and I climb into it. The room is dark and not at all quiet. The pipes groan and I can hear footsteps overhead. The city noise coming through the closed window never lets up.

Tomorrow, we go to a human school for the first time, and I can't sleep. Which is bad. I'm finally going to see Peter and I want to look my best.

Plus, it's kind of creepy, being alone in my room in the dark in Seventh. I snap my fingers and my fairy dust creates a little light.

Instead of comforting me, it casts eerie shadows against the bare walls. My chest tightens at the thought of remaining in this tiny room alone. I tread softly to Jangle's room and knock.

"Are you awake?" I whisper.

"Yes."

"Can I sleep with you?"

She rolls over, and I get the feeling she feels the same way about being alone tonight.

"Tomorrow will be better," I say when I get in. "You'll see."

I SQUAWK AWAKE the next morning, completely forgetting where I am and all of the events of the previous day. I scuttle away from the large form beside me in this strange bed and strange room, freaking out until a blue head pops up from under a pillow.

Then the whole thing washes over me like a wave in the Mermaid Lagoon.

I breathe deeply. It's just Jangle, and we're in Seventh not Neverland. I came here for Peter and once I find him, we'll go back to Neverland. Peter must be dying to return there. How could anyone want to stay in this horrible, loud, crowded place?

"Ugh," Jangle says, wiping her eyes. "The noise in Seventh is unbearable. How does anyone sleep here?"

I shiver in the morning chill as I pad to the latrine. I pause at the door, remembering why I don't like this room. It's dirty and stained and smells strange. I spray more of the cleaner we picked up last night. I turn the taps and marvel again at how the water instantly appears. In Neverland we have to collect our water from the well. The warm spray that sprinkles out over the tub almost makes up for the other funkiness.

I dress in one of the outfits Dylan chose for me—a short, dark blue skirt, a pink, lacy blouse and grey sweater—and meet Jangle in the kitchen.

She stares into an empty cupboard. "We should've bought some food."

"There's a food place next door."

"Right. Let's go there."

My toes pinch in my new shoes and I'm tempted to wear my fairy slippers.

Jangle pulls on my arm, "Come on, slow poke. I'm starving."

The shop sells tea and a whole lot of other drinks I've never heard of, like Americano, Macchiato, and Espresso.

We order two raspberry teas and two biscuits with butter. It's really busy in the shop and we're fortunate to find a table.

"At least the food in Seventh is pretty good," Jangle says.

My mouth is full so I just nod in agreement.

I sip my tea to clear my throat "I wonder where Dylan's school is," I say.

Jangle gawks at me. "I wonder *what* school is."

"Me, too. But it sounds like all humans Peter's age go to one."

"The Taxi might know."

"Good idea."

We leave the shop and stand by the curb to wait for a yellow machine to come by. I see one, fling one arm out, and whistle before shouting "Taxi!"

The yellow machine stops in front of us.

"You're a natural," Jangle says.

I ask the driver to take us to Central School. My stomach swirls with anticipation. This is it! I'm finally going to see Peter!

I close my eyes and dream of our reunion.

I call his name and when he turns to see me, it's actually him. He flicks his hair, dark and shiny, off his beautiful face. His blue eyes light up with happiness and his dimples pop up on both cheeks. He says my name and it sounds smooth and sweet, like honey.

He wraps me in his arms and I finally tell him what I should have told him long ago in the poppy meadow. That I love him. He kisses my forehead, then the tip of my nose and finally my lips, telling me he loves me, too...

A male voice pulls me out of my reverie. "This is it."

I stare past Jangle's blue head, out the Taxi window. The school has three levels, a mesh fence and lots and lots of teenaged humans flowing in and out the front doors.

The Taxi driver swivels his head to look at us and frowns. "This is the right school, no?"

"Yes," I say, handing him the money he asks for.

Jangle and I stand on the sidewalk in shock. With so many people, how will we ever find Peter? I don't even know where to start.

"Are you guys okay?"

The voice comes from a slight girl with brown hair and glasses.

"I'm not sure," I say.

"You must be new here."

Jangle and I both nod mutely.

"I'm Ivy. I'll take you to the office. You'll have to sign in."

"Thank you, Ivy," I say feeling very appreciative. "My name is, uh, Belle and this is my cousin, Jan."

Jangle and I huddle close together for fear of getting swallowed whole by these human teenagers. The halls are wide with grey, speckled floors, and long and narrow, yellow, metal containers along the walls. Kids open them to retrieve books and shut them with a loud bang.

Ivy escorts us into a room that is much calmer than the hallway we just passed through. Three ladies sit at desks behind a long counter. One of them rises to greet us.

"Mrs. Mullins," Ivy says. "These girls are new."

Mrs. Mullins is round with two chins, but her eyes are soft and she smiles at us kindly. "Well, then, let's get you registered."

We give her our address and use Mrs. Weeks as the name of our guardian, but are stumped when it comes to birth dates. We never thought this one through. As fairies, we've been alive for a long time in human years, but I'm not certain how old we are here.

"Month and date?" Mrs. Mullins asks again.

"May 12th?" I say.

Mrs. Mullins laughs. "You sound like you're not sure. And you're fifteen?" I nod and she writes down the corresponding year.

Jangle has a little time to think hers through. I wonder what she'll say.

"May 11th."

I shoot her a glare from the corner of my eye. One day before me? She just wants to be older.

"Oh, close cousins," Mrs. Mullins says happily. "You must have so much fun celebrating your birthdays together."

"Yes," I say, hoping I sound believable. "It's so much fun."

It takes forever and a day to get our classes sorted out, and I can't stop sneaking peaks out the windows, watching the teenagers moving along the hall. Some are happy and laughing with their friends. Others are alone, keeping their heads down and eyes on their feet.

No sign of Peter.

It's becoming clear exactly what school is. We're here to learn about the human world: its history, its literature, its science. I'm actually very intrigued.

Mrs. Mullins equips us with a school map with a pink line drawn to our first class.

"All the sophomore classes are on the first floor, the juniors are on the second and the seniors are on the third." She flashes a broad, sympathetic smile. "The gym and the cafeteria are also on the first floor, so just stay on this level and you'll be fine. I'm sure you'll have the place memorized by the end of the day."

She gives us each a small metal contraption along with a small piece of paper. "Here are your locks, their combinations and your locker numbers."

Then she shuttles us out into the hall and points us in the appropriate direction. Thankfully, Jangle and I are in all the same classes so we can stay together in this crazy place.

Despite the map, we stand in the hall like we can't read (we can!), forcing the teens to break around us like water in a stream splitting around a boulder. We're cemented to the spot, two useless fairies intimidated by their foreign surroundings.

We'd have probably become permanent statues there if not for Dylan spotting us.

"You made it!" he yells, pushing through the crowd.

"Dylan!" Jangle jumps, and I grab her sweater to keep her from throwing herself at him.

His eyes have that glint in them again. I'm happy we amuse him.

"Well, you guys look chipper," he says. "Let me see your class list."

I hand it to him and he hums. "We're in the same first class, history with Mrs. Winger. I'll take you there."

His eyes land on our empty arms. "Where are your things?"

"What things?" I say.

"You know, paper, pens?"

Jangle and I exchange worried looks. We are so unprepared for human school!

His eyebrow ring hitches up. "Where did you say you were from?"

"Neverl—," Jangle starts.

"We *never* said." I shoot Jangle a warning look. I swirl around hoping to distract him from his line of questioning. "Dylan, do we look hot again today?"

His eyes widen, and his mouth twitches. "Yeah, you do."

"Good. Let's go to class." I link one of his arms with mine and Jangle takes the other.

"By the way," Dylan says. "When are you going to tell me your real names?"

"Belle Fehr," I say.

Jangle giggles. "I'm Jan Fehr."

"You're related?"

We chirp together, "Cousins."

We come to a classroom and Dylan says, "This is it."

I barely hear him though. My ears clog, and the swoosh of my heart fills my head. I let go of Dylan's arm and the teens in the hallway blur into my peripheral vision. As far as I'm concerned, there are only two people left standing in the hallway, in this whole school, in the universe.

I see Peter.

His hair is shorter, but I'd recognize those blue eyes and dimples anywhere. He's taller and his shoulder's are, wow, broader and his bicep flexes when he runs his hand through his hair, causing my heart to screech to a stop. He's talking to someone, and laughing, and I'm momentarily confused. He seems *happy* here.

I review the fantasy I had on the ride over, the one where I run to him and throw myself into his embrace, and he holds me....

My legs are rooted to the floor, and my throat feels like it's stuffed with fluff from the silk forest trees.

I feel a sharp nudge in my side.

"That's him, right?" Jangle says. "What are you waiting for? Go."

Peter turns toward us at that moment, but his gaze moves fleetingly over our heads before he goes inside the classroom. He doesn't *recognize* me.

"*Belle,*" Jangles says. "Are you okay?"

I squeak out. "No."

A bell rings, and I nearly jump from my skin. Dylan pokes his head through the classroom door.

"You better get in here. You don't want to be marked late for your first class."

Jangle holds me up and pushes me in. The room is filled with desks situated in rows. Dylan points to two empty near the back, and I slide into one and stare blankly, like I'm comatose.

Peter sits three seats ahead of me. I can't peel my eyes off the back of his head.

I hear Dylan say to Jangle, "Is your cousin all right?"

I want to go to Peter, I do. He's the entire reason I'm here. But I'm afraid. Maybe he'll be mad that I came. What if he *rejects* me?

And then I see *her*, like she materialized out of thin air.

The person Peter's been talking to and laughing with this whole time sits in the desk beside him. A girl with red hair that falls in pretty curls down her back. A girl with a bright smile and dark eyes that never leave Peter's face.

A girl.

"Who's that?" I hiss. I turn to Dylan for the answer.

"Oh, I see what's going on. You're after that Peter Panelli guy. That's why you were asking about him."

"Who's that girl?" I press.

"That's his girlfriend, Wendy."

Girlfriend?

My vision blurs to black. I fall off my chair.

7

We're alone in the girls' restroom, missing our second class and I'm sobbing onto Jangle's shoulder.

"He has a *girlfriend.*"

I'm leaning against the counter, staring at my reflection in the mirror. My eyes are bloodshot and my wings droop woefully. I'm like a plant in dire need of water.

Jangle pats me tentatively on the back. "There, there."

"How long has he been back from Neverland?" I spit out. "A month? He sure didn't waste his time!"

I enter a stall to pluck off several tissues from the toilet paper roll and blow. "I came here for nothing, Jangle. *We* came for nothing."

She folds her arms across her chest and taps her toe, reminding me of her fairy self and how she used to do that all the time and how it used to bug me so much.

"What?" I say.

"I kind of like it here."

"You kind of like *Dylan* here."

"So what if I do? Just because things didn't work out for you, doesn't mean they can't for me."

"You think we should *stay*?"

She studies her nails. "For a little while. There's a lot to Seventh we haven't seen." Her eyes meet mine. "Besides, how exactly are we going to get back?"

I close my eyes and my lips tremble. I don't know. I didn't care about that part of the equation when I planned my escape from Neverland. I just wanted to find Peter, and now that I have, I realize my plan was horribly flawed.

"Tink?"

I look in the mirror at my bright red nose, and then catch her eyes in the reflection. Her wings flap impatiently.

"I haven't really figured that part out," I confess.

"You're kidding me, right?"

"I just figured that Peter got to Neverland on his own somehow, that it must be possible to get there again that way."

"And what way was *that*?"

I shrink into myself. "A green glow?"

She narrows her gaze. "A green glow."

I feel trapped by her interrogating tone. No one asked her to tag along. "Yes. A green glow. There was one on the horizon in Neverland the day we left."

Jangle unfolds her arms. "I remember seeing that. You think the green glow is some kind of portal?"

I haven't thought about it, but I'm not about to admit that to her. "Yeah. I do."

"But you don't know how to call up the green glow?"

I shake my head. "No. We just have to wait for it, I guess."

"Okay, well, that means we have time to explore Seventh a bit more, and have a little adventure." Her eyebrows dance. "Maybe a little romance?"

I sniffle. "For you, maybe."

"Tink, have a look around. There are plenty of fish in the Mermaid Lagoon."

Hrumph. Plenty of mermaids, too. And apparently Peter likes redheaded ones.

Try as I might I can't keep the tears from leaking out of my eyes. "Oh, Jangle, I'm such a blinking fool. Peter doesn't care about me at all."

Jangle turns to the mirror and works her fingers through her hair. "You know, *Belle,* maybe you're giving up too easily."

I hiccup. "What do you mean?"

She faces me. "Well, he's with Wendy right now, but that doesn't mean he'll be with her forever. It's not like they're married."

I hiccup again. "Are you suggesting I try to break them up?"

Jangle shrugs and turns back to the mirror. "It sounds horrid when you say it that way. More like, make Peter see why he should choose you instead of her. Make him want *you* more than he wants *her.*"

I stare hard at her. "Jangle, I'm glad you're my friend because I'd hate to have you as an enemy."

"Fine. Do nothing. Suit yourself."

I grumble. She has a point. Peter just thinks he likes that

Wendy girl because he hasn't met me yet. The human me. I nibble my lip. Maybe I *am* giving up too easily.

The door opens and Jangle tugs me away from the mirror before the girl catches a glimpse of our wings.

"Let's go see Mrs. Mullins," Jangle says. "Find out how we get back into class."

Mrs. Mullins's smile falls when we walk into the office.

"Why aren't you two in class?"

"We got horribly lost," Jangle says, "and then Belle had an emotional breakdown in the girls room."

I glare at her, but my red eyes must convince Mrs. Mullins to have pity. She scratches something on two small pieces of pink paper.

"Give these to Mrs. O'Brien." She points to a room on a school map lying on her desk. "Do you think you can find your way?"

"Yes," I say. "Thank you, Mrs. Mullins."

All the wrinkles in Mrs. O'Briens' face pull into a frown when we show up at her class. She takes our pink slips and flicks us away with her bony hand motioning for us to find a seat. My eyes scan the faces of the students looking for Peter, but he's not here. And neither is the redhead. I let out a quiet breath. I'm not ready to face them again so soon, and I'm grateful for the break.

The only face I recognize is the girl, Ivy, who helped us find the office this morning. She catches my eye and gives me a smile and a little finger wave. I smile back.

All I have is the notebook and pen that Dylan lent me in our first class. I lay it on my desk and look out the window. The sun is shining and I'm in New York and Seventh. I saw

Peter. I should be happy. I squeeze my eyes tight to keep the tears at bay.

Mrs. O'Brien goes on about a book and author I've never heard of. I stare blankly at a poster of a person reading, fixating on the tattered corner pulling away from a tack. She asks one of the kids to hand out small, paperback books. I flip through it with little curiosity. My mind is too cluttered and I can't focus on the words. Finally, the bell rings.

"Lunch!" Ivy says to me and Jangle. "Do you guys want to sit with me?"

"Sit where?" I say.

"In the cafeteria." She pushes her glasses higher on her nose. "You know, where kids go to eat lunch?"

"Sure," Jangle says. "Where is it?"

"I'll show you."

I'm glad we're taking a break to eat because I'm suddenly famished. My head pulses and I rub my temples. Being human is more taxing than I imagined. The kids here all seem to know each other and where they're going, and I feel lost and alone.

At least I have Jangle.

We enter a large room full of tables and join a lineup of kids. Ivy directs us to pick up a tray. Ladies on the other side of the counter wearing white coats and hair nets, dish out food.

"What is this?" I ask.

Ivy looks at me with big eyes. "Hello? It's mac and cheese."

The lady scoops the yellow noodles onto the plates on our trays and we pay at the register with our paper money.

Jangle and I follow Ivy to a table where they sit down. I, on the other hand, am paralyzed, standing still, tray in hand.

Peter walks into the room. Alone. A trill of excitement shoots through my body and I even feel a spark race through wings I know aren't visible. Phantom wings. My eyes lock in on him as he walks across the room. I will him to see me, to know me.

Finally, his eyes land on mine and he holds my gaze. My nerves crackle and I think I'm going to explode like fireworks, right here in the cafeteria. I mouth his name, Peter. He narrows his eyes, then looks away. He walks past me to his group of friends, like he doesn't know me at all.

I hear Ivy say, "Is there something wrong with your cousin?"

I turn back to them, and they're staring at me. The whole table is staring. I'm making such an idiot of myself. My knees buckle and I grab a chair, almost dropping my tray.

"Whoa." Dylan is suddenly at my side, rescuing my mac and cheese from a doleful encounter with the floor.

"Oh, thanks. Sorry. I don't know what came over me," I say.

"Or *who* came over you," he mutters, taking a seat beside Jangle.

I pick at my lunch, feeling defeated. Coming to New York was a bad idea. Peter doesn't know me. He has a new life. He's obviously forgotten all about Neverland.

Maybe that's what's wrong with him? Maybe he has *amnesia*?

If that's true, then all is lost.

I snap back to reality in time to catch Ivy introducing two kids who've joined our table."...and this is Miles and

Rita." Miles has orange hair parted to the side and a face full of freckles. Rita has dark skin and black, curly hair.

"Hi," I say. I force a smile, even though I can't remember being sadder than I am today. I don't want my new friends to think I'm unfriendly.

My eyes continue to dart to the table where Peter sits. I admit that sometimes I can be pretty clueless, but even I can tell my obsession with Peter is pathetic.

"Do you know him?" Rita says to me.

My attention is drawn back to the table. "Know who?"

"Peter Panelli? You keep staring at him."

My mouth drops and I'm not sure how to answer her.

Jangle jumps in. "Not really. Only by reputation."

"That's so weird that he was missing for two whole years," Miles says. Sandwich bits are stuck in his teeth. "And he still hasn't told anyone what happened to him."

"I heard he was kidnapped by terrorists for ransom." Rita sips her soda.

Miles wipes his mouth with the back of his hand. "I heard he was so upset about his parent's divorce, he ran away to live with relatives overseas. His father moved to London last year."

"Well, whatever happened, I'm sure he's traumatized," Ivy says. "He'll reveal it to his therapist eventually."

I look back at Peter and see him laughing at something one of his friends said. "He doesn't look traumatized to me."

"He's repressing it," Rita says. "Someday he'll snap and when he does, it's gonna be ugly. I just hope he snaps at home and not at school."

"Yikes," Dylan says. "You're casting a pretty dim light on the boy."

"I'm just saying, if I were Wendy's parents, I'd be worried."

My heart pinches at the mention of the redheaded girl's name. Why is Rita talking like that? She thinks Peter is bad?

"He's not like that," I say, feeling protective. "He's smart, and brave, and kind."

She gives me the stinky eye. "I thought you didn't know him."

I stall, realizing I've given myself away.

Rita puts her palms up. "Hey, I didn't mean anything by it. Just, you can't lose two years of your life and not be affected by it, that's all."

My eyes dart back to Peter. He tosses French fries into his mouth, and pats one of the guys on the back. He doesn't look dangerous, or repressed, whatever Rita meant by that.

He looks happy. Content.

Like he doesn't miss me or Neverland at all.

I should let him go. Leave him to live his happy human life. I'll go back to Neverland without him. I'll confess everything to the king, and face the consequences of my actions.

I feel my invisible wings hang down my back in humiliation. I'm such a bad fairy.

Jangle slaps my arm and whispers in my ear. "Snap out of it. You're like a black cloud over our table."

"I want to go home."

"We can't miss the afternoon classes. Apparently that is frowned upon."

"I mean I want to go back to Neve..."

Jangle presses a finger to my lips. "Don't say that word aloud here."

"Fine. But I do."

"I never pegged you as one to give up so easily."

I wrinkle my nose at her. It's easy for her to say. She's never lost at love.

"Aren't you at least going to talk to him before you leave?" Jangle stabs me with her elbow. "You did come all this way."

Then she nods over my shoulder and I know Peter's headed toward us.

8

The thought of talking to Peter makes my heart bounce around in my chest like a rubber ball. I turn slowly, steadying myself and zero in on his face. Bright eyes, chiseled features. Handsome. Very, very handsome. He's taking his tray to the receptacle, having left his friends talking loudly about something called football. He isn't looking at my face but he's going to walk past my table in two seconds.

This is my chance. I stand too abruptly, knocking my chair over. It rattles loudly against the floor and the whole cafeteria grows quiet.

Peter sees me again and his eyes squint in confusion. I muster up my nerve and take a step toward him.

"Peter!"

It's not my voice. I swivel around and the redheaded Wendy springs into the room, her curls bouncing with each step.

"There you are," she says taking his hand. "You were supposed to meet me in the choir room."

Peter rubs the back of his neck with his free hand. "Oh, man. I totally forgot. Got caught up in football talk." He presses close to her. "Can I make it up to you?"

Wendy looks up with a wide smile. "Of course."

They leave and I watch with my mouth hanging open, not believing how that Wendy girl just stole my thunder. Just blew in and swept my Peter away.

The bell rings and Ivy brushes passed me. "Man, Belle, you got it bad."

"Got what bad?" I ask, confused that she called me a man.

"The hots for Peter Panelli."

I fan my face with my hand. I do feel a little warm.

"You need to tone it down a notch." She stops to give me a stern look. "Or like, a thousand notches."

Rita joins Ivy and they turn to leave. "No kidding, sister."

"We're cousins!" I shout to her back.

Jangle stands by me. "I don't think that's what she meant. Let's go."

Dylan helps us find our next class. Algebra. Whatever that is.

"Are you in this class, too?" I ask hopefully. Dylan adds a measure of calm that I'm in dire need of.

He shakes his head. "Nope. Next one though. See you then."

I wonder what sort of evil this class has in store. Plenty it turns out. It's all about numbers and a few infrequently used letters. But the worst of it is the girl sitting at the desk to my right.

The Wendy girl. *Arg.*

She glares at me like I'm her biggest enemy.

Maybe I am.

Maybe she should be afraid.

I glare back.

The teacher, this one is called Mr. Wong, (blink, I hope I can remember all these new names), scratches something on the board that looks like a foreign language.

$2X(3Y+X)=Z$

What?

At least the other classes were in the English language. I swallow and glance at Jangle. Her face expresses the panic I'm feeling.

We should definitely stop coming to this class. Especially if *she's* going to be here every time.

Finally, the bell goes and she steps in front of me before I can make it out the door.

Her stare burns holes through me. "Keep your eyes and your hands off my boyfriend."

Even though she doesn't touch me, I feel slapped. She spins away leaving me shaking like a leaf.

"Did you hear that?" I say to Jangle.

She tugs on her hair. "Yes."

I storm out the classroom like I'm going to give the Wendy girl a piece of my mind, though I have no idea what that might be.

Peter is there, leaning against a locker, looking down on Wendy's head. She sees me standing across the hall and smirks.

Then she reaches for Peter's face, cups his chin with her hand, and plants a kiss right on his mouth!

I gasp and tremble.

I feel my feet taking me there, when a sharp tug pulls me back into the classroom.

Jangle gives me a look of warning. "I don't think confronting Peter in public is what Ivy meant by toning it down."

"She kissed him because she saw me looking. She did it to spite me."

"Don't let her think she's won. If you make a scene, she will."

I hate it when Jangle's right.

But this isn't over. I watch as Wendy leads Peter down the hall, holding tightly to his arm, turning her head to shoot darts at me with her eyes.

I shoot darts back.

This means war.

The end of Episode 2.

I hope you enjoyed *New York, New York*—I'd love it if you'd leave a review on Amazon. They are very helpful to authors and help readers find the books they love.

Read on for an excerpt from Episode 3, LOVE STINKS.

Elle Strauss
Love Stinks
episode 3

LOVE STINKS

LOVE, TINK - EPISODE 3

LOVE STINKS

Episode 3 in the Love, Tink Series

by
Lee Strauss

SUMMARY

LOVE STINKS, *the third episode in the Love, Tink novella series finds Tinkerbell enrolled in a New York City school as* Belle Fehr. *Peter Panelli finally notices her, but not in the way she would like. Wendy has her claws in deep and Peter appears devoted to her.*

Should "Belle" give up and go back to Neverland? How exactly is she to do that?

And what is with that man she spotted in Central Park who looks suspiciously like Captain Hook?

1

"Oh my fairy wings," Jangle says. "Your face is as rosy as a gem, and not at all appealing."

I'm watching Wendy the redhead clutching Peter's hand as she drags him down the hall. She squishes her face at me just as they turn the corner.

"Urg! That girl!" I spit out. "What does Peter see in her?"

"Uh, I don't know." Jangle's eyebrows arch. "She's female and pretty and not *mad*." She links my arm. "Come on. Let's find our next class."

"There's another one?" I whine.

"Actually, there's two more."

I groan into her shoulder. "You got to be kidding. This is the longest day ever."

Jangle is the map reader of the two of us—my disappointing non-meet up with Peter, and the *girlfriend* discovery—has rendered me useless. She navigates her way to the next classroom and announces to me that the subject of the hour is biology.

Good. Finally something I know about. In Neverland we learn all about cell structure, photosynthesis, anatomy, and plant and fairy reproduction. Another bonus is that there is no one in this class I know. Not Peter and the redhead, nor Ivy, Dylan, Miles or Rita. No one to judge me and I know they do. They think I'm silly, that I got the hots for Peter Panelli and that I need to *tone it down*.

I take in a long, deep breath. How in the king's name will I accomplish that? My Peter Panelli gauge is running high to burn out.

The teacher introduces himself to me and Jangle as Mr. Douglas. He's tall and very slim, like an elf. He has long, straight brown hair which is pulled back from a narrow face into a ponytail. His expression is blank as he hands out a multiple choice worksheet.

I work my way through the questions even though the image of Wendy kissing Peter—*her lips on his, they way they closed their eyes and moved their mouths, his hands on her waist*—is seared on my mind. I try to push it away but my emotions refuse to dislodge it. Anger, jealousy, sadness: they're all rolled up in one big nasty ball of fiery emotion.

Peter doesn't recognize me and I can't get past the Wendy barrier to tell him who I am. Plus, a small, no *big*, part of me is terrified that he'll be angry that I left Neverland to find him. Or worse, that he won't care at all.

I finish the biology questions before the bell rings and doodle on the side of the paper. My mind escapes to calmer, happier times. Just yesterday I woke up in my purple, canopy bed in

Neverland, with the morning sun shining warmly through my hut windows. The village outside my door was filled with fairies going about their business: working, playing, eating, laughing.

My hand moves quickly, filling up the white space along the edge of the page with small sketches of fairies with pointy wings.

The bell finally rings and I follow Jangle to Mr. Douglas's desk to hand in our work.

"Is this biology or art class?" he mutters as he receives my pages. I offer an apologetic shrug and he waves me away.

"Where to now?" I ask Jangle. I don't care where she leads me, as long as Peter isn't there. I don't have the fortitude to deal with him anymore. I just want to go back to our apartment and then figure out how to get back to Neverland. I'm sick of life in Seventh.

I follow Jangle through the crowded hallway with scooped shoulders and a heavy heart. Though I've given up on talking to Peter, my senses are constantly alert, and my eyes scan the faces as we push through. I sigh with a mix of relief and disappointment when I don't see him.

We pause at the entrance of the next room. It's different from the others. It's colorful, with walls covered with drawings and paintings, open shelves of art supplies, and instead of individual desks, there are rows of tables, each with two chairs tucked underneath.

Jangle tugs on her blue hair. "This looks fun."

It does, actually. Fairies are very creative, and this room shouted "make something."

"Where should we sit?" I ask.

We stand by the door, filled with uncertainty. A young teacher arrives. She wears a loose blouse with rows of beads around her neck and a flouncy skirt. Her brunette hair is up in a messy bun and she has leather sandals on her feet.

"You must be the new girls," she says with a friendly smile. "I'm Ms Janlinski. Welcome to my art class."

She gestures to the half empty room. "It's open seating, so sit wherever you like. Try not to sit in the same place every class. Change is good for creativity."

I walk mindlessly to an empty table by the window, sit and prop my chin in my hand. Outside there is a grassy field and a cement pad with two posts on either end. A few kids are throwing a big, orange ball into a net hanging from the top of one.

Jangle sits beside me and taps her fingers on the table. "This is so exciting. I wonder what we get to do."

She squeals softly and I look to see what brought on her expression of delight. Dylan, of course. His sneakers squeak on the white, marked up floor. His eyebrow ring arches up when he sees Jangle and the energy between them zings as she stares back. He sits at the table behind us motioning to the empty seat beside him. Jangle springs out of her seat and leaves me alone.

Traitor! I can't believe she'd abandon me like that. Especially since I'm obviously having a very trying day. I'm the one who's supposed to find love in New York! I'm the one whose object of affection doesn't even know I exist. I'm the one who's mocked and tormented by Peter's redheaded girlfriend!

I *hrumph* and go back to staring out the window. How unfair that Jangle is finding love while I'm so miserable. *She* wasn't even supposed to come to Peter's New York.

I hear her chair scrape across the floor and sense her

sitting down beside me, but I don't look at her. Maybe she feels bad for leaving me for Dylan. She should. I decide to just let her sit quietly and think about our friendship.

When she doesn't say anything or slap my arm, I swivel to check that she's still breathing.

And then I lose my breath.

It's not Jangle in the seat beside me. It's *Peter*.

2

Oh, blink!

My heart stops. I'm completely frozen in my seat. Every nerve ending buzzes from the tips of my toes to the edges of my taut, invisible wings. My lungs completely deflate and I dig my fingernails into my legs. Somehow I manage to glance over my shoulder at Jangle, my eyes wide and pleading for help. She and Dylan are smirking, and making silent laughing movements with open mouths.

I hate them.

A strangled sound escapes my lips and I clasp a hand over them.

"Are you okay?" Peter says. I'm mute but I nod, *yes*.

"You don't mind me sitting here do you?"

I shake my head, *no*.

A strange, uncomfortable expression takes over his face; like he wishes he could leave but is trapped. He explains, "It was the only seat left."

I turn my head sharply to the front of the room and place

my hands flat on the table, wishing desperately that Ms Janlinski would start speaking. Or singing or dancing. Anything to move this massive awkwardness between me and Peter to somewhere else.

"Close your eyes, everyone," Ms Janlinski's says from the front of the room. "And take deep cleansing breaths." She links her fingers and walks softly between the tables. "Just breathe."

I pinch my eyes shut.

Everyone is breathing softly except me.

I'm hyperventilating.

I can feel the heat from Peter's transformed, manly body, like a force field between us. I peek at him from the corner of my eye. His face is relaxed, peaceful, like he's completely unaware of me.

How nice to live in complete ignorant bliss!

I make puffing sounds from tight lips.

He whispers, "Are you okay?"

Peter's looking at me now. I zip my mouth, but the pressure in my skull is going to blow my eyeballs out.

My head moves up and down like a bouncy ball, and a little squeak pops from my mouth.

Peter's eyebrows furrow in doubt but he straightens in his chair and closes his eyes again.

Ms Janlinski continues in a low, soft voice. "Release the stress of the day's events and clear your mind until it's as blank as a white page."

Is she serious? Does she know what I've been through already? If I release the stress of the day's events into this room, everyone will be swimming in it.

And the day's only half over!

I twist my neck until I can see Jangle's face. It's calm and restful, like she's ready to fall asleep any minute.

I want to throw something at her.

"Now imagine a magical paintbrush," Ms Janlinski coos. "Let it create on the blank page."

A magical paintbrush? This I can do. I take a deep breath and release it slowly, focusing on my paintbrush and an imaginary blank page. *Relax, Tink.* I let the brush go. It paints Neverland and a younger Peter shooting arrows at red and yellow birds that are fortunate Peter's aim isn't very good. I remember our happy times and for a brief moment, I'm back there.

I smell the sweet scent of hibiscus and jasmine and hear the whistling of the wind through the broad leaves of the silk forest. I see the poppy fields in the meadow and brightly colored birds flying through clear, blue sky. The glittering fairy village overlooking the ocean. The king's palace sparkling like a gigantic jewel on the crest of Blue Mountain. Silver dolphins playing in Mermaid Lagoon.

I purposefully shut out Captain Hook, the pirates and the Lost Boys.

Also flirtatious mermaids.

"Take out your sketch pads," Ms Janlinski says, breaking the spell, "and draw the masterpiece on your mind."

Peter pulls up a large sketch pad he had balancing against the table leg. I feel dumb because, of course, I don't have any supplies. I turn back to Jangle. Dylan's peeling off a sheet from his pad to give to her, but they both seem to have forgotten me. They are so wrapped up in each other I can't get either one to look my way. Peter sees me squirm.

"Here, you can have one of mine." He pushes his paper to me and pulls off another sheet for himself.

I swallow dryly, then force my mouth to move. "Thanks."

Peter picks up his pencil and poises it over his page. I watch, fascinated. The strength of his fingers, the muscles tensing in his forearms, the crinkle of skin around his eyes as he focuses his concentration. The classroom disappears and it's just Peter and me, alone together.

He clears his throat and the room returns.

"You're making me nervous," he says without looking at me.

My face flushes hot with mortification. I shift in my chair and stare hard at my blank page. In the background, behind the roar of my pulse pounding in my ears, I hear the scratching sounds of pencils working feverously.

Focus, Tinkerbell. Draw something.

My hand moves on its own accord and before I know it, I've filled the midsection of my paper with fairies. I lose myself so completely; I'm free for a short while from the torment caused by Peter's nearness.

Peter places his colored pencils in the middle of the table, indicating with a small wave that I can use them, and I reach for a handful: blue, green, pink, purple. I color in the wings, and the hair.

"Fairies?"

Peter's voice makes me jump, and I cover my work with my hands.

He wrinkles his nose. "I don't know what it is with girls and fairies."

"You don't like fairies?" I squeak out.

I gulp. I finally have the nerve to speak to Peter and that's what I say? I'm worried about his answer.

Peter's blue eyes settle on mine. "I think fairies are cool."

He thinks fairies are cool. Is it a good thing, to be cool? But wouldn't that be the opposite of being hot? Could hot and cool both be good? Cool is the opposite of hot, so if hot is good, cool must be...not good.

My mind searches for a way to turn this around. I want to know how he really feels about Neverland.

"Do you miss it terribly?" I say.

He pulls back and frowns. "Miss what?"

"I mean, when you were gone, did you miss New York?" I know the answer to this question. Peter told me this himself. I only want to get him to open up to me. To trust me.

"Aren't you new here?" He pulls back and rubs his temple. "What do you know about me?"

I remember that he still doesn't know who I really am. "Just that, you were missing for a long time. Was it...awful?"

A shadow passes over Peter's face. "I don't like to talk about it." He shifts away from me, and plants his elbow on the table between us.

A barricade. A door. No trespassing.

My nosiness has pushed him far, far away.

I'm washed with pain. Peter didn't like Neverland and he doesn't like me.

3

The bell rings and the high pitched sound is immediately followed by the screeching of chair legs being pushed against the floor, the rustling of paper and the chatter of people around me. Peter leaves without saying a word to me. Jangle slides into his chair.

"So, did you tell him?"

I pierce her with an angry glare. "No."

"Well, I saw you guys talking. What'd you say?"

"Nothing," I mutter and pick up my pencil and notebook. "It was a disaster."

I race down the hall, dodging kids like salmon going upstream against the current. This has been the longest, most agonizing day ever, and it is finally over. At least the torturous school part. Somehow I find the front doors and barrel out.

"Whoa!" Jangle grabs my arm. "Where's the fire?"

I ignore her and keep skipping down the steps to the curb. Jangle stays close on my heels.

"Belle! Really, you need to get yourself together."

I stop short and bow my head, letting my yellow hair hang over my face. I feel a tear run down my cheek but I don't stop it. It drops and leaves a wet mark on my new purple shoes.

"Belle?"

I glance up at her through damp eyelashes. "I'm standing on the corner of mixed up and crazy, Jangle. I don't know what to do."

Jangle's face softens. "Oh, Belle. Let's go back to the apartment. We'll figure things out there." Jangle waves down a taxi and we climb in. "And you're going to tell me everything you said, word for word."

I'm in a daze the whole way back. My mind reviews the day's events: my early morning hopeful reunion with Peter, the redheaded girlfriend, Peter's unaffected reaction to me, and his apparent distain for everything that he experienced in Neverland, including me.

I've participated in every emotion known to fairies and humans in the course of one school day: hope, joy, disappointment, anger, despair, jealousy, hatred, love.

I let my head fall back against the headrest and close my eyes. I want to give in to the fatigue that encases me, and forget this day ever happened.

Jangle has to prop me up as we exit the taxi in front of our apartment building. Mrs. Weeks is sweeping the foyer when we walk in. She gives us a cautious nod and we lumber up the stairs. Jangle's purse has swallowed her key. I pull mine out as she digs hopelessly through hers.

"Why do humans lock their doors, anyway?" she says.

I turn the knob. "Humans are complicated creatures."

I toss my shoes off by the door and my feet pad down the worn carpet to my room, where I promptly flop onto my bed stomach first.

I hear Jangle's voice from the doorway. She sounds worried. "Do you need something? A cup of tea?"

I murmur into my pillow. "Just sleep."

"Okay, you have a nap. I'm going to buy us some school supplies for tomorrow, and when I get back we'll make dinner. Then you're talking."

I moan and wonder why on New York's good green earth would I ever step foot back in that school?

It grows dark by the time Jangle wakes me. "You better get up if you hope to sleep at all tonight."

My head is groggy and for two sweet seconds, I don't remember anything. I snap fairy dust with my fingers to bring on the light and regret it immediately. My eyes squish together in revolt at the sudden brightness. I snap again and am plunged into darkness. And then the horrors of the day flood back.

Oh, mercy.

I shuffle to the kitchen and watch as Jangle fiddles with the stove. "I'm not sure how this works. And for the record, Tink, don't expect me to wait on you hand and foot like this all the time."

"I won't." I know Jangle well enough to know this is an anomaly.

"Oh, fiddle," she says, then snaps her fingers. A blue light appears under the element. "I'll figure out how to do it the human way tomorrow."

She boils pasta in one pot and opens a jar of sauce into

another. After a short while, our apartment starts to smell pretty good.

I set the table for two and sit down. Jangle brings over a large, silver bowl filled with the stringy noodles and red sauce on top.

"This is called spaghetti."

"Interesting," I say.

She stares at image on the label on the empty jar. "Looks like you eat it this way." She says. "You use the fork to pick it up, then twist your fork against the spoon to gather it."

"Like a spool of wool," I say, copying her. I make "mmm" noises and we eat until our hunger is gone. I laugh a little at Jangle who has spaghetti sauce on her face. She points at me and laughs back. "You do, too."

I scrape the last bit from my plate then push is away. "I'm stuffed."

Jangle does the same. "Good. Now why don't you tell me what happened in art class."

I frown at her. I just got into a happy mood and with one sentence she strips it all away.

"You first," I say stalling. "You were so busy making googly eyes at Dylan, I couldn't even get your attention."

"I know, Tink. I kind of lost myself for a little while. It's just, he's just..." She props her elbow on the table and rests her chin in her hand. I notice her contoured reflection in the silver bowl, and see her wings flap like a flag in a strong wind.

"He's cute," she continues. "I like how his hair drapes across his forehead, and how when he smiles it's like he has a secret, or finds me entertaining but doesn't want me to know he's noticing me. I also like the shiny rings in his eyebrow and lip."

Her eyes sparkle as she looks up. "Especially the one in his lip."

"Jangle!"

"What? You never dreamed of kissing Peter?"

"That's different."

"How?"

I groan. "I don't know how. It doesn't matter anyway. I'm never going to kiss Peter." My heart beats a little faster as I remember the one *she* pasted on him in the hall. "He's got Wendy for that now."

Jangle tugs on her hair. "Yeah, I admit, the girl's an obstacle. But I thought you weren't going to give up. You were going to make Peter see what he's missing in you."

"How can I do that when I completely lose control of my senses whenever I'm around him? I'm a blinking misfit who can barely string together a single sentence, and my heart does this crazy dance and steals the blood from my limbs," I point to the strands of left over pasta in the bowl, "until they're as limp as that spaghetti."

With great remorse I relay the spectacular derailment of my encounter with Peter in art class.

Jangle's head nods in sympathy.

I pout. "It's hopeless."

"You can't give up until you at least tell him who you really are."

"What if he hates me?"

"Then he's an idiot. Tink, he's not going to hate you for coming to New York because you *like* him."

"What if he doesn't *like* me back?"

"You can't help how he feels. But how will *you* feel if you go back to Neverland without telling him the truth? You'll regret it forever."

"Ah, blink." I say, wiping my eyes. "Does this mean we're going back to that horrible place again tomorrow?"

~

I'm trembling when we enter Mrs. Winger's history class the next morning. Jangle gives me a little push through the door, then takes the empty seat beside Dylan, leaving me standing there like a dork (I heard that word used yesterday, and I believe it captures what I'm doing and what I look like, perfectly.)

Mrs. Winger sees me and waves me over to her desk. "Are you having trouble finding a place to sit?" She considers me with a kind look in her eyes.

Mrs. Winger has black, curly hair pulled back off her dark-toned face. She's pretty, even without make-up. She wears a dress that covers a large protrusion on her stomach. I can't believe I didn't notice this yesterday. Mrs. Winger is soon to be a mother.

Maybe this explains her maternal-like concern.

"I'm fine," I say, forcing my face into something less brooding so that she'll believe me. "I have a seat."

I take the same one as the day before, right behind Peter and diagonal from Wendy, and let out a tired sigh. This is going to be a long day.

At least this time I have my own paper and pencils. I open up the shiny pink binder Jangle bought for me (she has one just like it), and wait for Mrs. Winger's instructions. She's talking about something called the American civil war. There's a map on the wall and she points to a place called Virginia.

"Soldiers traveled from New York by train to the south until the Confederates started bombing out the bridges."

She points to an island next to a larger mass of land and my wings tingle with discovery. There is so much more to this earth than the island of New York. But then I feel sad. The humans war against themselves in a terrible way. Fairies bicker and argue, but never fight like this.

I'm beginning to understand how the pirates came to be so evil.

Mrs. Winger tells us to read from a textbook she hands out.

Wendy reaches for something in her backpack, and as she swivels around, our eyes meet. Her face stretches and she points her nose in the air. When she turns back she reaches over to Peter and strokes his arm. She smiles sweetly at him, and he smiles in return. When he turns back to his reading, she flashes me a nasty glare.

In Neverland there is this unspoken rule that fairy dust is only to be used for good, or at least not for evil. Benign acts like turning on lights or starting the fireplace are fine. Healing Peter when he was shot by One Eye Gus qualifies for acceptable use.

What I do with it next is greatly frowned upon.

I wave my fingers toward Wendy and a strand of her hair blows into her face. She wipes it away with her hand and keeps reading. I wave again. Her hair presses against her face. She flicks it away and then stares hard at Peter who is studiously reading.

"Stop that," she whispers.

He stares at her. "Stop what?"

"Stop blowing on me."

Peter screws up his face. "I'm not blowing on you."

Mrs. Winger's head rises up from whatever she's working on at her desk. "No talking, please."

Wendy resumes her reading and I wave again. This time her hair sticks stubbornly to her cheek and fans in front of her eyes.

She whacks at it like she's being attacked by bees.

"Stop it!"

The whole class inhales. A round of giggling breaks out at the back. Wendy's staring a Peter, her face flushed as red as her hair. She looks near to tears. She grabs her things and runs out.

I feel momentarily victorious.

Until Jangle nudges me. "What the blink was that?"

"I KNOW I shouldn't have done it," I explain to Jangle in the hallway on our way to the next class. But that girl just brings the worst out in me."

"I understand," Jangle says, "but you can't use your fairy dust like that. You have to do things the way a human would."

I move a strand of hair behind my ear and fiddle with my gold, hoop earring. "And how is that?"

Jangle shakes her head. "I'm not sure."

"What is our next class, anyway?" This is the subject we

missed yesterday, due to my having a colossal emotional meltdown in the girls room. Jangle examines the schedule.

"Something called Gym. It's this way, held in a place called a gymnasium."

We stutter to a stop when we go inside the cavernous room. The open beam ceiling is higher than four men stacked on each other's shoulders. The floor is wooden and there are steps to sit on along one wall.

"What goes on in here?" I say.

Jangle whispers, "I don't know."

A man dressed in shorts and a short-sleeved shirt approaches us, and Jangle and I skitter backwards against the wall. The man pauses and gives us a confused look.

"Are you the new girls who missed class yesterday? He stares down at a clipboard in his hands. "Belle Fehr and Jan Fehr."

We nod. This man with bare arms and legs must be the teacher.

"I'm Mr. Carlson. Come with me and I'll get you your gym clothes." He sees our befuddled looks. "You paid for them with your school fees."

The massive room becomes populated with kids dressed similarly to Mr. Carlson. Blue shorts and white t-shirts with a bird image on the back. The words *Central High Hawks* are written underneath.

We follow Mr. Carlson to a large closet along the side. He pulls a couple items off the shelf. "These look like they should fit."

He hands a shirt and a pair of shorts to each of us then points us to the girls changing room.

We push through a blue door that opens to a space with

walls lined with lockers and wooden slatted benches filling up the middle. An unpleasant smell like dirty socks and stale water lingers in the air.

I lower my voice. "We're supposed to change in front of everyone?"

None of the other girls seem to be bothered by this intimate situation. Jangle and I tuck ourselves into a corner, far away from the mirrors hanging along one wall, always careful to keep our wings hidden. We change quickly.

I notice the other girls wearing flat, thick-soled shoes tied with laces.

"I guess we go with bare feet," I say.

Jangle agrees. "More shopping to do after school."

We stay close to each other as we re-enter the big room. While we were changing, some of the kids had put up nets. They were playing with a white ball. By my observation, the idea was to keep the ball from hitting the ground.

Jangle nudges me and a little giggle escapes her lips.

I turn to where she's looking and all my blood drops to my feet. Peter is in shorts and a snug white t-shirt. The muscles in his arms and legs flex as he squats under the ball, keeping it in the air by grasping his hands together and meeting the ball with the inside of his straight arms. He's so strong and so...coordinated.

I feel faint.

Jangle giggles again and this time she's looking at Dylan. His shirt hangs on his bony shoulders, and his shorts ride low on narrow hips. I hardly recognize him when he's not in all black.

Mr. Carlson blows his whistle and splits us into teams.

He leaves me and Jangle together and the expression on his face makes me wonder if he thinks we'll shatter if separated.

If so, then he's very perceptive. At least *I* will shatter. Especially since Dylan and Peter are on our team.

I'd feel so much better if I only knew what is going on.

There are two other people on our team that I don't know: a guy with hair shaved so short he looks bald, and a really tall girl. Mr. Carlson blows the whistle. Someone on the other side hits the ball over the net to us. The tall girl bumps it with her arms the way I'd seen Peter do it. The ball comes toward me. I panic and jump out of the way and it hits the floor. The whistle blows.

Bald guy says, "What the heck was that?"

Tall girl says, "It's a volley ball. You're supposed to *volley* it."

I squirm and take a quick glance at Peter and Dylan. They don't look very happy.

"It's okay," Jangle says, coming close. "We'll figure it out."

Peter hits the ball over the net to the other team. I mimic his stance and bend my knees, crouching low. I watch as our opponents volley the ball. After two times, the front guy slams it down on our side. It hits the floor before the bald boy or tall girl can get it. Point for the other team.

I'm starting to understand. Our team rotates clockwise and Jangle and I end up in front of the net. The ball whooshes over the net toward us. Dylan volleys it to the tall girl, and the tall girl to me. I know what I have to do now. Jump and slam the ball down the other side. I'm not that tall, and pretty sure I can't jump that high.

But I *can* fly.

I use my wings to get a little extra height and slam the ball down.

"Nice jump!" Dylan says. "High five."

He raises his hand in the air, and I pick up that I'm supposed to slap it with mine. Tall girl and bald guy do the same.

Then Peter. He's actually smiling. His dimples pop and his blue eyes sparkle, threatening to trigger a full on swoon in me. When his palm hits mine, it's like being struck by lightning.

"Not bad, Belle," he says.

He knows my name. Well, my fake name.

I'm glad there aren't any mirrors in the room. My wings are flapping giddily.

Jangle's hands are on her hips and her right toe is tapping. She's the only one who knows what really happened.

I shrug and turn away from her. That high-five moment with Peter is the only good thing that's happened to me since arriving at Central High. I'm not sorry I did it.

4

Jangle gets the next volley and uses her wings, too. She's not one to be shown up, especially by me.

Dylan and Peter are amazed at our sudden, athletic prowess. A bubble of glee fizzes in my belly. My wings flap like flags in a strong wind, just thinking about how I've impressed them.

Before I know it Mr. Carlson blows his whistle three times indicating that the class is over. He assigns clean up to a few of the kids and the rest return to the changing rooms. Jangle and I lag behind.

"That was fun," I say with a skip to my step.

She spins around, checking to make sure we're alone. "That was cheating."

"I know," I say with a twinge of guilt. "We shouldn't do it again." I push her shoulder playfully. "But it *was* fun."

Jangle giggles. "Yes, it was. Did you see their faces?"

By *their*, I know she means Peter and Dylan.

"That was the best part."

"Well, Peter certainly knows who *Belle* is now." Jangle says with a smirk. "When's he going to find out about *Tink*?"

I sigh. "I don't know. Soon."

Most of the girls are finished changing by the time we huddle back into our corner.

Once the room empties, we change quickly into our jeans and blouses, and head to our next class.

I coast through English, spending ninety-nine percent of my time day-dreaming about the volleyball game and Peter's admiration. Things are turning around; I can feel it in my wings.

What a difference a day makes! Peter doesn't hate me, anymore. He thinks I'm a good athlete (even if I had a little fairy dust help). I feel warm and gooey inside, like soft honey, full of hope that Peter and I will have our happily ever after. I draw a little heart on the cover of my binder and scratch the words *Peter + Belle*.

"Aren't you in a good mood," Ivy says. She pushes her glasses up on her nose as she studies me.

"Hmm," I say.

I'm still in a post-volleyball euphoric state through lunch, especially since we decide to eat outside to watch the football practice, and Peter is playing.

"How can a guy who can't shoot an arrow to save his life, throw a ball in such a straight line?" Jangle says.

"I don't know but it's sure a vision," I say dreamily. "Isn't it?" Then it occurs to me that Peter might have missed the birds he shot at on *purpose*. He didn't want to hurt them. This new revelation of his sensitive nature just makes me melt even more.

My blissful mood remains as I glide into algebra after lunch and slip into my seat.

Jangled fingers are suddenly in my face. "Wakey, wakey"

"What?"

"You've been in a trance since Gym, or something. Belle's happy place."

I smile. So what if I am in my happy place. I have a right, don't I?

Apparently not. I'd forgotten all about Wendy being in this class. She looks past me when she takes her seat, like I'm invisible.

Fine. I close my eyes, determined to hold on to my happy place, but all I can see is Wendy's upturned nose and her self-righteousness. All my happiness seeps out as I brood about this one girl. Before Mr. Wong is finished handing out the assignment, my joy is a bland puddle at my feet.

Reality bonks me on the head. *Peter is with Wendy*. He's not mine. I consider my recent blissful emotional blunder and cringe at my weakness. I cover my face with my hands and moan. I find it impossible to focus as Mr. Wong explains how to do todays math problem. My mind glazes over and I find it hard to breathe.

I make little hiccupy sounds and Jangle gives me a strange look. I have to give her credit. It hasn't been easy to be my friend lately. I can't stop my body from reacting, and hold my hand over my mouth.

My hiccups get louder, enough to annoy perfect Wendy. She twists to give me a look of disgust.

"Miss Fehr," Mr. Wong says, "Do you need to get a drink of water?"

I nod. "Yes, please."

I head to the fountain in the hall and my hiccups echo through the long empty chamber. I can hear giggling in the classroom. This is so humiliating. I'm always falling apart around Wendy. It makes me feel so...so, I don't know. *Less than.*

I gulp back water. Hold my breath. Drink some more. Hold my breath again. Eventually I relax and my hiccups stop.

I enter the classroom just as Mr. Wong asks Wendy to collect the sheets. She gets to my desk before I do and stops. Her face grows hard like she wants to kill someone. That someone being me. I stop dead in my tracks because I know what she's looking at.

The heart I drew on my binder. The heart containing the inscription: *Peter + Belle.* Blood drains from my face in horror. How can I be so dumb?

After a moment she continues to collect the sheets, but when she sees me her eyes narrow to daggers, stabbing me.

I make it back to my desk, but my legs give out.

Jangle hovers over me. "What's wrong now?"

I cover the offending doodle with my hand. "Nothing." My humiliation turns to indignation. Who does Wendy think she is? She's been Peter's girlfriend for less than a month. I've known Peter for over two years. He's been to Neverland! I have just as much right to him as she does.

I gather my things and walk out with a straight spine and determination.

Jangle follows me. "I don't like the look on your face."

"That girl is just so infuriating."

"She does seem to dislike you. What set her off this time?" Jangle says. We're bumping shoulders with kids streaming down the hall and I lean in to show her my binder.

Her nose wrinkles and a low *ohh* escapes her lips.

"I know. It's stupid."

We're behind a group of tall boys so I don't see her until it's too late. I just glimpse her mane of red when she shoves my shoulder. She hisses, "Loser."

I stop, stunned. I don't know any derogatory words to say back, but before I can think it through, my arm acts on its own and pushes her back. My mouth shouts the only bad word I can think of. "Pirate!"

Someone shouts "catfight!"

I look for the cats but instead my eyes land on Peter. His expression registers disbelief and then morphs to disapproval. He didn't see what Wendy did to me, only my undignified response.

The fact that I've lost his favor is the worst kind of blow. I want to curl up and hide under a silk leaf and never come out.

Jangle grabs my elbow. "Let's go."

I'm completely dazed through all of biology. When Mr. Douglas inquires, Jangle whispers, "female problems," and that seems to keep him at bay. All I can think of is I have art for my next class and there's no way I can face Peter.

"I have to go home," I say to Jangle.

She takes one look at my stricken face and nods. "Okay."

Because I don't know how to get us back to Neverland and because Jangle and Dylan have a thing going on, we continue attending Central High. Days blend into one another and my goal for each day is to keep a low profile and stay as far away from Peter and Wendy as I can.

Truth is I'm ashamed of my behavior. I was so consumed with finding Peter and winning him over, that I completely lost myself. I don't hate, I don't push, and I don't call names. I'm not that kind of girl. Or that kind of fairy.

So, instead I hang around with Jangle and Dylan and eat lunch with Ivy, Miles and Rita. Whenever possible I take a seat so my back is to Peter, and in art I'm careful to come in after Peter and pick a chair as far away from him as possible.

I'm always searching the horizon for the mysterious green hue, in hopes that it will one day be my ticket home. The days grow shorter and cooler and the sky is often gray. No green hue in sight.

Sometimes, on the weekends Dylan takes Jangle and me to Times Square. I'd never been to anyplace like it. So many bright, flashy lights on the buildings and billboards reminding me of the abundance of gems in our fairy village. It's loud and busy, but after a couple weeks at Central High, I'm used to that.

On Saturday he takes us to see a play on Broadway and for those few hours I completely forget my own woes, catapulted into the fantastic world of imagination.

Jangle and Dylan hold hands as we wait for a taxi. They're staring at each other and I'm staring at them, feeling lonely and heartsick. Every so often Jangle's eyes cut to mine, but then immediately back to stroke Dylan's face with lovestruck, moon-eyes.

When she thinks I'm not looking, she leans into him for a kiss. My jaw drops as I watch their lips connect and the hole in my chest expands. I quickly look away before they catch me staring.

The ride home in the taxi is quiet. Jangle with hands clasped loosely on her knees, looking all glossy-eyed and dreamy, and me with my arms folded in tightly and my face pinched with emotional distress. I try to shake it off before Jangle notices my black mood. I don't want her to pity me.

"No offense, Belle," Jangle says when we enter our apartment, "but you're starting to feel like a third wheel."

I fiddle with my earring. "What do you mean?"

"I mean, sometimes I would like to be alone with Dylan. It's hard to grow a relationship when your roommate is always with you."

Her words cut me, but I understand. I close my eyes and let out a sorrowful sigh.

"Tinkerbell," Jangle says gently. "I didn't mean to hurt your feelings." She fills the teapot and puts it on the stove. Without looking at me she adds, "Maybe it's time for you to face Peter. It's the reason why we're here. Besides that, he deserves the truth."

5

I like Dylan. He's a nice guy and he's good to Jangle. But I think they're getting too close. He's starting to ask a lot of questions. *Where are our parents? Do we have siblings? Where are we from exactly, anyway?*

It's hard to keep putting him off with excuses and awkward distractions, so Jangle decides we need to make up a fake human history.

We're sitting in the computer lab. It's a normal sized classroom, but each desk has a monitor on it with a tower on the floor underneath.

I sit at the keyboard as Jangle watches over my shoulder. I'm amazed by this thing called Technology. We don't have it in Neverland, and I confess it's a lot to take in. Cyber space? World Wide Web? Texting?

I swear on the king's throne that Jangle and I are the only students at Central High without a cellular phone. We couldn't miss seeing the hand held devices everywhere. We try not to ask questions about things we don't understand anymore, it only draws attention to how different we are. When we first admitted to not knowing what email was, Dylan laughed, thinking we were joking around.

"Are you from Mars?" he asked. We wisely kept quiet, neither of us knowing if that was another place like Seventh or not.

Now we just watch and listen and try to piece the information together ourselves. Cell phones are for talking across space to other people with cell phones who aren't in the same room. Texting is mini typing and it's used between people with small devices no matter where they are. They can even be sitting next to each other, a behavior Jangle and I don't quite understand.

We decide to stay late after school one day to do what they call surfing the web. I type *map of the world* into the search box with my two pointing fingers. I glance around to make sure no one else is looking. The kids here type fast, and I don't want to get laughed at with my slowpoke ways. Fortunately, there are only a few stragglers using the computers for homework, and so I can continue pecking at the keys in peace.

We both hum when the map comes up. We've seen the world map hanging in our history class, but it still astounds us. Neverland is really small and easy to navigate in comparison.

I point to land across the large ocean. "Far away from New York is best."

Jangle nods. "Yes. A place kids from here wouldn't go to or even know."

"An island," I say to narrow it down. We are comfortable

with island living and so it won't sound like we're lying when we talk about it.

"Somewhere where it doesn't snow," Jangle adds. It's getting colder in New York and we've had frost in the mornings. I shiver as I recollect. It's never cold in Neverland.

"And where they speak English." I enter all the requirements into the search bar. A number of country names come up. After clicking through and reading up on a few we decide on Mauritius, a tiny island country southeast of the huge continent of Africa in the Indian Ocean.

"Okay," I say. "We're Mauritians."

"Why are we in New York without our parents?"

"They...are traveling?" I say.

"And we're here alone because?"

"I don't know." I tap my fingernails on the desk. "In Mauritius, you can live away from your parents at fifteen."

"You can?"

"I don't know. No one's going to care."

"And this," Jangle waves toward the window, "is where we wanted to go?"

"People from all over the world come here. Why not us?"

Jangle considers this. "Sounds good. And no siblings."

I flash her a wry grin. "Who needs a sister when I have you?"

Jangle lets out a long breath. "I can't wait to tell Dylan."

"Give it to him is small chunks, or else he might suspect we're making it up."

"Good idea." Jangle stands as I log off.

I'm about to join her, but then I catch sight of Peter and freeze to my chair. He just entered the room and chooses a desk. My eyes stay glued to the back of his head.

"What's he doing here?" I whisper.

Jangle shakes her head. "Maybe he needs to use a computer."

"No, he has one of those small, flat ones you carry around." I know this because I watch him *a lot*.

"Studying then." She sits back down. "You should go talk to him."

I hitch back. "Now?"

"Why not?"

I'm not prepared, that's why. I need a day, or a week, or an eon to psych myself up.

I grip the edge of the desk. Jangle is right. I need to talk to Peter. And he *is* sitting there all alone.

My heart beats erratically and sweat forms on my top lip. My wings reflect in the black computer monitor. They are stiff and quivering.

Jangle nudges me. "Go."

I make it half way across the space between Peter and me before I stop in my tracks. Wendy springs into the room, her red curls bouncing happily. She pulls a chair out beside Peter, and sees me just as she sits down. Her eyes narrow and she leans into Peter to whisper in his ear. He turns before I can move. His eyes scan my face and his brow furrows into a deep *V*. I wish for the ground to open up and swallow me, anything to get away from his disapproving gaze and her mocking grin. I nervously snap my fingers and the lights in the lab go out.

I escape through the darkness, feeling Jangle's hand on my arm as we leave. I hear her snap and the lights behind us come on again. The chatter in the room subsides, but the beating of my heart thunders loudly in my chest.

"Mauritius, huh?" Dylan says. We're standing by his locker the next day, waiting for him to grab his books. I'm there in body, but my mind is busy reliving my humiliation from the day before. Jangle wouldn't leave me alone this morning and forced me to come to school with her. She says it's for my benefit but I suspect she doesn't want to take on Central High alone, and Dylan isn't in all her classes like I am.

"Yeah," Jangle says leaning on the locker next to his. "Not many people have heard of it, so that's why we don't bother talking about it."

He closes his locker. "I've heard of it."

My eyes dart to Jangle's in alarm. Maybe Mauritius isn't as secluded as we thought. Maybe New Yorkers go there regularly on vacation?

Dylan faces us. "I saw it on a travel show on TV. It sounds like a made up science fiction movie name."

I let out a slow breath and we step into the crowd. I'm grateful it's too busy and noisy for him to question us further.

I follow Jangle through the morning classes, keeping my head down, and especially avoiding any eye contact with Peter or Wendy. We meet up with Ivy, Rita and Miles in the cafeteria. Miles and Rita are speaking to each other in a language called Spanish, practicing for a test they have in the next class. Ivy has a book open on her lap. Her glasses keep slipping down her nose and she pushes them up after each bite of her sandwich.

Dylan and Jangle are giggling. He shoves his tray away

when he's finished eating then says to Jangle, "Want to hang out in the gym?"

She giggles and nods, and without saying anything to me, leaves with Dylan.

"Hey?" I call after her, but they disappear out the door.

"What are they doing in the gym?" I ask the others. Jangle's not the sporty type, at least not without fairy dust help and I know she doesn't like doing that.

Ivy doesn't look up when she speaks. "Kids make out under the bleachers."

I level my eyes at her. "What do they make there?"

Rita's dark curls spring as she chokes on her juice. "You're pretty funny, Belle."

Then Miles makes smooching noises with his lips and I blush.

That's what it means to make out?

The burn of flush spreads from my face down my neck as I imagine Jangle and Dylan snuggling up together under the bleachers.

"Everyone does it," Ivy adds, her eyes still pouring over the words in her book.

Miles scoffs. "Not everyone."

Rita pats him on the back and laughs. "She means all the *cool* people do it. She wasn't talking about us."

"Is cool good?" I ask, remembering what Peter said about fairies being cool.

All three of them look up at me and I know I've said something dumb again.

"Yeah," Rita says. "Cool's good. Where'd did you say you were from again?"

I bite my lip. "Mauritius."

They nod at me like that is a really weird and unlikely place to come from. I stare down at my food.

They eventually become engrossed in a debate about global warming (is it real or not?), and I slip away without any fuss.

I wander down the halls toward my locker, wondering how long Jangle's going to be, and what *really* is going on under the bleachers.

And then I see Peter alone. I search the halls for any signs of an evil, redheaded girl, and see none.

This is my chance. Maybe if I tell Peter the truth, fate with reward me with a supernatural trip home to Neverland.

My heart skips and jumps and dies, but I forge ahead until I'm standing beside him. It takes me a nano-second to study his profile: his strong jaw with a trace of dark bristles on his chin; long lashes over studious eyes; his hair dark as coal, sweeping over his forehead. He reaches for a book and it falls unto the floor by my feet. I bend down impulsively and he does the same. Our hands reach for the book at the exact moment, his fingers brushing mine.

It's magical. Time stops. Our eyes lock and I stop breathing. I search the ocean blueness of his gaze, hoping for a glimmer of recognition. *Does he know me?*

"Peter!"

Wendy's shrill breaks the spell. Peter grips his book and stands. I straighten as well feeling sheepish.

Wendy pulls Peter away by the elbow. "I hate how she watches you all the time, like a stalker. It's weird."

"I dropped a book," Peter says. "She was just trying to help."

My heart swells a little at Peter's effort to defend me.

"She's not trying to help," Wendy says. Her voice pitches higher. "She's trying to break us up!"

Her eyes glass up and she grips Peter's shirt. A soft sob bubbles from her lips and Peter pulls her to his chest.

"Shh, Wendy," Peter says. "You know how I feel about you."

I'm quivering as I watch them walk away, arm in arm, until they disappear around the corner. My knees give out and I lean against the lockers, sliding down until I'm a plop of fairy mush on the floor.

6

I'm sitting on a bench close to the spot where Jangle and I first arrived in New York, in what I now know is called Central Park. Birds love it here, especially ones they call pigeons. They're not flashy and colorful like the birds in Neverland—but unassuming, dressed in humble grey.

When the sunlight hits them a rainbow shimmers delicately off their backs, and despite their lowly appearance their coo is lyrical and soothing.

I. feel an affinity with them as I observe the way they flutter about and look for food. Once a fanciful fairy creature living in an exotic land, I'm now banished to the streets of New York with nothing more than a grey fall jacket and a dying song in my heart.

I'm deep into nursing my melancholy mood when I see a man buying a hotdog from the stand Dylan works at. He's wearing a beige bomber jacket and baggy trousers, and when I catch his profile through the moving throng of bodies, I sink lower onto my bench, ducking half my face into my coat. My blood curdles at the sight of the man's bald head and large nose.

Hook!

Or is it? I slide off the end of the wooden bench and crouch behind it. If it's him, I can't risk being seen. My pulse races as I strain to see through the people snaking along the asphalt path. I will him to face my way so I can tell for sure, but he moves in the other direction. I leave my hiding spot to follow the man, but he's tall and his strides are long and he gets further away. I almost break into a run, but then he pauses to throw his garbage in the trash.

Is it him? Did he find a way out of Neverland? I squint and stare. No, it can't be. It's not him.

He tugs a wool cap down low on his head, then shoves his hands into his pockets and keeps walking. I almost collapse onto the dewy grass with relief. Just a lookalike.

Right?

With no other plans or way to pass the time, I continue on through the park and my thoughts return to my hapless situation.

I failed at my mission. Though I found Peter, he hasn't found me. His heart belongs to another, and I must satisfy myself with pecking at the ground for crumbs of affection, where ever they may come from.

And wait for a chance, though slim, to return to Neverland, even though it means facing up to my crimes and paying the penalty I deserve.

Jangle is worried because I refused to go to school with her today. She dragged me out of bed and I landed on the hard floor with a thump, but I put my heels in. I will not go back there. I assured her I'd be all right (and that she'd be all right), and told her she needed to go to make excuses for me. Besides, I know she wants to spend time with Dylan and this is a perfect chance for them to continue to be together without the *third wheel.*

I walk around the lake and watch grown men play with remote control boats. I continue on until I reach a body of water called Turtle Pond. My wings droop in the reflection. It's quieter here than in other areas of the park. I divert my wondering thoughts by observing the turtles.

At first I can't see them because they blend so well with the green-laden habitat, but once my eyes find one, it's like they pop into view everywhere. They are small and can easily fit in the palm of my hand. I squat to watch one on a mossy log. It has tiny red dots on the side of its head. When a bird swoops by, it tucks in its head, out of site.

Much like me. Wendy swoops in and I duck out of sight, hiding away in Central Park. It's for my own protection and the natural way of things.

My heart is heavy but I concede. I must bow out and leave Peter and Wendy alone. But I can't let my last memory of Peter be of me standing mutely in the hall with Wendy crying and spouting accusations.

I'll go back to say goodbye. If I leave the park now, I can arrive at the school in time for my last class.

Mrs. Mullins' doughy face brightens when she sees me come to the office.

"Are you feeling better dear? Jan told me you woke up with a fever."

I plaster on my agreeable face. "Yes, much better. Thank you."

"You know you only have one class left. You must like art?"

I almost choke up, knowing this will be my last time there. "I didn't want to miss it."

She gives me the slip and I make my way through the empty hallway. I'm early and the bell hasn't rung yet. It's strangely quiet and my shoes echo as I walk. I drag a finger along the wall and pause for a drink at the fountain. The basin is shiny aluminum and my wing tips peek out over my shoulders, shimmering in the reflection.

I'm reminded of my true nature: fairy. I don't belong here. It is right for me to leave. Or at least try to leave.

I wait outside the classroom door until the bell rings. It empties out in two minutes. I'm hiding around the corner, my eyes focused on the faces of the kids coming for the next class. I hide behind the door when I see Jangle walking down the hall with Dylan. I don't want her to call me out.

When I finally see Peter my heart jumps and I swallow. I slip in behind him like his shadow, taking the chair next to the one he chooses. I do this so quickly, he startles. A flash of shock registers in his eyes before he regains control.

He softens his shoulders and his lips pull up in a slight smile.

"You know," he murmurs, "Wendy's gonna freak out if she finds out we're sitting together."

"It's the last time," I say. "I promise."

Ms Janlinski calls the class to order.

"Today I want you to tell a story in pictures. Simple sketches, three sketches per row for two or three rows. All on one sheet."

The room fills with the rustle of paper and the search for pencils.

"Think this through a head of time." Ms Janlinski plays with her beaded necklace as she strolls through the class. "See it completed in your head before you begin."

This is easy for me. I'm the first one to start scratching at my paper, but I'm careful to keep it out of Peter's view.

My story is about Neverland. I sketch the Mermaid Lagoon with a boy lying on the beach, blood flowing from a wound and a fairy nearby. The next scene is the big tree in the middle of the silk forest and a boy sitting on a stump, whittling wood. The third scene is the poppy field where a boy and a fairy share a picnic lunch. The fourth is the view of the fairy village from the top of Blue Mountain, looking down on the castle and the waterfall.

The fifth has a boy with a knife fighting a bald pirate with a sword. A fairy flies overhead.

The sixth is a fairy all alone, with saggy wings and a very sad face.

I examine my work with satisfaction. Fairies have natural creative ability and my sketches are good.

I peek over my shoulder at Peter who is on his second diagram.

On the top of my page I write the words, *To Peter*. And at the bottom, *Love, Tink*.

I intend to sneak out of the room unnoticed, but stub my toe on the table leg.

It slips out, "Blink!"

Peter's head snaps up. Then he stares at my drawings. His face blanches and he sputters, "It can't be."

His jaw falls open as he takes me in. He studies my tear filled eyes. His are wide with bewilderment.

"Tink?" he whispers.

I swallow hard and force a small smile. Then I blow him a kiss. "Good bye, Peter."

The end of Episode 3.

I hope you enjoyed *Love Stinks*—I'd love it if you'd leave a review on Amazon. They are so helpful to Indie Authors like me and help readers find the books they love.

Read on for an excerpt from Episode 4, PETER PANELLI.

PETER PANELLI

LOVE, TINK - EPISODE 4

PETER PANELLI

Episode 4 in the Love, Tink Series

by
Lee Strauss

SUMMARY

Peter's back in New York City. He's grown used to his new, older body, his mom's inquisitiveness and the fact that his father still lives in London. He has his girlfriend, Wendy. She's safe, easy-going, reliable. And she doesn't know what happened to him the two years he was gone.

No one does.

Then the new girl, Belle, arrives and shakes everything up. Wendy doesn't like her, and weird things happen when she's around. Plus, she's cute and she's intent on getting Peter's attention.

She gets it.

Belle's true identity is revealed and now they're both in trouble. Hook's in town and he's after them. Peter has something he wants and if he delivers it, Hook promises to leave them alone.

If only it were so easy.

1

"Hello, Peter..." Wendy snaps her fingers in front of my face and narrows her eyes at me.

I'd spaced out, my mind drifting to a faraway place called Neverland, a place I can never tell her about. Never tell anyone about.

And Tinkerbell is *here*. In New York. But why? And how?

"Peter!"

"I'm sorry." I rub my face. "I can't seem to concentrate."

"I can see that." Her eyes soften and her lips pull up in a slight smile. "What's wrong? Are you thinking about...*them*?"

I know what she means by "them." The Lost Boys. Or, as they are known around here, the Missing Boys.

I *am* thinking about them, but only because I'm remembering my time in Neverland, and especially recalling a certain spry, yellow-haired fairy who has eyes as bright and green as emerald jewels.

"You know I don't like to talk about it," I say, averting my gaze.

"You have to talk about it some time." Wendy reaches across the couch and grabs my hand. "You've been home for over two months."

She shimmies closer, moving the textbooks that rest between us. "Why don't you tell me what happened to you?"

Her fingers tighten, but I can't squeeze back. My hand hangs limply between us.

"I can't," I choke out. My words seem to echo through the high ceilings of the townhome I share with my mom.

Wendy flips her hair behind her shoulder and tilts her head. "Peter. You have to talk about it. Maybe something you know would help the police find the boys. They're our friends. Don't you want to help them?"

I swallow the lump that always forms in my throat when we talk about the boys. Yes, I want to help them. They're the ones who don't want to be helped. They weren't interested in coming back. How do I explain that to their families?

"Let's just go back to studying, okay?" I say instead.

She leans over, closes her eyes and parts her lips. I meet her, relieved that her curiosity is curbed for now and that she'll be satisfied with a kiss. Her lips are tender and sweet, but I'm responding by instinct. I'm a guy. I like to kiss girls, and kissing Wendy is nice, but it doesn't give me the thrill you'd think.

I've known Wendy since I was five when she sat at the desk next to mine on our first day of kindergarten. She's sat beside me ever since, and it's been nice and comfortable and easy.

But not exciting. Not thrilling. Not new.

I pull away and give her the smile she expects and then open my books, staring hard and pretending that I'm reading the words there.

But the letters blur because I'm thinking about the way Belle Fehr, *Tink,* blew me a kiss in art class. Now that was *thrilling*.

It all makes sense now. The strange behavior of the "new girl." The way she keeps staring at me, following me and freaking Wendy out.

"Don't you find Belle Fehr to be super annoying?" Wendy says. I jump at the co-incidence. Can she tell I'm thinking about her? Girls have a weird sixth sense that way.

She gnaws on the end of a pen. "Where did she come from anyway? She and her cousin, what's her name? Jan? I mean, what's with those two?"

I shrug and stare out the window. Our brick townhouse faces a busy vehicle corridor that has wide sidewalks filled with pedestrians. I watch a man walking a large, brown dog until he disappears from view.

"They're new," I finally say. "You've never been anywhere new, so you don't know how stressful it can be."

I risk a glance from the corner of my eye and see the deep frown I knew I'd find there.

"I've been places."

"I don't mean on vacation, Wendy. I mean move."

Her glare returns.

"So, they're new. Doesn't mean I have to like them. Belle creeps me out with the way she stares at us all the time. It's like she's been obsessed with you from day one."

"I don't know what to say."

She drops her pen. "Say you agree with me. Say you

think her possessive behavior is weird, too."

"Why? What difference does it make?"

She's one to talk about being possessive. She's practically been my shadow since I returned to New York. My disappearing off the face of the earth for two years messed with her mind big time. Not that we were *together* before then. We were twelve. We kissed once in a game of truth or dare. But I knew she liked me as more than a friend. And I didn't mind that she liked me. She was cute.

Now that I'm back, she's clear about us being more than friends, and again I don't fight it. Having her in the girlfriend slot makes a lot of things at school easier. At least it was until Belle arrived. Now Wendy doesn't want to let me out of her sight.

And she certainly doesn't want to share me.

"It makes a big difference." Her eyes bore down on me with a glaze of anger. I reach over and weave my fingers through hers, hoping to defuse it. "You worry too much."

It works. Her gaze softens and she leans in for another kiss. We break apart quickly when we hear the front door open.

"Peter?"

It's Mom.

"I'm home." She walks through the living room with two bags of groceries in her arms and stops when she sees us.

"Hi, Wendy," she says. "Are you staying for supper?"

Wendy packs up her things. "I can't, Mrs. Panelli, I have dance class tonight. But thanks for asking."

I walk Wendy to the door. The bus stop is one block down from my house and the next one is about to arrive any minute.

She gives me another kiss. "See you tomorrow."

I nod. "See you."

I help Mom make supper.

"How was your day?" she asks as she fries up the chicken.

I pour the pasta into a pot of water and set it to boil. "Fine."

She pushes her dark hair behind her ears and zeros in on me with questioning eyes. People say we look alike and I can see the resemblance.

"You know I hate that answer," she says.

"Okay, it was good."

Surprising is a better word, but I can't share my encounter with Tinkerbell with her.

Wendy's not the only one who wants me to talk. I catch Mom staring at me with wistful eyes, wishing I would open up to her. Or a counselor or psychiatrist. I refused, for obvious reasons, to say a word about my time away. But at least I'm back and that's the main thing. And I'm doing okay at school. I'm not running with gangs or causing trouble. I think she's accepting that having me home is better than having answers.

I stir the pasta and think again about the last class of my day. Tink's drawing is safely stashed away in my locker. She left abruptly before the end of art without turning her poster in. It's a picture story of my life in Neverland and is signed to me. I don't regret taking it.

I looked for her after class but she was already gone. I wonder if Belle Fehr will come back to school tomorrow.

I hope so. I really, really hope so.

2

I'm eager to get to school the next morning. I wake up before my alarm—which never happens—shower, dress, eat, brush my teeth and shout bye to Mom before she leaves for work. She raises her eyebrows at my unusual hurry, but simply waves me out the door.

It's cold out. I flick the hood of my hoodie over my head and turn away from the wind as I wait for the bus. Red and brown leaves fall from the trees that line the street and tumble along the sidewalk and into the ditch.

At school I scan the yard and the hallway looking for Belle Fehr's blonde head and the blue-haired chick she's always with. I'm tall so I can see over the heads of most of the people, but I don't spot them, and disappointment rushes through me.

There's a tug on my shoulder and quick as lightning the thought flashes that Belle has found me. I turn, but it's not her.

"Hi, Wendy," I say, forcing a smile.

She smiles back. "Hi, gorgeous."

We walk side by side through the crowds, stopping at my locker first, then hers, but my eyes never stop searching.

Wendy wrinkles her forehead. "Are you okay?"

I reassure her by wrapping my arm around her shoulder like I always do, and try not to feel guilty that I'm searching for another girl the whole time we head down the hall.

I break away from Wendy before we enter the room. Mrs. Winger normally greets all the students as we walk in, but today she's noticeably missing. Odd.

My eyes dart to the empty desks behind mine. I take my seat but can't stop my eyes from checking the back door of the room waiting for Belle to enter. That guy they hang out with, Dylan, saunters in just as the bell rings, but she's not with him.

I let out a frustrated sign when I realize Belle's not coming. Then I have a worse thought: maybe she's gone back to Neverland somehow. Maybe I've missed my chance to talk to her, to ask her all the questions burning in my gut. In a strange way I miss Neverland. Not that I want to go back, but I would like to hear about it again. Talk to someone who *knows*.

I want to know *why* she came. It kills me that I was too dense to figure out who she was before now.

Wendy pokes me. "Are you okay?"

I wish she'd stop asking me that. "Yeah, I'm fine."

Mrs. Winger still hasn't shown up. I take the opportunity to look over my shoulder, in the opposite direction of Wendy. Dylan sees me staring and frowns. I point to the empty desks normally occupied by Belle and her cousin. He gets my meaning and shrugs.

I can't tell if he doesn't know, or thinks it isn't my business.

The class grows quiet and I face the front. A man is standing at the board writing something.

He's as tall as me with broad shoulders and a bald head. Something inside my gut twists.

"Mrs. Winger is in the hospital having her baby," he says.

The hairs on the back of my neck stand and my blood freezes. I know that voice.

The man faces the class, but his dark eyes zero in on me. "I'm your substitute teacher. You can call me Mr. Hookley."

I swallow a dry lump. It's Hook.

3

How did he find me?

My eyes twitch and sweat beads on my forehead and the back of my neck. My saliva disappears and my tongue feels like a dried biscuit. My knuckles turn white from gripping the desktop.

Wendy pokes me. "What's the matter with you?"

How can I explain to her, to anyone, just how *wrong* this is? Hook should not be here in this classroom. There is only one reason why and it has to do with me. He wants me dead.

Hook takes attendance, reciting names until he gets to mine.

He pauses. "Peter Panelli?"

I slowly raise my hand. A dry whisper passes through my lips. "Here."

Hook smirks, the skin around his dark eyes and big hook nose crinkling. He breaks his gaze with me and continues.

"And is Belle Fehr not here?"

Dylan answers, "No. She and Jan Fehr are home. They're sick."

Hook hums. "I see."

He spreads his hands wide, addressing the class. "Why do people go to war?" he says. He tents his hands together and taps his fingers. "Why does one man track down another?"

My blood pumps in high speed, my heart thudding out of control. I think I'm going to have a seizure.

Wendy leans over. "Do you need to go to the nurse? You look awful."

I shake my head. I'd love to leave, but I don't want to talk to Hook. I can't ask to go see the nurse, he'd know it is because of him. Last thing I want is to look weak.

"Are you sure?" Wendy persisted.

"Yes!" I say. "I'm fine."

Someone raises his hand and answers Hook's questions. I don't pay attention. My mind can think of one thing only.

I have to find Tinkerbell. I have to warn her.

THE BELL RINGS and I'm standing and running out of the classroom like my seat is on fire. I see Wendy's shocked expression, but I don't waste time looking back at Hook.

I imagine him chasing me down with long strides as I hide myself in the crowd of kids in the hall. I escape into a janitor's closet and close the door. I'm encased by sudden darkness and my nerves shoot off like I'm being bitten by fire ants.

I try to calm myself with long, slow breaths. My mind immediately takes me back to the time in Neverland, when Hook had me flat on my back. The look of hatred in his eyes, the glint of the blade on my neck. How I'd almost crapped my pants.

The memory is so vivid, it's like I'm there again. The watery smell of the silk forest; the crazy loud birds and annoying buzzing insects; the hot sun burning my nose.

The scent of my fear burning my nostrils. Hook's rancid breath.

My chest tightens. I'm certain I wouldn't have lived to see another day in Neverland, much less a new day in New York if it hadn't been for a small, feisty fairy. If it hadn't been for Tinkerbell.

I have to find her.

I mix in with the other students crowding the hall. I make sure Hook is nowhere in sight and then I search for Dylan. He's the only one here who probably knows where she lives.

I feel a tug on my arm and almost jump out of my skin.

"What is wrong with you?" Wendy arches her eyebrows and her dark eyes bore into me. "Do you have Post Traumatic Stress Syndrome?"

"No. Yes. Maybe," I answer. "I don't know. But I have to go."

I leave her standing dumbfounded in the hall. I know she won't follow me because she can't stand to be late for class, and I need to get to the gym for mine. Dylan will be there. I rush to find him.

I round the corner past a set of exit doors, and catch a

glimpse of a lanky guy dressed in all black exiting the building. I chase after him.

"Dylan!"

He ducks behind a bush. "Shhh," he says. "They don't know I'm leaving."

"Where are you going?"

"What's it to you?" he asks.

"Do you know where Belle Fehr lives?"

Dylan starts walking. "You have bad timing, man."

"What do you mean?" I hope I'm not too late. "Is she okay?"

His eyes dart to the side, taking me in. "Why wouldn't she be?"

"I don't know. She's...not in school."

Dylan shakes his head. "You finally noticed her, huh?"

"I noticed her on the first day."

"Of course. You have a girlfriend. I get it."

I cringe. "That's not it. It's just...I have to talk to her. Do you know where she lives?"

"I do. In fact. That's where I'm going now."

"Can I tag along?" I say, keeping pace beside him. He flashes me a look like he'd rather I didn't.

"I can't afford a cab," he says. "It's a long walk."

He can't be worried I'll have trouble keeping up with him, so I assume he'd like me to hail a cab for us both. I wave an arm at the next taxi and it stops.

Dylan gives the cabbie an address on 7th, and then we sit in awkward silence together in the backseat. He probably wants to ask me the same thing everyone does: Where was I for the last two years?

I want to ask him if it hurt to pierce his face like that. Neither of us say anything.

The cab stops in front of a multi-story apartment building that could use a makeover. The manager lady gives Dylan and me the evil eye when we pass her in the dingy foyer. I follow Dylan up a flight of stairs and we stop in front of the number 4.

He knocks and my body breaks out in a shimmer of cool sweat.

The blue-haired girl opens the door.

"Dylan?" she asks. Her eyes widen when she sees me.

"Are you guys okay?" Dylan asks. "You looked shaken when you left school yesterday. And since you don't have a phone..."

The girl motions for us to come in. "We're fine," she says. Then her eyes land on me and she tugs on her spiky hair. "I think."

The apartment is small, with a tiny corner kitchen that shares the living room space. My eyes land on Belle who is sitting on the sofa with a tissue in her hand. Her eyes are red, like she's been crying and when she sees me, all the color leaves her face.

An uncomfortable quiet settles on the room.

Finally, the blue-haired girl stretches her hand toward me. "I don't think we've officially met. I'm Jan."

I shake her hand. "I'm Peter."

"Oh, I know."

"I'm here to talk to Belle," I say, looking across the room at her.

She gulps and her eyes fly to Jan's like she's pleading for help. I think Jan mistakes her message because instead of setting herself firmly on the sofa beside Belle to protect her from me, she links Dylan's arm.

"Let's go for a walk," she says to him.

Two minutes later, I'm alone in the room with Belle Fehr, aka, Tinkerbell.

4

"I'm not sure what to call you." I cringe. Lame opening line.

She wipes the corners of her eyes with her damp tissue, then says, "It's probably best if you stick to Belle. It's my New York name."

I pull out a kitchen chair and sit facing Belle. I run two hands through my hair while I stare at her face. She looks so different but somehow the same. Her blonde hair is hanging loose over slender shoulders, her face is less round and more heart-shape. Overall she's much bigger—human-sized. Her eyes are still large and bright green. They're the feature that looks the most like the fairy version.

"This is just so crazy," I say. "You're Tinkerbell?"

Belle presses her lips together and nods.

There's so much I want to ask her, but I don't even know where to start.

"Why did you come?"

Her face flushes red. She tucks her legs under her and

gazes out the window. Instead of answering, she asks, "Do you remember when we went on a picnic in the poppy fields?"

I smile for the first time in days. "Yeah. That's one of my better memories."

She looks at me under long eyelashes. "Really?"

"Yeah, really."

"Mine, too," she says. "I was nervous because I had big plans to tell you how I felt."

I squint at her. "About what?"

Her lips tug up slightly. "About you."

I suddenly find it hard to swallow. "Me?" My voice raises a couple octaves. "But, you're a fairy?"

Her expression sours. "Believe me, I'm aware."

"I don't mean that like it sounded. You're hot. Now that you're not a fairy. Strictly speaking."

I'm a babbling idiot. I've no idea if she's still a fairy, and even though she is hot as a human, it's majorly dumb for me to say so. At least to her face.

She folds her arms. "Well, strictly speaking, I am still a fairy. And I came for you, which makes me an utterly stupid fairy."

I lean back in the chair feeling dazed. I really had no idea. I mean, I was a pretty clueless thirteen year old at the time. And now, at almost sixteen, I'm still no expert on girls. Fairy or otherwise.

"It's not stupid," I say. "I'm flattered."

"How nice for you."

I see the feistiness and spunk remains in Tinkerbell's human form. I hold back a grin. Her mouth purses into a look of scorn. It's cute, and I find myself staring at her lips.

Then I shake myself. I have Wendy, and she's going to kill me when she finds out I've skipped school to come here.

"The reason I came to see you," I look back at her, keeping my eyes trained on hers, "is because of Hook."

"Hook?" Her jaw goes slack. "As in Captain Hook?"

I lean forward with my elbows on my knees. "He's Mrs. Winger's substitute."

"He's a teacher?" Belle stands and paces the small rug. "That *was* him, then. I thought I'd spotted him in Central Park yesterday."

"What I want to know," I say, "is how did he get here?

Belle stops and stares into space. "The green hue. It was growing on the horizon in Neverland before I left."

"That's how the Lost Boys got there," I say. "We were caught up in a strange green storm."

"But the Captain's been stuck in Neverland for years," Belle says. "Why could he get out now?"

"Maybe he's been waiting for the green phenomena to hit again."

Belle's stands straight and I can almost imagine her wings zinging stiff. Her cheeks drain of color. "Do you think he's looking for me?"

"I think he's looking for me."

"But why?" Belle sits back down and presses her hands between her knees. "I can see why he'd be angry I took off, but why does he care so much about you?"

"I'm not sure. But you should've seen the way he looked at me. Like he wanted to finish the job he started in Neverland. I'm just glad there weren't any sharp weapons around."

"So, you're worried?"

I steady my gaze on her. "Yes, for both of us. 'Mr. Hookley' is a dangerous man."

Belle springs off the sofa. "Would you like some tea?"

Before I can say anything, she's filling a kettle. I know I shouldn't stay, but I hear myself say, "Sure, okay."

Her bright eyes dart to me and then back to the kettle. She pushes her hair behind her ears, and a strand gets caught in her hoop earring. I grin. I remember this habit from Neverland, when she was in fairy form.

She leans on the counter. "I have questions for you."

"Shoot."

Her eyebrows furrow in an incredibly cute manner. "Shoot what?"

"I mean, ask me whatever you want."

"Okay. Are you glad you left Neverland?"

"It's more like I'm glad to be back in New York. I never hated Neverland. I just didn't like feeling trapped. I'm glad to be aging properly." I chuckle. "Though it was a shock to suddenly have an older, taller body and a deeper voice."

She busies herself with adding tea leaves to a pot and pouring the steaming water over it.

"Milk and honey?" she asks.

I haven't had tea since Neverland, and I'm eager to taste it the way Tink makes it again. "That sounds good."

She sits on the chair beside mine and blows over her tea. The way her lips purse together is so adorable. Wendy's chastising face flashes to mind and I look away.

"Tell me about Wendy," she says.

What is it with girls and mind reading?

"What do you want to know?"

"Well, it seems like you just left Neverland and boom,

you have a girlfriend. It's not my business, of course." She glances away and plays with her earring. "I'm just surprised at how fast it happened."

I sip my tea and pull back sharply with a burnt tongue.

"Wendy has always kind of been around. She was my first crush in fifth grade. When I disappeared it broke her heart. She always held out hope that I'd return, even when others thought I was long dead and buried.

"When I came back, she was over-the-top happy and clingy. I couldn't push her away."

Belle places her teacup down. "Will you excuse me?"

I nod and she pads down the hall and disappears into one of the rooms.

My phone's been buzzing non-stop and I take the opportunity to check it. I have six missed texts from Wendy wondering where I am. There's one from my mom asking why my school called. I have some damage control to do when I get home.

Belle returns looking fresher and more composed.

"Thanks for the tea," I say. "I have to go. My mom's expecting me."

A flash of disappointment crosses her face, but she recovers with a smile. She walks me to the door and I pause before leaving.

"This is so strange," I say. It's hard for me to wrap my brain around it. Tink the fairy from Neverland is now one hot New York girl.

"Yeah," Belle agrees.

"Will you be in school tomorrow?" I ask.

She nibbles her lip and I find myself holding my breath waiting for her to answer.

Finally she says, "I suppose I could come. Someone needs to protect you from 'Mr. Hookley'."

"Great," I say, relieved. "See you tomorrow."

I rush down the steps to the sidewalk outside feeling pretty good. I hail a cab and give directions to my house.

My phone buzzes again. Another text from my mom. I read it and my heart stops.

Are you on your way home? Your teacher is here. Mr. Hookley.

5

I sprint to the front door of my house almost kicking it open.

"Mom! Mom!"

"Peter?"

"Are you okay?"

"Of course." She looks up from the magazine she's reading on the sofa. "What's the matter?

"I got your text about Hookley."

She laughs. "You're worried that you're in trouble with your teacher?"

"No, it's just..." I scan the townhouse, looking for him.

"You can relax." She sets her magazine down beside her. "He left already."

My knees weaken with relief that my mom's okay, I collapse in a heap in the wing-back chair across from her.

"Did he say what he wanted?" I'm horrified he knows where we live and that he'd been alone with my mother.

"He said you looked troubled and skipped school," she

flashes me a stern look. "Which was verified by a call from the school office."

I don't know what to say about that, so I keep quiet. It works, she starts talking again.

"He'd heard about... your *disappearance*, and wanted to make sure you were okay."

I rub my hands along my legs. "That's above and beyond the call of duty, wouldn't you say?"

"Well, Peter, it turns out that Mr. Hookley knows your father."

My eyebrows shoot up in surprise.

"They went to college together."

I don't believe it. "Dad never mentioned him."

"No. But there are lots of people he knew from college that he didn't mention in passing."

I'd call Dad to check this but since it's the middle of the night in London, I let it go.

"Which brings me to another...issue," Mom says tentatively.

"What's that?"

She links her fingers together, a move she does when she's nervous. "Well, you know how your dad has a new girlfriend?"

I know and it makes my stomach clench. Mom never talks about it so I'm curious as to why she's bringing it up now.

"Yeah?"

"Mr. Hookley asked me to dinner," she says quickly. "I said yes."

I choke on my saliva.

"Peter, really. It's just dinner."

"I know, Mom, and I'm fine with you dating if you want to, just not with him."

"Why? Because he's your teacher?"

Good idea. "Yes! No dating my teachers!"

"Ronald said he was just substituting. You can look at him as a friend of your father's and not as your teacher."

Ronald? "Pick someone else."

"Why?"

"I don't trust him."

"You don't even know him. A one-hour history class hardly counts."

She reaches for my hand and squeezes. "You have Wendy. Dad has Lilly. I just want to go on one date."

I'm going to kill Hook. My heart races, I feel my pulse in my ears. I can't breathe. A sheen of sweat breaks out over my whole body. This must be what it feels like to have a panic attack.

What does Hook want from me? Whatever it is, he better leave my mother out of it.

My phone buzzes again. I pull it out already knowing who it is. Wendy. I do something I haven't done once since returning from Neverland. I don't answer her.

The only person I care to see in school the next day is Belle. I search the faces of the people streaming up and down the hall, but don't spot her blond head.

Wendy nudges me from behind. "Why did you blow me off yesterday? Don't you know I was worried?"

Normally, I would wrap an arm around her shoulders,

kiss her reassuringly on the cheek. I can't this time. I open my locker and pull the books out I need for the first class. "I didn't blow you off. I just had other things to deal with."

Wendy folds her arms. "Yeah, like Belle Fehr?"

My head snaps to her then back to my books.

She doesn't wait for me to answer. "Lane Cooper told me she sat with you in Art yesterday. That she left suddenly after *blowing you a kiss.*"

"It's not what it looks like," I say feeling annoyed. Wendy's jealousy is *not* what I need right now.

"What it looks like, is that you and Belle have something going on that you won't tell me about."

She's right about that. I go to close my locker, but Belle's poster falls out. Wendy grabs it before I can.

"What's this?" She scowls as she examines it. "To Peter? A gift? And who is Tink?"

I snatch it back and toss it into my locker before closing it. "It's none of your business."

"None of my business? Are you kidding me? If a girl gives you a gift and that girl's not me, then it's my business." Her hand goes to her throat. "Oh, it's her, isn't it? *Tink* is Belle Fehr."

"Just leave it alone." I slam my locker shut and turn my back on her.

"Fine!" she shouts after me.

"Fine," I say wishing my first class didn't have both Belle and Wendy in it. I want Belle to show, but if she does, it will be really uncomfortable.

She does.

And it's really uncomfortable.

Wendy's sitting stiff, looking straight ahead, lips in a

tight line, and anger radiating off her like heat in every direction.

Belle sits behind me, and I try not to twist my head to look at her. Primarily because I still value my life and I wouldn't put it past Wendy to clock me in the nose if she saw me. I do manage one sneak peak. Her face is wide with shock as she stares past me to her former employer, Captain Hook.

Fortunately, Hook doesn't seem to recognize her. How would he know she was here, and even if he did, Belle doesn't look like Tink unless you observe closely.

Hook leans on the front of his desk, blabbing away. His eyes continually dart to mine and his mouth tugs up in that wicked grin I know so well.

With Belle and Wendy *and* Hook, the room is a cauldron, and I'm the poor sucker burning in it.

When the class ends, he makes an announcement. "Peter Panelli, will you please see me after class?"

Wendy marches out in a huff, and I wait for the room to clear before I go to Hook's desk. Belle is the last one to leave. She hangs at the back door of the room, her eyes wide with question. I mouth that I'll be fine and wave for her to go. I don't want Hook to put two and two together.

"What do you want?" I spit out when I reach him. He's sitting behind Mrs. Winger's desk.

"Oh, Peter, Peter, Peter." He puts his feet on the desk and crosses his ankles like he doesn't have a care in the world. "Still short-tempered and headstrong, I see."

"Just answer the question." I press both hands on the desk and lean in. "Why are you *here*?"

"You have something I want."

My heart stalls. He's after Tink and there's no way I'm delivering her to him. "What?"

He removes his feet from the desk and leans toward me. Our noses are only inches apart.

"Ask your father."

"My father? What does he have to do with this?"

"Everything. And he has something that's mine. I want it back."

I step away, flushing with confusion. "I don't know what you're talking about."

Hook huffs. "You know what? I believe you. Doesn't change the fact that you're the only one who can give me what I want."

"And if I refuse?"

"Well, then, I may have to go on more than one date with your mother." He smirks. "Such a lovely lady."

"You stay away from her!"

His beady eyes narrow and my skin breaks out in goosebumps. The warning bell sounds and the class fills before we can finish. He holds his right hand to his head like a phone and mouths, "your dad."

I storm out with murderous thoughts filling my mind followed by questions about my dad. What kind of trouble is he in and what does he have that Hook wants?

And how am I going to get it?

6

In the hallway I lean up against the wall and close my eyes. A groan escapes my lips and my mind races for answers to basic questions like, what should I do now? Go to class? Find my mother? Phone my dad?

"Peter?"

I open my eyes to Belle's cute, worried face.

"What did he say?"

I push off from the wall and start walking, motioning with a nod of my head for her to follow.

"My dad has something he wants."

"Your dad? That's...surprising. What is it?"

"I don't know. The bell went off before I could get it out of him."

We both had gym next so we walked there together.

"Thanks for coming to school today. It might not seem like much, but it means a lot that you're here." I manage a smile and she rewards me with one of her own. "Who else can possibly understand what's at stake?"

"Just me," she admits. "Oh, and Jangle."

"Who's Jangle?"

Her eyes flutter like she made a slip. "You might as well know." She lowers her voice and I have to duck down to hear her. "My 'cousin' Jan, is another fairy from Neverland. Her real name is Jangle."

"How many of you are here?"

"Just the two of us. She kind of tagged along for the ride."

"Does Dylan know?"

Belle shakes her head dramatically. "No. And you can't tell him."

"Don't worry," I say. "I'm an expert at keeping secrets." Jan and Dylan walk ahead of us, close with shoulders touching. "They seem to really like each other."

"Yeah. They do."

We reach the gym and I hold open the door.

"By the way," Belle begins shyly, "I'm sorry for causing trouble for you with Wendy. I'll hold back from now on." She offers a sad smile before disappearing into the girls changing room.

A strange twist works its way from my heart to my gut and I realize with a shock that I don't want her to hold back.

During the lunch break, I find a quiet hallway and try to call my dad. My frustration grows with each ring. *Pick up!* It's early evening London time, but maybe he's teaching a late class. Dad's a science professor at University College London. He accepted a position there after he and mom broke up; *after* I disappeared and it seemed like I was never coming back.

When I did return from Neverland, he moved back to New York and for a short while, maybe a day, I'd hoped things could go back to the way they were before I left. But he'd changed too much for it to work. We all had. It was like we'd lost the ability to talk to one another. The three of us were like turtles living in a glass cage with our heads tucked in. Dad went back to London after only two weeks.

To be honest, it was a relief. Mom and I tentatively poked our heads out from our shells shortly afterwards and settled into a life together. Things started to feel normal.

Until Belle showed up.

And then Hook.

I hang up and dial again. Still nothing. Someone taps me on the shoulder and I jump.

"Did I scare you?" Hook peers down his crooked nose at me.

"N-no." I won't admit it to him, but my knees are quivering. I *am* afraid of Hook.

"Our conversation was cut short this morning. Let's go somewhere..." he glances around at the kids moving down the hallway, casually passing the time until the lunch period ends. "...quieter, to continue it."

The present company is no match for Hook, but I want them as witnesses in case he's tempted to get physical. "I'd rather just continue talking here, if you don't mind."

"Fine. Your father has something that belongs to me."

"Yeah, you've mentioned." I cross my arms and keep my expression blank. "What exactly?"

"It's an...artifact."

My jaw slackens. "An artifact?"

"Yes. An ancient box."

"A box?"

"Are you deaf, boy? Stop repeating everything I say."

I hold up my palms. "I just don't get it. Is it valuable?"

He smirks. "You could say that."

If Hook wants a dumb box, I'll get him a dumb box. "If I get you this artifact, you'll leave me and my mother alone?"

"Yes."

I don't know if I can believe him, but I don't have a choice. "I'll look for it."

"Good. And as an incentive for you to find it, I've booked reservations for two at the Italian restaurant down the street from your house. I'm picking your mother up at seven."

I curl my fingers into fists and scowl, but he just walks away, chuckling.

I FINALLY REACH my dad after school.

"Dad, I've been calling all day." I hear the frustration in my voice. "Why don't you answer your phone?"

"Sorry, Peter. I was working. Is something wrong? Is your mum..." He's picked up a British accent and I snarl silently.

"She's fine." At least for now.

"And you're okay, I'm assuming?"

"Yeah, I'm fine."

"Well, what's got your knickers in a knot?"

"Do you know a man called Hook?"

"No. Why?"

"He claims to know you. From college. Bald head, hook nose. He says you have something he wants."

Silence. "Dad? Are you still there?"

"Hookley."

The way dad says his name, breathy with a hitch of fear, makes my skin crawl.

"He wants a box you have, and I think we should give it to him. Where is it?"

"Stall, Peter. Make him believe you're looking for it. I'm catching the next flight to New York."

Dad hangs up before I can get another word in. I stare at the phone in my hand and almost push redial.

I don't see the point. He isn't going to talk. The only thing I know for sure is that whatever is in that box scares him.

7

As soon as Belle enters the art room I wave her over to sit beside me.

"Are you sure this is a good idea?" She stands beside the empty chair, arms wrapped tightly around her books. "What if Wendy finds out?"

"It's fine," I whisper urgently.

She sits and lays her books on the table. "Is everything okay?"

I lean in closer. "Hook asked my mother out to dinner."

She frowns. "Like, on a date?"

"She thinks it's a date. He's using her as leverage, so I'll do what he wants."

"And what does he want?"

"An artifact. A box. At first I thought Dad might've taken it with him, but then, why would he catch the next flight back. It must still be here somewhere. I'll look for it after school."

Her frown deepens. "Will you give it to him?"

"If it means he'll leave my mom alone."

Belle furrows her brow. "I wonder what it is."

"I don't know. But I'm not letting my mother out of my sight."

"You're going to follow them?"

I nod. "Do you want to come with me?"

Her bright eyes widen. "I sure do."

I give Belle my address and she agrees to meet me at six-thirty. After school I head home. My dad still has an office on the second floor. He cleared out most of his things when he left for England, but Mom let him store stuff he couldn't or didn't want to take with him. Their split was cool that way. Mom and I never go in there, but today will be an exception. Maybe I'll find the box there, or at least a clue to where it is. And what it is.

Wendy intercepts me before I make it to the bus stop.

"If you want to break up, just tell me. But don't treat me like I'm invisible." She's crying and I feel like crap.

"I'm sorry, Wendy. I just have a lot of stuff going on."

She strokes my arm. "Then tell me about it. Let me in."

I can't let her in because it's too dangerous. I don't want her to get involved with whatever Hook is up to.

"Wendy."

"It's her, isn't it?"

"Huh?"

"Belle Fehr. You're interested in her now. It's pretty obvious to anyone with eyes."

"That's not it."

It's not all of it, anyway. Truth is, I am interested in Belle

Fehr. But she's a fairy from Neverland. It's never going to happen. I need her to help me get rid of Hook, that's all.

"Sure, lie to me, Peter. Lie to yourself. We're through." She spins on her heels and storms away. I can tell by how her shoulders shake that she's crying, and I know I should run after her, but I can't. It's better this way.

Still, I feel terrible. Wendy's been nothing but supportive to me. She stood by me on my return even though I refused to tell her anything. It was nice to have someone to lean on, someone to take the pressure off when the questions became too intense. I don't think I could've faced going back to school if she hadn't been there to hold my hand. Literally.

My gut feels hollow with regret, but deep down I know I did the right thing by letting her go. As much as I.ve appreciated having her with me, my motives haven't been right. I don't like Wendy as more than a friend. Not the way she likes me. It's a convenience and nothing more.

She's a good person and I'm sorry I hurt her.

Mom gets home early from work. She's humming, something I haven't heard her do since I've been back. I'm worried by her uncharacteristic happiness. Hook is bad news I'm afraid for her.

Her eyes land on me and the humming stops.

"Is everything okay?" she asks.

I force a smile. "I'm fine."

"Peter?"

Right, she hates that word. "I'm great, okay. Everything is great."

She narrows her eyes at my outburst. "Good to hear. There's leftover lasagna in the fridge." She heads upstairs.

My stomach growls. Despite all of the recent stress, I'm starving. I remove the cold lasagna from the fridge, put a large piece on a plate and heat it up in the microwave.

Modern pleasures. Things like lasagna and microwaves are a couple of the many things I missed in Neverland. Sure it was fun for a while, like an endless camping trip. I got bored. Plus, I wanted to grow up.

Now I'm not sure what my hurry was. I wonder about the other boys, Curly, Nibs and Tubs. Are they still glad they stayed?

I do my homework and finish eating. I try to focus on my geometry assignment but find that I'm constantly checking my phone for the time.

Then at six-thirty on the dot, the doorbell rings.

I skid on my socks on the hardwood floor to the door pausing for a moment to get composed.

I open it and Belle waits on the other side. She's wearing jeans and a thigh-length wool jacket cinched at the waist with a belt. Her blonde hair falls around her shoulders in waves and her signature golden hoop earring stick out. Her green eyes are bright and hopeful. She holds her hands together in front of her.

"Are you going to invite me in?"

"Oh, yeah." I feel like an idiot. "Come in."

My mom calls down from upstairs. "Is it Ronald? Tell him I'm almost ready."

"No, it's for me," I shout back.

"Ronald?" Belle asks with arched brows.

"Ronald Hookley," I answer, nodding.

Belle removes her boots and coat and I lead her to the living room. I spread out school books on the couch and coffee table. "I want them to think we're studying," I explain.

"Good. What are we studying?"

"History?"

"Sounds reasonable, considering."

Belle sits on the couch on the other end from me, where Wendy usually sits. It's strange and I have to look away. I've never invited another girl to my house before.

Mom comes down the stairs wearing a pink dress and pearl earrings. I think she's overdoing it, but instead of mentioning it I say, "You look nice."

"Thanks." She stops short when she sees Belle. Her eyes dart to mine and I know she's wondering what happened to Wendy.

"Mom, this is my friend, Belle. She's new to our school."

Mom finally smiles. "Hello."

"Hello, Mrs. Panelli. It's great to meet you."

Mom slips on her heels. "You kids studying tonight?"

"Yeah. History test coming up. Mr. Hookley's a hard taskmaster."

Mom doesn't laugh.

She has her coat on and is ready to go when the doorbell rings again. She shouts out a quick goodbye and I hear the door click closed. I don't think she wanted to face the awkwardness that would be sure to follow if she'd brought him in, and I'm glad he didn't see me with Belle. I don't want him to connect the dots.

Belle fiddles with her earring. "What now?"

I spring to my feet. "Let's follow them."

I know the restaurant well. *Bellisio*'s is where we celebrated my thirteenth birthday, just days before the green storm whisked me away to Neverland. It's walking distance from our house.

We are overwhelmed by the scent of garlic, tomato sauce and oregano the second we enter the restaurant. A small crowd waits by a sign that says, "Please wait to be seated."

The restaurant has a lot of wood, red velvet and wrought iron in its décor. Italian music pumps softly from the speakers imbedded in the ceiling. A hip-high wooden plant stand, about four feet wide, acts as a divider between the foyer and the restaurant. Belle and I duck behind it and I can see Mom and Hook being seated at a table for two by the window. She's laughing at something he said, and my stomach knots.

A voice calls over, "Table for two?" The small crowd has dispersed and it's just me and Belle standing there. The hostess smiles, picks up two menus and motions for us to follow.

"We're waiting for people," I blurt.

She nods and thankfully is distracted by new arrivals.

Hook tells the waitress something and soon afterward she arrives with two glasses of white wine.

I don't want my mom to drink alcohol. She can't have her defenses down around this guy.

Belle tugs on my arm. "Do you want me to do something?"

I stare down at her, and for the first time it occurs to me that maybe her fairy dust powers work here.

"Can you?"

"If you want."

"I want."

Belle snaps her fingers and Hook's wine mysteriously

spills onto his lap. He jumps to his feet, wiping at his crotch with a white linen napkin. My mom covers her gaping mouth with a hand.

I chuckle and catch Belle's eye. "Nice one."

"I'm only supposed to use the dust for good, and normally this wouldn't qualify."

"I think it does," I say. Anything that stops Hook from using my mother is enough for me.

Apparently, looking like he wet his pants isn't enough to pull Hook from the date. He smiles and waves a hand like he's brushing the incident off. My mom studies the menu.

The foyer has emptied again. The hostess catches my eye, and I tap at the imaginary watch at my wrist and shrug. *Still waiting.*

I miss the part where they order. Hook and Mom are chatting about something. I can't remember seeing her so talkative. She looks happy, and I almost feel bad that I'm there with Belle wanting to sabotage her date.

Their meals arrive and I look at Belle. "Do you have anything else up your sleeve?"

"How bad do you want it?"

"Bad enough to end the date. It's gone on long enough."

She snaps her fingers and waves her hand. In an instant, the candle flickers and the silk flowers burst into flame. Mom gasps and pulls back as Hook starts smacking it with the linen cloth from his lap. Mom's on her feet. The other patrons are staring. Those at nearby tables stand and yell. A waiter runs over with a fire extinguisher, but not before the overhead sprinkler start. The fire goes out but everyone is already on their feet and rushing toward the door.

I pull Belle down behind the planter as Mom and Hook

move past. Mom's on the other side of Hook and doesn't see us, but Hook catches sight of us from the corner of his eye. His glare rests heavily on me and then on Belle. A flicker of understanding flashes. He looks back at me with a grin.

He *knows*. He knows Belle Fehr is Tink.

8

Belle and I race back to my place. We slip in through the back sliding door I'd left unlocked and barely get settled into our spots on the couch when I hear the key in the front door and my mom walks in.

"Home already?" I shout out.

She pads in to the living room in stocking feet, holding her shoes by the straps in one hand.

"There was a bit of a situation at the restaurant."

"Really?" I say, then play it up. "You're all wet. What happened?"

"A small fire and the sprinkler system set off. Anyway, I'm going to change."

She doesn't mention that the fire started at their table. She also doesn't say anything about a second date, so maybe our intervention worked.

"Thank you," I say to Belle. If it wasn't for her fairy dust, the date would've gone on much longer and my mother might be a lot happier than she is right now.

"I hope it helped," she says. "But did you see the way he stared at me? I think he figured out who I am."

I sigh. "You might be right. I'm sorry. I've gotten you into trouble with Hook again. It's the last thing you need."

"That's okay. We're destined to be enemies, I think. At least your mom is out of harm's way for a while."

She smiles a little and straightens the books on the table in front of us.

"Did you come in on the green hue?" I ask her, suddenly curious.

Her eyes move to me and then to the floor and she whispers, "No."

"Fairy dust, then?"

Her face registers shame and I don't understand. "What's wrong?"

"I used the queen's fairy dust." Her eyes land on mine and she stares hard at me. "I had to steal it. From the king. I'm a thief."

Then it dawns on me. She stole it to send me home.

"Oh, Tink." It's a slip. I haven't called her that since she told me to use her New York name.

She closes her eyes and lowers her chin. "I'm going to go back and face my punishment."

"Why? You can stay."

"What is here for me?"

I'm here, but she doesn't know that I've broken up with Wendy. Her big green eyes latch onto mine. "I have to do the right thing. I have to go back and confess."

"But what will happen to you there?"

"I don't know. No one's ever stolen from the king before. I'm the first."

She looks so sad and forlorn; I just want to squeeze her.

"I should go," she says. She puts on her coat and I grab mine.

"I'm going with you." I'm worried about Hook being out there, maybe watching our house.

"That's not necessary. I'll take a taxi straight there."

"It's no problem." It's the least I can do to repay her for coming with me tonight and willing to use her fairy dust for my purposes.

I wave down a taxi and we shove into the back seat together. Belle's careful to keep from sitting too close to me. She tilts her head to stare out at the bright lights of New York City against the dark sky.

"I'm starting to get used to it," she says.

"The lights?"

"And the noise and the bustle."

"It's very different here, than in..."

Her eyes cut to mine and I hold her gaze steady. I can't stop myself from reaching over and weaving my fingers through hers.

Her eyes widen, but she doesn't pull away.

"Thank you, again," I say.

Before I know it, we're pulling up in front of her apartment on 7th. I want to tell her Wendy and I aren't a couple anymore. The urgency to get it out before she leaves the taxi surges through me.

She pulls her hand free from mine and opens the door.

"Belle."

She pauses and I search for the right words. "Wendy..."

Belle puts a finger to my lips and an electric current rushes through my whole body, paralyzing me.

"It's okay, Peter. You don't need to say it."

She slips away and I watch her enter the front door of her building. *Don't need to say what?* Does she know about me and Wendy breaking up? How? Or does she mean she was fine with me staying with Wendy?

"Where to?" the cabbie says.

I tell him to take me back to the place we started, and spend the trip home wondering how I managed to make such a mess of things.

Mom's sitting in the living room wearing her bathrobe and sipping a cup of tea.

"Where'd you go?" she says when I enter.

"I took Belle home."

"What happened with Wendy?"

I avoid looking at her. I take my time removing my coat. "We broke up."

"What happened?"

I shrug. "Not much. Wendy's been a good friend..."

Mom tilts her head. "And a good girlfriend."

"Yes. But I never asked her to be that. She just kind of assumed, and I let her."

"I see. And now there's Belle."

I let out an exasperated sigh. "It's not like that."

"I get it. Matters of the heart are complicated." Mom gets up, pulling her robe closed around her legs. "I'm going to bed now. See you in the morning."

"Good night."

I do homework until I'm certain Mom's in bed for good. I

pack my books in my bag for school in the morning, make sure the doors and windows are locked and turn off the lights before heading upstairs.

I walk past my bedroom to the closed door at the end of the hall. Dad's old office. I slip inside. It's weird being in here again, especially without Dad sitting in the leather office chair behind his desk. I flick on the light.

A film of dust covers the surface of everything. I'll have to be super careful if I hope to hide the fact that I'm snooping in here.

I start with the desk drawers. They've been emptied out with the exception of a few pens, empty file folders. A scientific calculator.

Dad used to work at NYU. I thought having a professor dad was cool until he started going all mad scientist. He was so obsessed with his work and new experiments, that it became his whole life. All he would tell us was that he was on the verge of a great breakthrough that would make him and his work famous, something so secret he couldn't tell me or Mom. He spent less and less time at home, and even though they didn't talk divorce in front of me, I could tell things were rocky. My parents went days without speaking, weeks even.

I go through his filing cabinet next. Mostly empty files. He must've taken the contents with him to England.

The bottom drawer won't budge. Dad emptied the others, why not this one? And why leave it locked?

I begin a mad search for the key, totally forgetting about dust and that I'm leaving telltale signs of my intrusion. Dad is somewhere over the Atlantic on his way here, and I have a feeling that if I'm going to get to the bottom of things, I have to do it before he arrives. Dad doesn't have a history of sharing the truth and I don't expect him to start now.

I check the desk drawers again and under the large calendar mat on the desktop. I peek behind a sketch of the Tower Bridge in London with the edition number 102/500 etched at the bottom hanging on the wall. A bookshelf holds a number of heavy tombs on topics like quantum physics and general relativity. There's a compass and a screwdriver, but no key.

The floor is covered in wall-to-wall carpeting, and securely fastened under the baseboards, so no hope of a secret panel under wood floors.

Where else can you hide a key in this room assuming it's in here? There's no other way in outside of physically breaking the lock on the file drawer, and I don't want to do that. Snooping through my dad's office is one thing, vandalizing it is another.

I'm ready to give up. I decide to erase evidence of my trespass here by *dusting* the room. I'll tell Dad I did it as a welcome home gesture. I'm wearing a blue T-shirt over an undershirt. I take it off and use it as a dust rag. When I'm satisfied the room is dust free, I leave, flicking out the light.

Then I stop. My eyes rest on the screw that holds the switch plate. It rests flat against the wall, but a slender key could easily fit in.

Is that why Dad has a screwdriver on his shelves?

I flick the light back on and race for the tool. I loosen the screw.

A key falls to the floor.

Bingo.

9

The key slips into the bottom file cabinet drawer and it opens with ease. My breath stops at the title of the lone, thick file hanging there. TOP SECRET.

I slip it out carefully and tuck it under my arm. I have a feeling this is going to take time to wade through and I want to do it in the comfort of my own room. As long as I have it back and locked up before Dad returns, I'm fine.

I toss my dirty shirt into the laundry and then lean up against the wall on my bed. I rummage through the file, and it's like Dad's talking in a foreign language. It's all science-speak and weird diagrams.

I pick out phrases like *particle physics* and *string theory*. Stranger terms like *bosons* and *fermions*. Because I shared a home with my father for thirteen years, I've heard of them and though I don't understand what they are exactly, I do know they are very, very small. Like smaller than an atom's neurons and protons.

Basically, I take after my mother when it comes to

science, meaning, I don't really get it. Sure I've memorized the periodic table, and understand the basics of how atoms work. I get how the human body is put together, and the cell structure of plants and animals.

When it comes to physics, well, I don't take physics. It stretches my brain and turns it to mush. When Dad lived here he loved to watch shows featuring theoretical physicists like Stephen Hawking and Edward Witten. I'd glaze over after two minutes of talking about the mystery of the black hole.

Black hole. I see the word in Dad's notes. Along with the words *quantum field theory* and *space time gravity*.

And this: *inter dimensional travel*.

The words fritz in my brain like static electricity between my sheets. Tearing, pulling, clinging.

The pieces start clicking together. Hook and I both ended up in Neverland, a place that exists in *another dimension*. We both know my dad. Dad was involved in researching the possibility of inter-dimensional travel. Was he experimenting, too?

I read on looking for notes on the artifact Hook wants. It has to have something to do with this. I find an address for a warehouse in the industrial section near my house. I shiver when I read it. The alley behind it is exactly where the boys and I were hanging out when the green storm happened.

My gut instinct tells me my dad had something to do with that event, but what? Now I wish I'd talked to him about it. He tried to get info from me, but I thought he was like all the others. I didn't think he'd believe me.

I move stealthily past my mom's bedroom door and down the steps. I put on my coat and shoes, tuck my cell phone into my pocket and the file under my arm, and slip out the front door. I close it slowly until I hear a soft click.

It's dark and cold, but the city is alive with people, like it's the middle of the day. I walk toward the industrial district with my head high. I keep a scowl on my face and refuse to make eye-contact.

My heart rate picks up as I turn off the main road onto a quieter side street. By the time I reach the alley, I'm alone. The emptiness of the block frightens me, every shadow a potential enemy.

I'm in the alley where the green storm swooped me and the boys away. I remember it clearly, like it was yesterday. We were all complaining about our crummy lives; troubles at home and school. Bad grades and groundings.

My heart had almost stopped when it happened. My mind couldn't comprehend what I was seeing and feeling. I thought I must've died, and was on my way to the afterlife.

Next thing I knew we were falling out of the sky and landed, quite miraculously, unharmed in a poppy field in Neverland.

An island in another dimension.

I speed up as I get closer to the address of the warehouse, questioning if coming here at night by myself was the wisest thing to do.

I arrive at the door and turn the knob. Locked. Of course it would be. I eye a numbered keypad—what was the passcode?

I have no idea.

I flick on the flashlight app on my phone and read through the file notes. Dad must've left it written somewhere. He's brilliant, but that doesn't mean he remembers everything he does. Otherwise why would he bother to write anything down?

I search for an obvious entry, such as warehouse passcode and a number. Dad wasn't that blatant.

I try the first date listed on the document at the front, the date noted as the first day of experimentation. Then I try the date of when the experiment *failed.* I wonder what that means? How did the experiment fail?

I pinch my eyes closed. *Think, think, think.* I remember standing at the door of dad's office, feeling the same way when trying to find the key. I see the picture hanging on the wall by the switch. The edition numbers 102/500 sketched there.

I open my eyes and enter the numbers.

The door clicks open.

I grin a little. There is a piece of my dad in me somewhere.

Inside is dark and eerie. I call out, "hello?" As if anyone is here. As if anyone would answer me if they were here.

The door swings shut behind me with a slam, and I almost crap my pants. For a split second I think someone is here. I flash my phone light across the door and the room, but see no one. The wind must've sucked it shut.

My eyes begin to adjust to the darkness. Once I can confirm I'm alone and that there aren't any corpses hanging from the ceiling or zombies in the cupboards, my pulse slows.

Mostly I'm surprised by what I'm not seeing. I'd imagined some kind of mad scientist laboratory, with tons of Petri dishes, glass tubes and Bunsen burners. The place is oddly bare. A long stainless steel table, cleared off. Empty shelves on the opposite wall. An emergency exit at the back of the room.

I'm not sure what I'm looking for, but I have a sinking feeling that whatever it is was removed from these premises long ago. I open a couple of closet doors, slowly at first just to make sure my zombie theory is correct.

Maybe I'm looking for the wrong thing. Hook said he wanted a box, an artifact. I scan the place looking now for anything shaped like a box, big or small. I see something, but it's only an old phone book.

I hear a squeak from the rafters and a bat flies away through a broken window panel high above.

I'm looking up when I see it. A plain looking box tied to the top of one of the metal rafters, near the wall. It's tucked into the shadow of the slanting roof and if it weren't for the bat, I would've missed it.

I look for something to climb and see a ladder folded flat against the wall at the back. I manage to move the awkward object without destroying the place and set it up under the rafter with the box.

It's wobbly and on the short side. If I stand on the top step I may be able to reach it. The ground below looks far away and I'm sure a fall will be more than unpleasant. I decide it's worth the risk. The ladder shimmies and I work to keep my balance. My heart lurches. Once I'm stable I reach up. I have to use both hands in order to undo the knot. Sweat beads on my forehead and I push back at the mental image of the ladder falling away from under me.

The knot releases and the thin rope falls to the ground. I tap at the box and grab it before it topples.

It's plain, about the size of a shoebox. No ornate carvings. Heavier than a pair of shoes but not so heavy that I can't manage it with one hand as I make my way down the ladder.

I'm not quite at the floor when I hear his voice.

"I see you've found my box."

My head snaps up to see Hook's ghoulish-looking face in the front door. I jump the rest of the way to the floor and run for the emergency exit.

10

I hear the cocking of a gun and Hook's gravelly voice. "I wouldn't do that if I were you."

I stop in my tracks. I wouldn't put it past Hook to kill me.

"Just give me the box, and I won't shoot."

"Why should I believe you?"

"I don't know. Maybe you can't. But I'm the one with the gun, so hand it over."

I'm not sure why I resist. If I toss the box, I'll make it to the back door before Hook can retrieve it. But there's something about this artifact my dad was willing to jump on a plane for. Somehow, I know it will be bad for everyone if Hook walks away with it.

I opt for a stall tactic.

"Can I at least take a look inside first? I mean, I'm super curious."

One side of Hook's mouth hitches up. "Sure."

That's when I know he means to kill me, no matter what I do.

"I'm going to set it on the table," I say. Hook nods and I take careful steps toward the stainless steel surface, wishing I had Belle's fairy dust to knock the gun out of Hook's hand. The table sits between me and hm. I open the lid of the box. Inside is a panel with several small levels. I expected more. It's not very impressive at first glance.

"That's it? This is what all the fuss is about?"

"Just close the lid. Carefully." Hook wipes his bald head with his free hand.

I close the lid.

He motions with his gun. "Now step away."

Instead of stepping back, I slide the box along the length of the table.

"Hey!" Hook shouts. I duck just as the gun goes off.

The box comes to a stop on the edge of the table, like a car about to fall off a bridge. Hook decides the box is worth more than I am and he races to catch it before it falls.

There's no way I'm letting him have it. I attack him from behind. The gun flies from his hand and slides along the floor out of reach.

We wrestle along the dirty floor. Hook spits in my face. "You little brat!"

He tries to push me off, but I won't let go. I don't know why. I don't really have a plan except to keep Hook from getting the artifact.

We bump into the table, our eyes staring up at the box teetering above our heads. It falls and we both reach up to claim it. Hook's meaty arm ends up whacking it like a bat. The box shimmies across the floor. We crawl over each other to get it. I reach it first and hold it tight to my chest like it's the winning ball in a Super Bowl game. Hook tackles me from behind, his weight almost knocking the breath out of me.

"Get off!" I wheeze.

"Give me the box!"

Suddenly everything goes green. It's oozing from under my body, and drapes itself over me and Hook's bulk above me.

"Let go of it!" Hook shouts. I can feel him trying to get off of me, and I want to toss him off, but it's like we are magnetized together. The entire warehouse fills with the green hue which burns my eyes. I close them tight.

I feel nauseous, like I'm spinning through space. I want to throw up. I've got déjà vu.

My body jolts and everything goes dark.

When I awake, I'm staring at the dirty, youthful faces of the Lost Boys.

I'm back in Neverland.

End of Episode 4

I hope you enjoyed *Peter Panelli*—I'd love it if you'd leave a review on Amazon . They are very helpful to authors and help readers find the books they love.

Read on for an excerpt of DAZED & BEFUDDLED.

Elle Strauss
Dazed & Befuddled
episode 5

DAZED & BEFUDDLED

LOVE THINK - EPISODE 5

DAZED & BEFUDDLED

Episode 5 in the Love, Tink Series

by
Lee Strauss

SUMMARY

Tinkerbell and Jangle search in vain for Peter after he disappears. They have reason to believe Hook managed to take them both back to Neverland. Is it time for them to return, too? It means Belle will have to face the king and the consequences of her crimes against the kingdom, but she's prepared to fulfill her sentence if it means saving Peter once again.

She has no idea what that's actually going to cost her.

1

I'm excited to go to school for the first time since arriving to New York. I choose my clothes carefully, going for skinny jeans, wedged heels, and a striped long-sleeved t-shirt with a boat-slip collar. I play with my hair wondering if I should wear it up or down. A hum escapes my lips.

Jangle leans against my bedroom doorframe and folds her arms. "Someone's happy today."

I can't stop a huge smile from stretching across my face. "Maybe."

Her left eyebrow raises disappearing behind a lock of short blue hair. "You were with Peter yesterday, weren't you?"

I giggle. "I'm sorry, Jangle. I didn't say anything because I was too busy pinching myself. After all this time, Peter and I..."

Jangles other eyebrow springs up. "You what?"

"Oh, nothing like *that*." I'm mortified that Jangle might

think Peter and I did something other than just hang out. "We studied at his place together. I met his mom."

"That's pretty cool." Jangle steps into my room and gives me a hug. "I'm so happy for you. I know how badly you've wanted this."

I squeeze her back and feel just a teensy weensy bit bad that I didn't tell her everything, including how I'd helped Peter sabotage his mother's date with Hook. But I know how much Jangle frowns on my using my fairy dust for anything but the noblest of reasons.

Peter thinks ruining Hook's chance at bewitching his mother is a noble reason, and I agree. But I don't want to get into an argument with Jangle over it. It's mine and Peter's secret.

A little thrill runs up my back. Peter and I share a lot of secrets, a fact that makes me very happy. My wings snap and shiver in my reflection in the mirror. I apply my cherry lip gloss and smack my lips.

I collect my books and put on my warm, chocolate-brown jacket and cinch the belt. "We need to go, Jangle," I call out.

Her stilettos tap along the wood floor. "My, aren't we in a hurry." Her lips pull up in a knowing grin.

"Let's just go. I'm sure you're eager to see Dylan, too." I wait for the swooning face I've come to expect from Jangle every time Dylan's name is mentioned, but it doesn't appear. "Is everything okay?"

She grabs my arm. "It's fine." We navigate the steps carefully in our heels and wave down a taxi once we're outside.

I'm looking for Peter's dark head the minute we arrive at school. I can't see him anywhere outside or in the hall when we walk to our lockers. Dylan is waiting for Jangle when we get there.

"Mornin' ladies." He bends to give Jangle a kiss. I scan the crowd, but still no Peter. I see Wendy's red head and glance away quickly before she catches me staring. I push down a sliver of guilt, though I didn't do anything wrong.

I don't think.

We walk to first class and my stomach spins and flips. In just a few moments I'll see Peter. I wonder what he'll do or say when he sees me. Oh *blink*. What should *I* do or say? I nibble my lip. I never thought this through. Should I stop and say hi, or go directly to my desk? What is the proper protocol? It's not like we went on a date last night. We're just friends. So, how am I to act as his friend now? A bubble of panic floats to the surface.

Peter's not in class when we arrive and a sense of relief spreads through me. He can make the first move when he sees me sitting at my desk. I'll take my cues from him.

A warning bell rings and the class floods with kids. Wendy sits without acknowledging my presence, which is fine by me. Dylan and Jangle take their usual seats. I turn to Jangle and she gives me a look that says, *where is he?*

I shrug. The final bell rings and that's when I notice we're missing the teacher. Mr. Hookley's not here, either. A tremble of fear washes over me. Both Peter and Hookley gone? This can only be bad news.

2

The chatter volume increases like an invisible hand is slowly turning a knob. A paper airplane shoots across the room. A "snowball" fight breaks out, white paper crumpled in the fists of the throwers as they lob them. Someone sharpens a pencil.

My heart thumps in my chest. Peter is missing. Again. Some kind of fairy intuition tells me Hook is responsible and I feel terrible because I wasn't careful enough. I'm sure Hook figured out it was me who caused the fire and the sprinkling system to go off in the restaurant while he was trying to have dinner with Peter's mom. Hook did this to get back at me, and I feel immobilized. I don't know what to do, how I can save Peter now.

The noise in the class in unbearable. I pinch my eyes closed, pressing down on the anxiety and worry. Without thinking I snap the fingers on both of my hands and put my palms up. Silence. Finally. I slump in my seat and breathe out long and slow.

"*Blink*, Tinkerbell!"

My eyes snap open at Jangle's use of my real name. Then my jaw drops. Every single person in my history class is frozen stiff, like a large diorama. Mouths open in laughter, arms in mid-pitch. Wendy sitting stiff-backed with her eyes staring at Peter's empty chair.

"I'm sorry, Jangle, I wasn't thinking."

She's staring in horror at Dylan's solid form. "Just undo it!"

I snap but nothing happens. Jangle's eyes are wide with question. I snap again. Still nothing. "I don't know what's wrong," I say, freaking out. We hear the principal's voice on the other side of the closed door.

"Hurry!" Jangle says.

I snap again and still nothing. "Something's wrong with my fairy dust!"

Jangle double snaps both hands and the room comes to life again. Everyone's blissfully unaware that I've just robbed them of thirty seconds of their lives.

Mrs. Johnson walks in wearing a pencil skirt and sensible shoes. She stands at the front of the room. "Mr. Hookley can't make it this morning. I will be your substitute. Please open your textbooks to page 254."

Jangle pulls me aside the moment Dylan leaves for his locker.

"What the heck happened in there?"

"I don't know. It was just so loud and I'm really, really worried about Peter. Hook's done something to him, I just know it."

"You were with him last night. Did he say anything about Hook? Has Hook tried to contact him?"

"Oh, Jangle, I haven't been fully truthful."

Jangle guides me to a quieter alcove. She lowers her voice. "What happened Tink? If we're going to help Peter, you have to tell me everything."

I swallow a sob and begin. "Peter's dad has something Hook wants."

"What?"

"Peter didn't know. Hook said it was an artifact, some kind of box. When Peter wouldn't help him, Hook asked Mrs. Panelli out for dinner."

Jangle tugs on her hair. "Why would he do that?"

"To get at Peter."

"Why would Mrs. Panelli say *yes*?"

I shrug. "I have no idea."

"So, Hook and Mrs. Panelli went on a date. What happened?"

I stare at the floor, feeling sheepish. "I kind of used my fairy dust to break it up."

Jangle pokes me. "Kind of?"

"I did it for Peter. His mother doesn't know how dangerous Hook is."

The warning bell rings and we have to run to make it to gym. I stop short before going through the doors. "I'm not staying, Jangle. I have to look for Peter."

"I'll come with you."

"Are you sure? I don't want you to get in trouble with the principal."

"Peter's life is more important."

We sneak out a side door and stay hidden behind shrubs and hedges until we make it to the road. Jangle hails a taxi and I give the driver Peter's address.

"Nice place," Jangle says studying the three-story brick and stone townhouse.

We aren't the only ones to visit Mrs. Panelli. A police car is parked in front. I'm worried Mrs. Panelli won't answer the doorbell, but a few seconds after it rings, she's standing there. Her hair is rumpled and dark rings sit under bloodshot eyes. She's been crying.

"Oh... Belle," she says like it's just coming to her that she met me for the first time the day before.

"Hi, Mrs. Panelli. This is my cousin, Jan. Peter didn't show up for school today. Is he here?"

She presses a tissue to her nose. "No. I'm afraid he's... missing." She steadies her bloodshot eyes on me. "Do you know anything?"

My throat thickens. I do know something; I just don't know what to tell her.

"Come in," she says when I don't answer. "Please."

There are two officers, a tall one and a short one. There's another man standing in the corner, average height, glasses on his nose. He has a tortured expression and I know it's Peter's father. He made it here from London.

The police shoot Mrs. Panelli a questioning look when they see us.

"This is Peter's friend, Belle. She was here last night studying with him when I went to bed. She might've been the last person to see Peter before..." Mrs. Panelli chokes up and I want to put my arms around her and comfort her, tell her everything will be okay.

Except that I don't know if everything will be okay. My knees weaken and I sit on the edge of a chair. Jangle sits on the arm rest beside me. "I'm Jan, Belle's cousin."

The tall officer asks me what Peter and I did the night before.

"Just studied. For history." My cheeks burn with my lie. I can't tell them that we spied on Mrs. Panelli on her date with Hook.

"Has Peter tried to contact you?"

I shake my head. "If he had, I'd tell you."

"What do you know about Mr. Hookley?"

I gulp. "Nothing. He's my history teacher."

"Seems Ronald is missing, too," Mrs. Panelli says softly. "He's not answering his phone."

The shorter officer shifts his weight. "It could just be a coincidence, but we do find it strange that the missing boy's teacher didn't come in for work. The principal confirms he didn't call in for a substitution."

"Because of that, we sent a team to check in on him," the taller officer says. "Ronald Hookley's apartment is empty and his bed wasn't slept in last night." He turns to Peter's parents. "Do you think he might have something to do with your son's disappearance?"

Mrs. Panelli bursts into tears. "I should've listened to Peter. He tried to warn me off him. Told me to date anyone but him. I thought he was just turned off by the fact Ronald was his teacher, but now I can see there was more to it." She looks up with imploring eyes. "Why didn't Peter tell me what it was?"

Mr. Panelli places a hand on her shoulder. "It's not your fault. You didn't know."

"Who did know?" she snaps. She stares up at him. "Did you?"

Mr. Panelli removes his hand from his wife's shoulder and turns to stare blankly out the window.

The shorter officer speaks again. "There was a disturbance reported last night in the warehouse district." He rattles off an address and looks at Peter's parents. "Are either of you familiar with this location?"

"I used to do research there," Mr. Panelli says.

The officer's eyes don't leave Mr. Panelli's face. "It's also the area the missing boys were last seen before they disappeared."

My ears perk up. Mr. Panelli's jaw twitches.

"Do you think it's connected?" Mrs. Panelli asks.

"Don't know, ma'am," the officer says. "Do you?"

Mr. and Mrs. Panelli don't answer, but I'm suddenly certain they are connected. Jan and I say our goodbyes, promising to let Peter's parents and the police know if we hear anything. We head straight for the warehouse district.

3

Though it's the middle of the day, brooding dark clouds hang low over Manhattan making it feel like nightfall is approaching. Wind blows litter along the alley and Jangle and I both wrap our arms tightly across our chests. I hold my collar tight to my neck wishing I'd thought to wear a scarf.

"Are you sure this is the right place?" Jangle asks.

I glance at the address I scribbled on my hand. "Yes, this is what the officer said."

I pull on the door and it doesn't budge. "I'm sorry. I don't know what I thought we'd find by coming here."

Jangle looks up and down the dingy alley. "This is where the green hue picked up the Lost Boys?"

My hair is blowing in my face and I brush it with my hand, removing a strand from my mouth. "Apparently."

I tug on the door once more, and let out a groan. "Where is he, Jangle? I'm so worried."

"The police said there was a disturbance reported here, yesterday. Did they mention a green hue?"

"No, they didn't mention the color green. But what if... *Blink*, Jangle! Do you think he's been sent back to Neverland?"

Jangle shivers. "I don't know. But where else would he be?"

"Hook took him. He could be anywhere."

"Maybe Hook is back in Neverland, too."

"How can we be sure?"

I pull a piece of hair that got tangled up in my earring by the wind. "The only way we can be sure, is if we go back and look for ourselves."

We walk to the main road, and after an eternity we finally see a taxi and wave it down. We're too cold to talk about what it would mean to go back to Neverland. Things best left said over a cup of hot raspberry tea.

I put the kettle on the second we walk through our apartment door, and hold my hands over the steam until they warm up. I fill the tea ball with loose raspberry leaves, conveniently purchase from the café in the shop on the corner, and place it in the teapot. When the kettle whistles I pour it in.

"Jangle," I call. "We need to talk about this."

I'm warm enough to remove my coat. I pour two cups of tea, adding honey to each. Jangle enters the room and I hand her the cup with the butterflies on it because I know it's her favorite.

"Jangle," I begin. "Maybe it's time to go back to Neverland."

"But, we're not sure that Peter's even there."

"It's the only way to be sure."

Jangle tugs on her blue hair. "What about Dylan?"

"You could stay," I say. "I'd understand."

Jangle stares out the window and sips her tea.

"No, if you go, I'll go. I like Dylan, but, I don't think we're meant to be anything long term."

"Are you sure?"

"Yeah, it's been fun, but, well, he doesn't know the real me."

"Does that mean you miss Neverland?"

She smiles. "A little. Okay, a lot. This has been an exciting adventure, but I'm feeling homesick."

"Then let's go back," I say. My heart drops several floors at the thought. I'm not looking forward to going back. It means I have to face the king and confess my crime. But if it means saving Peter, I'll do it.

Jangle sets her empty cup down on the table. "How do we get back? The queen's fairy dust was a one way ticket wasn't it? And unless we can summon the mysterious green storm..."

My breath leaves me. How *do* we get back?

4

Fairies aren't known for planning ahead.

Jangle frowns. "We've really painted ourselves in a corner this time, haven't we?"

"Maybe we're jumping to conclusions. Maybe Peter is still in New York. We should wait awhile before we do anything rash."

"In that case, we should probably keep going to school." Jangle reaches for her bag. "We don't want the police showing up here, looking for us next."

We arrive back at New York Central in between one of the afternoon classes. Students are huddled in groups along the hall, talking in hushed tones. My eyes dart to Jangle. Dylan sees us and rushes over.

"Where did you guys go?" he asks. "I looked everywhere for you."

"We had to leave for a little while," I say.

He lowers his voice. "Have you heard the news, then? About Peter Panelli?"

My heart skitters like a stone across the surface of Turtle Pond. "Have they found him?"

Dylan shakes his head. "No. And the weird thing is that Mr. Hookley's missing, too."

He opens his phone and brings up a news report. "They're saying their disappearance could be connected and that it looks suspicious."

The bell rings and we walk toward our next class. Wendy passes us in the hall. She has a friend on either side, and it looks like they're propping her up. Tears streak down her pale face and I feel sorry for her.

Until she stops and waves a long finger in my face. "You have something to do with this don't you, Belle Fehr. Everything was fine until you showed up."

I stand still, shocked by her outburst.

"Never mind her," Dylan says as Wendy continues down the hall. "She's just looking for someone to blame."

She's not wrong. It is my fault. If I hadn't left Neverland, Hook wouldn't have followed me. And Peter would be safe.

Peter and Hook remain missing and in the news, and by the next evening, I'm frantic.

"If Hook really did find a way to take Peter back to Neverland, he's probably trying to kill him as we speak! We need to go back."

I snap my fingers. Nothing happens. "Oh, no!

My heart is so swollen with concern for Peter that my fairy dust problem feels like more than I can bear. My bottom lip slides out in a pout.

"Breathe," Jangle says. "It's going to be okay."

I take a long slow breath and sit down.

"Let's think this through," Jangle says. "What is so special about the queen's fairy dust?"

I look up at her. "She's the queen?"

"So?"

"It makes her dust...special."

"But how?" Jangle crosses her arms and taps a toe. "She was an ordinary fairy until she married the king."

"I don't know. It's just the fairy way."

Jangle stares back at me. "Are you sure you even want to try to go back?"

I exhale loudly. "I am if you are."

"I am."

"But, what about Dylan?"

She tugs her hair and gazes out the window. "I broke up with him after school today."

I move to her side, and lay a hand on her arm. "How did that go?"

"He was upset, but I saw him talking to another girl shortly afterward. I think he'll move on."

I don't know what to say, so I just give her a big hug. She pulls back and takes my hand.

"Maybe our dust and our strong wishes mixed together will work." She snaps her fingers and shouts, "Take us to Neverland!"

Nothing.

"Oh, Jangle, I think we're stuck here!"

A bright star flickers in the northern sky.

"I don't remember seeing that before," I say.

Jangle peers at it. "Me either."

We gawk at it intently. Where did that star come from?

"Do you think..." Jangle began.

"Yes!" I feel a tickle of excitement. "We must wish upon a star!"

I grab her hands and we stare hard at the bright, sparkling light in the sky. "We wish upon a star to go back to Neverland!"

The light in the sky grows so bright it's blinding. I pinch my eyes shut against the glare. And when I open them, we're in Neverland.

5

I gape at Jangle, and blink. She's back in her much smaller fairy form, wings zinging straight out from her back in full view.

"Tinkerbell?" Jangle's voice has changed, too. Higher, with a melodious ring.

I gaze at my small, thin arms and spin my head to stare over my shoulders at my wings. Bright, white, and plain to see.

I feel like I can't catch my breath. My knees give, and I lower myself into the mossy bottom of the silk tree forest. Broad leaves flap overhead in a warm breeze. A purple and yellow Sassy Bird sings as it flies above us and lands in the branches. Sunlight streams through the lush green canopy.

"We're back," I say, stating the obvious.

A tear runs down Jangle's face.

"Are you okay?" I ask.

She runs a finger under her eye. "I'm fine. I'm just surprised. And shocked. And really happy to be back."

I share her surprise and shock, but not her happiness. Nervous fireworks shoot off in my stomach.

I stand and wipe the dew off my backside.

Jangle stands with me. "What are you going to do?"

"I have to find Peter, make sure he's okay." And figure out a way to send him back to New York. Again.

I start walking and Jangle springs into step beside me. "We don't even know if he's here for sure."

"He's here, Jangle. I can feel it in my wings."

I'm almost sprinting, the way to the boys' hideout imprinted on me like instinct, but I slow as I get closer.

I'm about to see Peter again, only this time he's a *hot* teenage boy, and I'm a small, plain fairy. I'm ashamed that for a moment I'm more concerned about what Peter will think of my appearance when he sees me, than I am about his safety.

I hide behind a silk leaf and stare. Peter is there, like I knew he would be. He's with the Lost Boys and they're looking at him like they're seeing a ghost. This version of Peter is much different than the one who'd left.

"Wow, Peter," says Curly. "You've changed."

"I know. It's what happens when you grow up."

Curly wrinkles his forehead. "Maybe growing up isn't such a bad thing."

"Shut up, Curly!" snaps Nibs. "We don't want to grow up. We agreed."

"Why'd you come back, anyway?" Tubs asks. "We were doing fine here without you. Hook didn't even bother us."

"That's because he was in New York with me."

"And it was great. Why'd you bring him back, Peter?"

"I didn't mean to. It was an accident."

"Yeah, well thanks for nothing." The boys disappeared into their home in the hole of the root system of the great tree. Peter sits on a log and cups his face with his hands.

Poor, Peter. So unhappy already.

I call out, "Peter?"

He jerks upright and stares in my direction. "Tinkerbell? Is that you?"

Jangle pushes me into the open.

"I'm here. I'm back, too."

He runs to me and before I know what's happening, he's on his knees and his arms are wrapped around me. He smacks Jangle out of the way, quite by accident. I forget for a moment, that he can't see her here. I have the distinct trait of being the only fairy the humans can see as a result of the deal the fairy king made with Hook when I inadvertently allowed him to see the fairy kingdom. It was meant to be a punishment—free labor from me in exchange for Hook's promise that he'd stop looking for other fairies—but with everything that happened with Peter, I see it differently now. My visibility is more of a blessing than a curse.

"I'm so happy to see you, Belle."

He called me "Belle." A little string of happiness floats through me. Peter still sees me as Belle, the pretty human girl.

"I'm happy to see you, too. I'm so glad you're all right."

His smile falters.

"I mean. You're not hurt. I know you want to go back to New York."

"Can you help me again?"

Truth is, I don't know. "I'll try. But first, can you tell me what happened?"

He takes my hand, and my wings flutter like crazy. I'm embarrassed that Peter can see what his touch does to me.

I wave to Jangle and she disappears. I know she's going to the fairy village, and I don't want to think about the uproar her reappearance will cause. The fairies will be full of questions. I think belatedly that it's a mistake to let her go back alone.

I can't make myself leave Peter. I'm so relieved he's not hurt; I just want to bask in this moment. We walk until we enter the poppy meadow.

"I have good memories of this place," Peter says with a smile. I feel the corners of my mouth pull up, too, and look away shyly.

I sit in front of him so I can see his face. "What happened? How did you get back here?"

Peter lets out a long sigh. "My dad invented a machine."

I screw my nose up in confusion, but stay silent.

"He created a way for humans to travel across dimensions. Hook had something to do with it and I think their experimentation went wrong and that's how Hook ended up stuck here for so long."

"Who are the other pirates, then?"

"My dad and Hook had rented a yacht. For some reason they thought it would be safer to try the experiment off shore. The pirates are just unfortunate yacht rental staff."

Peter scrubs his face and begins again. "My dad tried frantically to get Hook back, this time from his warehouse lab. I was with my friends in the alley when the experiment went wrong again. The green hue was energy from the experiment. It swooped us up along the way."

"Why didn't your father get pulled in?"

"Apparently the energy fans out in one direction, and my father is always on the "safe" side of the box."

"The box?"

"Yeah, the artifact dad hides the invention in."

I pluck a stem of grass and twist it between my fingers. "And you know all this, how?"

Peter huffs. "Hook and I had a not-so-friendly chat after we arrived."

"I suppose you can go back whenever you want," I take a small, sad breath. "Now that you have the box?"

"Maybe if I could figure out how to use it. I'm afraid Hook has the answer to that."

I have to push down the rush of joy that springs up. I'm happy to have Peter for a little while longer. "Where is Hook now?"

"He's having a reunion party with his boat mates, and probably planning my funeral."

I stare hard into his eyes. "Why does he hate you so much?"

"Because he hates my dad and I'm a way to hurt him."

I reach over to squeeze his hand but stop when I see how much smaller mine is now than his. Peter sees me pull back.

"This is weird," he says. "I know you are Belle, that Belle is you, but..."

"I'm a fairy. I belong in Neverland."

"Do you think... "

Before Peter can finish his thought, we're interrupted by gruff voices in the adjoining forest. We instantly lay prostrate in the poppies to hide ourselves.

"He's got to be here somewhere," Hook's voice says. I see the reflection of the sun off his bald head. One Eye Gus is with him. "We have to find him. He has the box. It's our ticket back."

"I'll help you find him, but you better not leave me here again."

I gasp. I've never heard One Eye speak to Hook that way before.

"I think Hook is losing his power hold on the other pirates," Peter whispers.

They disappear back into the silk forest and I exhale. "I'm sorry, Peter."

"For what?"

"If I hadn't come to New York, Hook wouldn't have tried to find me."

Peter gently lifts my chin with his finger and stares compassionately into my eyes. My wings quiver and I almost coo.

"Tinkerbell, we're caught in a feud between my dad and Hook. This would've happened whether you came to New York or not."

I love him so much for saying that. I wish I could kiss him, but I know we're only friends, even when I was in my human form.

Peter stands up. I flap my wings and lift off the ground until my lips reach his cheek. I press them to his skin gently.

"I have to go, Peter."

I fly away, and when I'm out of the poppy field I touch ground. A glance over my shoulder confirms that Peter is staring after me. My heart is heavy, knowing our time together is short and that I have to find a way to help Peter get back to New York. Then we will say good-bye forever.

6

I knew I shouldn't have let Jangle go back to the village without me. She's standing in the square surrounded by fairies demanding answers.

"Where were you?"

"How did you get out of Neverland?

"There's only one way we know of, and it's a crime!"

Jangle looks unnerved. At least Knobs is standing with her. Then someone spots me and a hush descends. The fairy circle around Jangle breaks open, creating a path for me to enter. It's the first time in months that I've walked on the gemstone streets of the fairy village, and my legs tremble. In the distance I see the castle jutting out of Blue Mountain toward the sea. The king is standing on his balcony, a staff of gold in his right hand. I can't see his face, but I'm sure he's scowling.

Someone points a finger. "It was her, wasn't it? She's the rebel fairy. She pulled you along didn't she, Jangle?"

Jangle opens her mouth to speak but I cut in. "Yes. It's all my doing. Jangle was pulled away by accident."

Her eyelids flicker like she's debating what to say. I shake my head subtly. "I need to see the king."

The circle opens on the other end, and I walk through the village, a trail of curious fairies behind me. I pass the waterfall and my little hut. I long to go inside, climb under the covers of my purple canopy bed and sleep this all away. Instead I jut out my chin and continue on. A castle keeper answers my knock, opening the tall, heavy door.

"I'm here to make my confession to the king," I say.

"He's expecting you."

He leads me down a long, ornate hallway lit with burning torches hanging on the walls. We enter an atrium with a rock fountain in the middle. Lush green vines grow up the walls and parrots fly free in the dome of the glass ceiling.

"He wants to speak with me here?" I ask, unable to contain my surprise.

The castle keeper doesn't reply, just bows and leaves the room. I expected to be taken to a plain room to be questioned or even to the dungeon to serve out a punishment without a trial.

A bell rings and the king enters. He's dressed in a regal robe with a golden sash. His hair is parted down the middle and hangs long over his shoulders. His beard is cut short and his eyes are narrowed, examining me. I feel small and transparent, like the king can read my mind. Like he already knows what I'm going to say.

"Tinkerbell," he says with his low baritone voice. His tone is gentle and I feel confused and unworthy.

I bow. "Your majesty."

"I understand that you have something you'd like to tell me."

"I do, your majesty."

The king sits in a high back wooden chair carved with intricate designs of flowers and birds. He motions for me to sit in a similar, smaller one. I almost choke. It's the queen's chair.

I shake my head. "No, sir, thank you, but I'll stand."

"Please, for my sake, sit."

His eyes flash with kindness and a small smile forms on his lips. I'm shaking, and do as he says.

Once I tell him the truth he's bound to toss me out on my fairy behind, shouting at me with a righteous roar to never grace his presence again. I blink back tears.

"Tinkerbell, it's been a long time since you've come to see me. Please, tell me what is burdening your heart."

"I've done a grave wrong," I say. "Though I did it for a noble purpose."

"A grave wrong for a noble purpose? Either the wrong is not so grave or the purpose is not so noble."

"I'll let you decide, your majesty."

"Tell me your story."

"One of the lost boys, Peter, wanted to leave Neverland, to go to his New York."

The king knits his bushy brows. "Where is this New York?"

I swallow. "It's in another dimension."

The king nods. "I see. And did the boy succeed?"

"He did, with my help." I feel I need to explain the direness of his situation more clearly. "Hook wanted to do him harm. If I didn't help Peter, I feared things would not go well for him here."

"You wanted to spare his life?"

"Yes."

"I would say that is a noble reason." I hold back from telling the king the full truth. That I was only willing to help because of my strong affection for Peter.

"So, what did you do to help your human friend?"

His gaze bore so deeply into me, I can't help but squirm. I can tell that he knows, he has to. Everyone knows there's only one way to leave Neverland.

"I stole the queen's fairy dust."

A heavy silence fills the atrium. Even the birds stop chirping.

"I see. And you also went to Peter's New York? You and Jangle? You've both been missing for many weeks."

I can't bear to look at him any longer and move my gaze to the floor. "Yes. We went, too. But Jangle, her coming was an accident. I thought..."

"You thought what?"

"I thought I was in love."

"With a human boy?"

"Yes, your majesty. "I'm so sorry."

"Is this Peter safely returned to his home?"

"He was, but then Hook came."

"Captain Hook?" The king strokes his beard. "That explains why things were so quiet here."

"Yes, and he did something, and now they're back in Neverland."

"The both of them?"

I nod.

"And this is why you've returned also? To help Peter once again?"

My voice is small and tight. "Yes."

"I see." The king sits tall and straightens his shoulders. "You understand you've committed a crime against me and my kingdom by sneaking into the queen's private chambers and stealing her fairy dust?"

"I do."

"As noble as your reasons may be, a debt must be paid."

My stomach swirls and I wonder what my punishment will be. "Please, your majesty, I'll do anything, just don't make me go back to work for Captain Hook."

"I believe you've paid adequately for your previous demeanor. I will need some time to consider an appropriate service for you for this one."

I play with my hoop earring. "You're not going to throw me into the dungeon?"

The king's lips tighten like he's trying to keep from smiling. "No. You may go home. I will summon you at dawn."

A castle keeper shows me out and I cup my eyes against the reflection of the setting sun on the ocean. The fairies must've gotten bored of waiting because only a scattered few remain to witness my unshackled departure. I move toward my hut as if I'm in a dream. This morning I awoke in Peter's New York. I had a human body. I had *homework*.

My hut is exactly the way I'd left it except coated in an inch of dust. I snap my fingers and instantly the dust is gone. I grin with the awareness that my return to Neverland somehow restored my fairy dust. I go through the motions of making tea, noting that my stock is old and that I'll need to get new supplies in the morning. I sit in the rocking chair beside the fireplace and consider my good fortune. At least for today. Tomorrow, when the verdict comes, I may not feel so lucky. I wonder what kind of punishment the king is considering for me, and why he hasn't already decided on something.

I've almost fallen asleep sitting up, when I'm startled upright by hard knocking on the door. At first I think the king's men have come for me, but the king's men wouldn't knock.

Whoever it is knocks again.

"Come in," I call.

To my surprise, it's Knobs.

"What is it?" I ask.

He fidgets his tunic with his fingers, and his concerned expression scares me.

"Is Jangle all right?" I ask.

"She's fine. She's the one who sent me. She told me to tell you that Peter's in trouble."

7

I spring out of my rocking chair. "What kind of trouble?"

"Captain Hook and his gang have captured the Lost Boys."

I'm flying out the front door, racing out of the village, before I realize I don't know where I'm going. I turn to Knobs. "Are they on the ship?"

"No. Hook found their tree fort. The boys are being held captive there."

I spend all my energy flying to the tree fort in the middle of the silk forest. I see Jangle perched in a tree branch and it's all I can do to fly myself up to her. There's a reason fairies walk most of the time and not fly. Flying is hard work.

"Jangle!"

"Oh, Tink! Hook has the boys trapped in the tree."

Knobs joins us and I notice how he takes a spot on the other side of Jangle, pressing in close.

Hmm.

Hook paces at the entrance of the tree fort. One Eye Gus has a gun pointed inside. The other pirates surround the place.

"Oh, *blink*," I say. "Peter."

I flap my wings and Jangle grabs my arm. "You can't go in. They'll see you. I'll go."

I hate it that I can't go to Peter, but Jangle's right. I hold back.

Jangle flies above Hook's head just as he stretches out in a yawn. His bulky arm brushes Jangles wings and sets her into a spin toward the ground. I gasp and Knobs whispers, "Oh, no."

It looks like Jangle's going to crash, but her wings flap hard and she regains her momentum. Then she disappears inside.

Time slows down.

"I'm glad you're back," Knobs says. I glance sharply at him. His purple hair hangs loosely around his face, his hazel eyes staring ahead to the spot where Jangle disappeared.

"I didn't think you'd miss us," I say.

"I did, and no offence, I was especially worried about Jangle."

I look at him sharply. "Is there something going on between you that I don't know about?"

He hangs his head. "She wanted more than I did. She was tired of waiting for me and that's why she left. I was so stupid, and now, I think she's changed her mind about me."

Is this why she was so eager to leave Neverland with me? She was angry at Knobs? I was so involved with my own problems with Hook and my feelings for Peter I hadn't even noticed.

Knobs' face etches with worry. "What's taking her so long?"

"I don't know."

Just when I'm about to send Knobs in after her, Jangle's blue head pops out. She flies back to us and wilts against the trunk. Knob puts a reassuring arm around her. "What did you see?"

"The boys are tied up."

"All of them?" I ask. "Peter?"

She nods. "Yes."

"What are we going to do?" I ask. Growing panic makes my skin twitch. "Even if we sneak in and untie them, Hook and his guys are still there, armed. They won't hesitate to shoot."

Jangle points above our heads. "We can use that."

I look up and then grab onto Jangle's arms in fright. An Orangeback spider is nesting in her web. Her body is the size of a fairy's fist, with long black legs and a black underbelly. Her back is orange and from a distance, especially when she's curled up, she looks like a common sweet fruit. Her silk has an adverse reaction to skin, causing itchy hives. Her bite is deadly poisonous.

My stomach lurches.

Jangle pokes me and raises her brows. "You collect the silk," she says, "and Knob's and I will scatter it."

"Oh, Jangle, it's an *Orangeback*."

"Do it for Peter."

Of course. I'll do it for Peter.

I wish there were room in the branches for more than just me, but I accept my solo mission. I breathe in deeply and think. I need a way to gather it. An idea forms. I pull at the vines around me and quickly weave a small basket. Jangle plucks a silk tree leave and wraps it around my right hand. "Fill the basket, Tink."

I stare up at the Orangeback and swallow. I can do this.

I engage my wings and lift off until I'm even with the spider's web. I grab a fistful of silk and the Orangeback moves quickly toward the disturbance. Toward me. I shriek and let myself fall back to the branch below. I'm panting and Jangle pats me on the back. "You're okay. You have some."

I whimper. "It's not enough."

"It's a start," Knobs adds. "Go to the other side now."

I inhale and muster my courage. I repeat the performance on the other side, including another shriek as the Orangeback races toward me again.

I lower to the branch and stare at the silk in my basket. "Is it enough?"

"One more time," Jangle says.

I'm trembling as I stare up at the Orangeback. She's angry now, and waiting for me, I can feel it. I gulp and flap my wings. They're sluggish and weak. I muster up all my energy and fly to what's left of the web, opposite to were the spider waits.

I whip away a palm full of silk, and the spider dodges. My wings flail and then collapse. I fall, a scream escaping my mouth. I'm waiting for the thud of the hard ground to shatter my body but I'm suddenly hovering over the earth.

"We got you," Jangle says. I see the tips of her and Knobs' wings flapping rapidly from underneath me. They set me on my feet and whisk the silk away.

I hide behind the trunk. I'm certain my screams were

heard by Hook's men. One Eye Gus moves toward me, gun raised and at the ready. I take a tentative step back.

"Here, fairy, fairy," he says. I stumble on an exposed tree root and fall. His free hand swipes the air and he grasps my wings, lifting me like a cat holding her kitten by the scruff of the neck. I yell out and One Eye laughs. "Look what I caught, boss!"

I kick and squirm and search for Jangle and Knobs. I can't see them anywhere.

The weight on my wings causes a searing pain in my back, making my eyes water. One Eye holds me up like a trophy to Hook.

His dark eyes glint and he lets out a dry chuckle. "Tinkerbell," he says. "Or is it Belle? It's nice to see you again."

"I wish I could say the same."

He clasps his hands together, giddy, like a madman. "I'm so happy we can have this little reunion." Then his smile fades. He points inside. "Tie her up."

One Eye tugs me by the wings and I cry out.

"Tink!" Peter sees me hanging like a planter from Eye One's hand and I feel humiliated and powerless.

"Leave her alone!" He wrestles against the rope around his wrists and ankles. "She's got nothing to do with this."

One Eye points his pistol at Peter. "Don't try anything stupid."

Peter's eyes lock on mine and I whisper, "I'm okay."

One Eye sits me on the table and ties me to a heavy wooden candle stick. He levels his good-eye on Peter. "Try anything, and I light the candle."

8

"Belle, are you okay?" Peter's eyes are sad and soft. "I'm sorry you got pulled into this."

I'm stuck on the way Peter alternately calls me Tink and Belle.

"Tinkerbell?"

"I'm fine," I say, forcing a smile. My wings could use a massage, but everyone in the room is tied up and uncomfortable so I don't complain. I take in my surroundings. The hollow tree root system is big enough to house four boys. Curly is pressed up against a twisty root, Tubs to another across the room. Nibs and Peter are sitting on the two lone chairs made by weaving vines to driftwood, Peter looking particularly oversized on his. It's strange to see him so much bigger and older than the other boys now.

The Lost Boys aren't happy to see me. The three of them frown and scowl.

"She's just going to bring us more trouble," Curly mutters.

Peter snaps, "Leave her alone." A swirl of happiness fills me when he comes to my defense.

"What's Hook going to do to us?" asks Nibs.

"I want to go home," Tubs whimpers. His lips tighten and his faces flushes like he's trying hard not to burst into tears.

Curly twists his neck. "Don't you dare wimp out now."

"Just be patient," I say. "My friends will help us."

Curly laughs. "What friends? There's no one else on this deserted island but us."

"If you believe that," Peter says, winking at me, "you're stupider than I thought."

Hook ducks in. "Too much talking going on here." He stuffs his hands in his pockets like he doesn't have a care in the world. He saunters over to the table. "Aren't you a cute little ornament?"

"Let me go," I say. He leans in close and I choke on his foul breath.

"I don't think so." He reaches toward me like he's going to stroke my hair, like I'm his pet. I spit at him.

He pulls back and slowly wipes his face with his sleeves, never letting his eyes off me. "You shouldn't've done that." He reaches into his pocket and pulls out a lighter. "A souvenir," he says with a humorless grin. "From New York."

He ignites the lighter and holds it over the candle flame. "This might hurt a little."

Peter calls out. "No, wait! I'll do what you want."

Hook snuffs out the lighter and a slimy smile, like he knows he won a game by cheating, crosses his face. "I thought you'd see things my way."

"Don't Peter," I say. "Don't give it to him."

I know Hook wants the box. He wants to control inter-dimensional travel. A tool that will make him powerful in a way a guy like Hook should never be.

"I have to, Tink. I can't let him hurt you."

Where are Jangle and Knobs? I crane my neck to see past Hook but his body blocks my view of the entrance.

Peter begins, "I buried it..."

"No!" I shout. "Wait!"

Hook gives me the evil eye, but then his attention is caught by a commotion outside. His men are yelping and a smile tugs up on my lips. Jangle and Knobs are at work dropping Orangeback silk on our enemies. Hook leaves to investigate.

"What's going on?" Peter says, eyeing me. "Your friends?"

I nod happily, especially because Jangle and Knobs have arrived with triumphant smiles on their faces.

"It's about time," I say.

"Who are you talking to?" Curly asks. I ignore him.

"The big boys are running to Mermaid Lagoon like babies," Jangles says with a sparkle in her eye. I burst out laughing. Salt water is going to make their problems so much worse.

"She's nuts," Curly adds. To them I'm talking and laughing to myself. Jangle cuts me free and my sudden, unexplained escape gets the notice of the boys.

Jangle and Knobs work on freeing them and I tend to Peter.

"What happened?" he asks as he rubs the circulation back into his wrists. I tell him about the Orangeback silk and how Hook is probably a nice shade of red and covered in hives right now.

"Good work, Tink!" Peter's smile and affirmation have the same effect on me here as they did in New York. Except this time Peter can see my wings sizzle and zing. A blush rushes up my neck, and I look to the ground.

Peter lifts my chin gently with his finger, and I'm afraid my wings are going to pop right off.

"You're so cute when you're embarrassed."

Peter just called me cute! I think I might just die of happiness.

"See you later, love birds," Jangle says.

I wave and Peter waves, too. "Bye Jangle."

She stops and her eyes widen with shock. "Can he see me?"

I laugh. "No. He knows you're there, though. I told him."

"Okay, tell him I say bye."

"She says bye."

"What's next, Peter?" Tubs asks.

"Why are you asking him?" Curly snaps. "I'm the leader here now."

Tubs crosses his arms. "Fine, what's next, Curly?"

I don't think Curly thought that far ahead. "Um, I...we... I'm..."

"I know a place you can hide," I say.

9

Peter searches my face. "Where?"

"There's a cave on the other side of Blue Mountain. It's kind of out of the way, and you have to do a bit of climbing."

Peter smiles. "Sounds perfect." He rolls up his sleeping mat, and packs a hand-made sack of woven vines with the candle, a dish, and a spoon. He digs under one of the roots and produces a sword packed in its sheath. He pulls the sword free and admires the blade. "I didn't have a chance to dig this up before Hook and his men arrived."

I stare at him in alarm. "Peter."

"Don't worry, Belle. It's just for looks."

The other boys pack up their things.

"Let's see this cave," Curly says.

I float to the floor and Peter takes my hand. "Lead the way."

I point north and they follow me. The forest thickens before we reach the foot of the mountain. We have to tread carefully not to trip over roots and need to draw away vines to find passage. All the while I'm completely focused on the sensation of Peter's hand wrapped over mine. I'm filled with the desire to be bigger. I'm the size of a two year-old human child and I feel completely inadequate with my little palm raised high to grip his. I pull it away, not because I don't want to hold his hand but because I do. As Belle, not Tink. I hold in a frustrated sigh.

"Is everything all right, Tink?"

I hate how he's defaulted to my fairy name again. "I'm fine."

The boys lag behind, bickering over something, Food, I think. They're hungry.

I'm about to tell Peter we can stop and pick passion fruit and huckleberries, but he ducks a little to look at my face before I open my mouth. "Have you seen the king?"

With all the current excitement, I'd momentarily forgotten about the morning meeting I'd had with the king. I nod.

"What did he say?"

"He's going to summon me in the morning to announce my punishment."

"Are you frightened?"

"Not really. The king is just, but he's also kind. My punishment will fit the crime. I really only want to serve my sentence, whatever it is, and get it over with."

"You'll let me know, won't you?"

I don't really want to share any further humiliation with Peter but I say, "Sure."

It's my turn to ask questions. "Did you really hide the box?"

"Yep."

"Where?"

Peter hesitates. "I don't want you to get in the middle of my hassle with Hook."

"I think I'm already in the middle of it."

He shrugs. "It doesn't work, anyway."

I stop short. "What do you mean? It worked to get you here."

"I fiddled with it before I buried it. Tried everything. I don't know what I'm missing, but I'm missing something."

"Can we eat?" Tubs says loudly from behind. "I'm starved."

We're at the base of the mountain with a long climb ahead. I point. "The cave is up there. Might be a good idea to stop to eat now."

Peter removes his sword and uses it to hack open a couple coconuts. I'm fixated by the way his bicep bulges. His eyes move to mine and I'm mortified he caught me staring. He smiles then hands me one. I'm dying of thirst and take a long drink.

After we're finished, Peter says, "We should get going. It's almost dusk and Tinkerbell still needs to get home."

I love the tenderness I hear in Peter's voice, how he's concerned for my safety and wellbeing. It energizes me and I show the boys the trail. Peter hacks at the overgrowth with his sword and we climb.

"How do we know she's not leading us on a wild goose chase?" Curly says when we're half way up.

"Why would I do that?" I say, feeling indignant. "Do you want a hiding place from the pirates or not?"

"He's just lazy." Peter stops. "You're out of shape Curly. Got too lax with Hook being gone, have you?"

"Shut up!" Curly says.

Peter stares down hard at him, his bigger body looking even more imposing being on the upside of the hill. "Or you'll what?"

Curly mutters, "Never mind."

We keep hiking and finally we reach the cave. It's huge for me, but the boys have to duck a little to walk around. At least it's wide enough for them to sleep in. The view from the opening is vast. You can see the whole north side of the island all the way to the ocean.

"This is great, Tink," Peter says.

"I have to go home now." My wings droop. It's time to say goodbye to Peter, and I don't know when or even *if* I'll see him again.

"I know your village is on the other side of the ridge," Peter says. "I'll walk you."

"You don't have to."

"I know. I want to."

There is a spectacular sunset painting the sky purple and pink at the top of the ridge. Peter and I stand and breathe in its beauty.

The fairy village is below, and I know that only I can see how the gems in the path and in the brickwork of the huts sparkle in the setting sunlight, and how the king's castle explodes with beauty in its brightness. Peter can't hear how the waterfall laughs as it falls and the chatter of the fairies working and playing rings like a melodious flute.

"It's down there, isn't it?" Peter says.

I nod.

"Can I... will you...let me see it again?"

I remember last time I opened Peter's eyes to see my village. I'm ashamed because my motives were ignoble. I'd hope to entice Peter to stay. It didn't work and he'd gotten angry. He'd stormed away and that's when Hook cornered and attacked him.

I want to redeem those memories. I nod. "Okay. But there's something I failed to tell you last time. Open eyes give you access."

"What does that mean?"

There's a reason why you and the boys, Hook and his men, never enter the village. It's protected. Only those who can see it can enter.

"I thought Hook saw it? Isn't that what got you into trouble in the first place?"

I sigh. "Yes. The king had to seal it again, to keep him out."

"I won't go there," Peter says. "I just want to see it one last time before..."

I understand. Before I get punished and he finds a way back to New York.

I snap my fingers and blow the fairy dust in Peter's face. He closes his eyes and when he opens them again he gasps.

"It's so beautiful." Peter inhales and lets out a long breath. "Thank you for letting me see it again." He gets down on his knees, a move that makes me catch my breath. "You are a very special fairy. A very special person, Belle." He leans down and kisses me on the forehead, then disappears over the ridge into the dark of night.

A tear runs down my cheek.

I know Peter just said good-bye.

10

I feel numb and alone as I lay in the dark on my pretty, purple canopy bed. My thoughts flip through the events of this impossibly long day. Waking up in New York, looking for Peter, traveling back to Neverland with Jangle. Facing the king and rescuing Peter. Saying good-bye without saying a word.

I stare at the small version of my human hand. In one way I'm glad to be back. This is what I am. This is where I belong.

I think.

I'm surprised at how much I miss my human body. How much I miss my wardrobe. Even the craziness of 7th and Central Park. I miss my apartment and wonder what will happen to it when we don't pay the rent at the end of the month. Mrs. Weeks will probably clear out our stuff and hand it over to someone new.

I'm so confused by my feelings. And I'm not used to

being alone. Jangle has practically been my shadow these last two months in New York. Or, maybe I've been hers.

I slip out of bed and put on a robe. I hope she doesn't mind that I'm about to wake her in the middle of the night. I open my front door, jump back and scream.

"Jangle!"

"Tink! You scared me half to death." She brushes past me and heads straight for my rocking chair. I snap my fingers and the fireplace alights.

"I'll make tea."

Minutes later I'm handing Jangle her cup.

"It's just weird, you know?" she says, looking up at me from under her blue bangs.

"Yeah. Do you miss it?"

"A little."

I raise my brows in question. "So, Knobs?"

"Knobs what?"

"Do you like him?"

"Sure. What?" Her eyes brighten with understanding. "No!"

"I think he likes you."

"He does not."

I chuckle. "If you say so."

"I say so." She taps her teacup with her fingernails. "What about you? What's happening next?"

I sit in a chair opposite her and take another sip. "The king is summoning me tomorrow to announce my punishment."

"Are you sorry you came?" she asks softly. "I mean, if you could go back, would you?"

Good question. What is in New York if I don't have Peter?

"Probably not."

We both finish our tea and yawn at the same time.

"I don't want to be alone," I say.

"Me neither."

"Good. I get the right side of the bed."

I awake to the sun shining through my bedroom window and a knocking on the front door. Jangle moans. "Can you get that?"

I pad to the door and open it a crack. It's one of the king's men.

"I'll need a few minutes," I say.

"The king says to take your time and to wear a dress."

Wear a dress? To my sentencing?

"Why does his majesty want me to wear a dress?"

"I don't question the king." The guard nods. "I'll wait outside."

I walk back to my room in a daze. Jangle sits up and wipes her eyes with her fists. "I'm sorry, Tink. I forgot that this is...an important day. I'll come to support you."

"He wants me to wear a dress."

Jangle stares with a furrowed brow.

"Why would the king want me in a dress?" I say. "Is he going to make a spectacle of me? In one of those head and wrist locks like we learned the human's used in history class?"

I'm filled with dread and despair. I shouldn't be surprised. *I stole from the king*. I deserved as much.

"No, no, it can't be that." Jangle jumps out of bed and

paces the small foot rug. "How long do you have to get ready?"

"The guard said I could take my time."

Jangle wrinkles her nose and tugs on her hair. "That doesn't make any sense."

"I'm going to wash up," I say, still stunned.

Jangle sprints to the kitchen and yells over her shoulder. "I'll make breakfast. And then I'll help you make yourself beautiful for the king."

When she says that, I'm suddenly terrified.

11

"Look at it this way," Jangle says as she creates thin braids and pins up my hair. "He's bound to give you a lighter sentence if you blow him away with your beauty."

I almost scoff, but when I watch Jangle place tiny pink gems in my hair, my jaw drops. I *do* look pretty.

Jangle steps back to examine her handiwork. "Those weeks in New York really paid off."

I smile. Jangle did have a knack for fashion. She moves to my closet and opens the door. "Hmm, I think we might have a problem."

I join her and groan. "I'm not much of a dress person." I remember all the skirts and dresses Dylan helped me pick out in New York. "Well, at least I wasn't. What are we going to do?"

Jangle links her arm through mine. "I don't know. Maybe we should go visit the seamstress?"

"She'll need more than a minute's notice to sew up something nice."

Someone taps on the door. My heart drops to the floor. "Oh, no, Jangle. It's the summons and I'm not ready!"

"I'll stall. Choose your best dress."

My pulse is hammering. Not because I don't have the right dress, but because I'm about to face the king and hear my sentence. My biggest fear is that he'll banish me from the village.

"Tinkerbell!" Jangle calls. I hear the light clapping of her slippered feet on my hut floor racing toward me. "The king sent you a gift!"

She has a box in her arms.

My expression reflects the one on Jangle's face: surprise, intrigue and confusion.

"Open it," she says holding the box out for me.

I lift the lid and a soft gasp escapes my lips. The most beautiful fabric I've ever seen is folded inside. I lift it carefully and pull it out. It's shimmering pink with white lace framing a scooped collar. A black silk band wraps around the waist.

"What's going on, Jangle?"

"I don't know, but you better put it on."

My robe falls to the floor and I slip into the soft, silky dress. I look at my reflection in the mirror and I'm speechless. My first thought is that I'm beautiful. My second thought is that I wish Peter could see me. My third thought is the king is playing with my head. My situation is worse than I thought.

"I guess I'm ready to go," I say.

The king's guard leads me back to the castle. The village fairies see me—how could they not!—and I feel conspicuous and on display. The murmuring grows and I know they're talking about me. *I'd* be talking about me.

The large wooden doors of the castle open before I'm close enough to knock. My heart thumps in my chest. The guard leads me to the king's chambers, a private area where I've never been before. My anxiety level is as high as New York City's Chrysler building.

The king is seated on an ornate, high back chair—his throne. His lips twitch when he sees me, but he doesn't smile. The guards hold back and I stand before him. I wonder if I should kneel, but I opt for a curtsy and let my arms hang loose at my side.

"Tinkerbell, I've had time to consider your punishment."

My stomach clenches at his words.

"These are the crimes you are accused of: You trespassed in forbidden rooms of my home. You stole property belonging to the former queen. You left the fairy kingdom through forbidden means. You provided passage, via this forbidden means, to an alternate dimension for a member of this fairy kingdom, and for an alien to invade our kingdom."

He steadies his blue eyes on me. "How do you plead?"

I swallow hard. I feel like passing out from fear. "Guilty, your majesty."

"Tinkerbell, I'm taking into account the extenuating circumstances. Had we not been invaded by unfriendly aliens from another dimension, the temptations you faced would never have existed. My agreement with Captain Hook, established to keep the peace on Neverland, exposed you to the deceitful and cunning ways of the aliens. You are gullible and easily corrupted."

I frown a little at his assessment, but work hard to keep my face blank. I want him to get to it. What is my sentence?

"There is only one way I know of to rid Neverland of the aliens once and for all. The magic of a fairy queen's dust. Since you are the fairy guilty of ridding us of our only resource, you will assist in our acquiring it again."

My eyelids flutter and I shake my head. "How your majesty?"

"You must become the next queen."

My mind swirls at his words. The king rises from his throne and kneels in front of me. My heart stops.

"Tinkerbell, you're the strongest, bravest, and most intelligent fairy I know, important attributes for the next queen of our great fairy kingdom. You are also very beautiful. Please become my wife."

I'm dazed, dumbfounded, or as they say in New York, freaked out. Peter's face flashes through my mind. I don't love the king, but I know I don't have a choice. This is my punishment.

I feel disembodied, but I hear my voice say, "I will."

The End of Episode 5

I hope you enjoyed *Daze & Befuddled*—I'd love it if you'd

leave a review on Amazon. They are so helpful to Indie Authors like me and help readers find the books they love.

Read on for an excerpt of the final episode, FAIRY MADNESS.

FAIRY MADNESS

LOVE, TINK - EPISODE 6

FAIRY MADNESS

Episode 6 in the Love, Tink Series

by
Lee Strauss

SUMMARY

In the final episode of the Love, Tink series, Tinkerbell must face the consequences of her crimes and become the next queen of the fairy kingdom in order to send all the humans out of Neverland for good. She doesn't love the king, but it's her punishment to bear.

Turns out Peter doesn't see it that way. And he's not the only one.

1

I'm sitting in the living room of my hut, having tea with Jangle. The logs in the fire are snapping and my rocking chair is creaking. Jangle makes a strangled-sounding sipping noise. We're not alone. Sitting in the kitchen are my new personal guard and handmaiden.

Jangle whispers, "Will I have to call you your majesty?"

"Jangle!"

"But will I?"

"I don't know. Oh, what a mess." My eyes dart to my new companions and I clear my throat. I have to be careful what I say around them.

"At least he's good looking."

"The king? You think so?" I've always found the king to be pleasant, in looks and manner, but I'd never considered him to be good looking.

"Yeah," Jangle says, tugging her hair. "He's not *hot,* but he's very attractive in a regal sort of way. You could do worse."

"I don't love him."

"You can learn to love him. Besides, you got off easy as far as punishments go. Half the girls here would die to be the new queen."

"Would you?"

Jangle hedges. "It's not about me, Tink. This is you." She squeals a little. "You're going to be the next queen!"

I can't find the happiness she's looking for. I stare into the flames.

"You're thinking about him, aren't you?"

"He's here. How can I not?"

"He's here until you send him and all the humans away with your fairy dust when you become queen. Then it will be best if you forget about Peter and New York and everything except what you have to do to fulfill your duties to the fairy kingdom."

She's right, I know. I nod and force a small smile.

Jangle leaves and I'm left alone with my new companions. I know they're here to help and protect me, but I feel watched and guarded. The king wants to make the announcement of our engagement tomorrow and the wedding will take place in three days. I'm not sure what the rush is, but I expect the king is ready to rid Neverland of the humans once and for all. And he's lonely. I hope I can make him happy.

I go to bed early, before the sun has set and darkness falls because I don't know what else to do. I can't wander the village without being questioned about my sentencing and I vowed not to say a word until the morning's announcement. The guard will sleep on a mat by my front door and my handmaiden on a cot in my room. I lie on my bed and stare at the purple silk canopy floating above. In three days the castle will be my new home. I'll miss my little hut.

It's been an emotionally exhausting day. I quickly doze off but wake to a rumbling sound of thunder. I bolt upright. My room is dark and I wait for the flash of lightening that doesn't come. My eyes adjust and I make out my handmaiden's form lying prostrate on her cot.

I hear the thunder again. Its sounds melodious and oddly like my New York name: Belle.

Bbbbeeellleee!

I jump out of bed, and tiptoe softly past my maiden and my guard. Outside I hear it again. I see a boy's silhouette on the ridge. It's Peter. He's calling me.

2

Peter's in trouble.

I engage my wings and fly as fast and as hard as I can, over the tree tops, finding my way by the light of the moon. I'm exhausted when I land at his feet, and work to keep from puffing like an old dog. Peter bends down.

"Are you okay?"

"I'm fine," I say, catching my breath. "Are you? Is something wrong?"

Peter places his hand on my shoulder. "I frightened you, didn't I? I'm sorry."

"So, you're okay? Nothing's wrong?"

"I'm okay, but I wouldn't say nothing's wrong."

He sits on the moss, hands braced on the top of his knees. I sit cross-legged beside him.

"I couldn't stop thinking about you, and your...meeting with the king. What did he say? Is he sending you back to Hook?"

My chest floods with happiness. Peter is concerned about me. He cares.

"No, I don't have to work for Hook again."

He exhales. "That's good. What then?"

"He wants all the humans gone from Neverland."

"I'd like that, too, but what does that have to do with your punishment."

I play with my earring and wince when I tug too hard. "All he needs to accomplish that is the queen's fairy dust."

"But," Peter furrows his brow. "I thought you used it all."

"I did. He needs new fairy dust, which means he needs a new queen." I pause, hating what I have to say next. "I'm going to marry him in three days."

Peter's eyes cut to mine. The moonlight reflects off his sharp features. His gaze narrows and his jaw tightens. "You're only fifteen."

I sigh. "I'm not really fifteen, Peter."

"How old are you?"

"I don't know. We don't celebrate birthdays here."

"Do you love him?"

I shake my head. "No. If I did, it wouldn't be much of a punishment, would it?"

"Why does the king want you? Can't he find another fairy chick who'd want to marry him?"

"Despite my flaws, or maybe because of them, the king has taken an interest in me. He thinks I'm brave, and intelligent. And beautiful."

Peter strokes my face. "He's right."

I'm stunned by his forthrightness. I glance down feeling embarrassed.

"What if I could get the box to work? Then you wouldn't have to use fairy dust to get rid of us."

I look up daring to hope. "Do you think you could do it?"

"I'll try."

"I'd still have to be punished somehow." The small flicker of hope goes out. "Maybe in a way that would be worse than marrying the king."

"But, if I got the box to work, you could come back with us."

"Back to New York?" If I did that, I really would be banished from Neverland. "I don't know."

We sit in silence and I wish we could be together, safe under the light of the Neverland moon forever. Finally, Peter speaks. "So, you're really going to go through with it. You're going to marry someone you don't love?"

It sounds awful when he says it that way. Tears burn behind my eyelids and I pinch them closed. "It's my punishment."

3

The sun is stroking Neverland with long, orange fingers when I tap lightly on Jangle's hut door. She doesn't answer, so I tap louder.

"Jangle, it's me."

She cracks the door open. Her blue hair is sticking up at all angles and she stifles a yawn. "Tinkerbell?"

"Can I come in?" I'm already through the entrance before I finish asking the question.

Jangle closes the door and turns to me. "What's wrong?"

"I just saw Peter."

"I thought you were going to stay away from him?"

"He called me from the ridge. He's worried about me. And he doesn't understand."

Jangle sighs and puts on a kettle for tea.

"I know, I know," I moan. "I just wish..."

"Wish what?"

"That things were different."

"Well, they're not. You're lucky you haven't been banished to the dungeons. As they say in New York, you need to suck it up."

Sometimes I hate her.

Her face softens. "Look. Think of it this way. You get to have a big party thrown in your honor and you get to live in a castle. It's not so bad."

"Will you be my maid of honor?"

Jangle's face breaks into a broad smile. "How could I pass a chance to stand one person away from the king?"

I pass on the tea and sneak back inside my hut. The guard snorts and I freeze. He resumes his regular breathing and I trod past him softly. It's not like I really need a guard. The fairies may not like me much anymore, but they're not violent. I'm not in any physical danger.

Getting past my handmaiden isn't as easy. She looks like she's asleep, but the moment I lie down and pull the covers up to my chin, she speaks. "Where were you?"

"With my friend, Jangle." Not a lie, just not the whole truth. Besides, she's *my* handmaiden, I'm not hers. I roll over so my back is toward her. She apparently gets the message since she doesn't probe any further.

I fall into a deep sleep, which is a good thing because it's not long. The roosters crow and I groan.

"You must rise," my maiden says. "The king awaits."

She wants to help me get ready, but I'm uncomfortable undressing with her around. I send her to fetch Jangle for me instead. I need her support to help get me through whatever I must face today.

Jangle clings to my arm as we accompany my guard and

maiden to the castle. The villagers stare. I keep my eyes down, but Jangle stares back with a phony smile and waves. "Just wait until they hear the news," she says snickering.

I'm worried about what they'll do. Fairies don't get physical, but that doesn't mean they don't have strong opinions. They do and they're not afraid to make them known.

Jangle giggles as we reach the tall, wooden doors. "I've never been inside the castle before."

I smile. I'm happy to share this experience with her.

A castle keeper greets us and my guard and maiden fall behind until it's just Jangle and me following him to the courtyard. A tea party for two has been prepared, but when the king's servants see I've brought Jangle they quickly present a third chair and place settings. The courtyard is beautiful, full of colorful flowers and luscious greenery. The patio is made up of crystal and white gemstone, and white exotic birds fly freely and chatter overhead. I spot a little monkey eating a sweetfruit.

Jangle gapes. "This is spectacular." She's right, it is.

The king arrives, dressed in a royal blue tunic with a golden belt hanging loosely on his hips. His wings are straight and tall, pointing out beyond his head and shimmering in the sunlight. Jangle and I curtsy. I never used to curtsy, maybe because I always wore trousers when I visited to make my reports on Hook, but now, with this new situation, I can't imagine not.

The king folds both of his hands over mine. "Tinkerbell." Then he kisses my cheek.

I blush at this affectionate gesture. I motion to Jangle. "This is my friend, Jangle. She's agreed to be my maid of honor."

The king shakes her hand and I'm surprised by her sophisticated composure. "It's a pleasure to meet you face to face, your majesty," she says.

The servants pour the tea and produce tiered platters filled with pastries and chocolates.

"Please," the king says, "help yourself."

I take one to be polite, but my stomach is churning too much to actually eat. I'm engaged. To. The. King. My tongue feels like it's stuck to the roof of my mouth. I'm thankful Jangle doesn't share my nerves.

"This is so beautiful," she says. "I love the smell of the flora."

"Thank you," the king replies. "And I'm sure you've seen many lovely things...in your travels."

I almost choke on my tea.

"Do you mean New York?" Jangle asks, bravely.

"I do."

"New York is fascinating, I won't lie." She goes on to tell him all about 7th and how frightened we were at first, but that after awhile we figured out how to live and thrive there. The king looks duly impressed.

"I'm surprised you returned to Neverland after such an exciting escapade."

"It was fun, and different, and I'm really glad I got to go." She catches herself. "Even though it wasn't supposed to happen. But I'm really happy to be back. There's no place like Neverland."

The king smiles at her and holds her gaze. "I'm happy to hear that." Then he turns to me. "Are you happy, also?"

I swallow and force a smile. And then I lie. "Of course."

After tea, the king leads me to his balcony that overlooks

the village. His trumpeter blows the horn, calling all the villagers to the square to hear a royal announcement. My legs tremble with nerves and I look over my shoulder at Jangle who gives me a thumbs up.

The murmurs begin the moment they spot me standing beside the king.

"My people," he begins. "I come to you with joyous news. In two days there will be a wedding celebration. Allow me to introduce my bride-to-be. Tinkerbell."

A hush descends on the crowd, followed by a slow, reluctant applause. Then someone shouts out, "Long live the queen," and I want to burst into tears.

I DREAM that Peter is calling again.

I sit upright and strain to hear. Is it real or a dream?

Bbbbeeellleee!

I tiptoe pass my maiden and around the guard until I'm outside. I see Peter's silhouette and groan. Why is he calling me again? He knows I can't see him. I go back to bed and ignore his call. I worry that he might really be in trouble. I can't live with the thought that Peter might need my help and I refused to give it. I slip out again and fly to the ridge.

"Peter, what is it?"

"I'm sorry, Belle. I know you're not supposed to see me, but I need your help."

"What happened?"

"The box is gone."

"Gone? How?"

Hook found me digging it up. He had all his men with him and I was alone."

"Oh no."

"He has the box. We have to get it back."

4

I follow Peter down Blue Mountain. My wings are too tired to fly, so I'm forced to walk. Peter has longer legs than he did last time and I struggle to keep up. I slip on the shale and pebbles roll down the mountain, hitting the back of Peter's legs. He stops and sees how far behind I am.

"I'm sorry," he says. "Let's try this."

Before I have my breath I'm losing it again because Peter's strong arms have lifted me over his head and onto his back.

"Hang on."

He races down the hill and I hold onto his muscular shoulders, my legs gripping his narrow waist and my heart beating from the thrill of touching him this closely. My wings zing and flitter and I feel a silly grin spread across my face.

The moonlight is bright, like a gigantic spotlight on Neverland, lighting the way for Peter's rapid steps.

I speak into his ear. "Where are we going?"

"The lagoon."

Peter doesn't slow down and I realize how high the level of his anxiety is. Peter is very worried about Hook having this box. We reach the beach and Peter gently lifts me off his back and lowers me to the ground. A flare of disappointment shoots through me.

He points to Hook's ship. "It's with him on his yacht."

I take in the Mermaid Lagoon and the soft, rhythmic slapping of waves hitting the shore. The salty smell of the sea fills my lungs. I flinch when my eyes land on the cave door entrance to Hook's office. Polly sits in the window, preening herself.

Hook's ship gently bobs in the harbor.

"What should we do?" I ask.

"I was hoping you could answer that question. Do you have some spare fairy dust?"

"Say I do? Then what?"

"You could create a diversion?"

"I could, but I think I have a better idea."

"What's that?"

"Recruit a fairy Hook *can't* see."

Peter waits for me as I rush back to the village and tap three times on Jangle's door. When she doesn't answer, I tap more urgently. Finally, she cracks it open and stares at me through puffy eyes. "Tink, you have to stop waking me up in the middle of the night. I need my beauty sleep."

"Peter needs our help."

She raises an eyebrow and waves me in. "I thought we weren't seeing Peter anymore. You know, because of your new fiancé?"

I haven't even thought of the king once since Peter called for me, and I blush as I recall my recent pony back ride with him.

"Please, just one more time. Hook stole his box."

Her wings spring to attention. "The magic inter-dimension traveling box?"

"That's the one."

"Let me change my clothes."

Five minutes later, I'm standing with Jangle in front of Peter at the beach.

"She's here?" Peter says looking at my right side.

Jangle stands on my left. I point. "She's over here."

"Does she still have blue hair?"

I nod.

"Cool. And she's into this?"

Jangle folds her arms and taps a toe. "I hate how he talks about me like I'm not here"

I throw her a glance. "He can't see you." I turn to Peter. "She's into it."

She tugs on her hair. "Only because I despise Hookley."

Peter's eyes move to my left to what is just an empty space to him.

"I wish I could see you, Jangle. Thanks for coming."

Jangle huffs. "Fine. What's the plan?"

"What's the plan?" I repeat.

Peter gets on his knees and tells us. When he's finished he says, "What'd you guys think? Will it work?"

5

"Why don't I just walk on board and take the box?" Jangle asks.

"Because, even though the pirates can't see you, they can see it," I answer. "If the box mysteriously floats itself out the door, they're going to know there's a fairy underneath it."

"Okay, we'll do it Peter's way. But only because getting the box is for the greater good."

We creep close to the shore but remain in the shadows so that the sleeping goon supposedly guarding the yacht doesn't see us when he startles awake. Jangle walks along the ramp onto the boat and inches carefully by him. Her task is to find the box and hide it on the yacht.

Peter and I exchange worried looks. As long as Jangle can locate the box and move it without anyone seeing it move away by itself, she'll be fine. We wait for Jangle to signal from the deck. She appears and flaps her arm.

I snap the fingers on both of my hands and wave at the yacht. It tilts back and forth like its caught in a storm, except the sky is clear and the wind is calm. The goon wakes up and yells. In short order Hook is standing at the helm, the moonlight reflecting off his shiny bald head like a beacon.

I stop the "storm."

"Who's out there?" Hook shouts.

Peter steps into view. He's holding a fake box, the size and shape of the real thing and waves it in the air. "Looking for this?"

Hook disappears inside and we know he's looking for his box. If Jangle did her job, he won't find it.

Moments later Hook reappears and shouts to his men, pointing in Peter's direction.

"Are you sure they won't catch you?" I ask.

Peter smirks. "I can run laps around those old guys."

The pirates sprint down the ramp.

"Now's your time to prove it," I say. I bury myself in the bushes and hold my breath as Hook and his men rush by in hot pursuit of Peter. Jangle is on deck with the box. Unfortunately, she's not alone like she expected. The goon is still there.

His voice carries over the water. "What the heck?" He's sees the box floating in midair. Jangle tries to dodge him, but the goon stays positioned in front of her, grasping at the air toward Jangle. She fakes right; he stays in front. She runs and he chases, guessing her position and dives for her legs. She falls and I scream.

I run up the plank and grab his neck from behind. His hands leave Jangle to grab at me. I release him, but not before he grips my wing. He may not be able to see Jangle, but he can see me. I yelp in pain as he tosses me through the air. I grab hold of the rail as I pass over it, avoiding a midnight swim. Jangle picks up the box.

"Throw it here!" I shout. I'm back on the deck and I lift my hands.

The box goes high, over my head. I flap my wings to catch it, but I'm slammed by the goon's body. He topples over the rail, missing the box. I'm stuck underneath him and barely get a breath before plunging into the salty water.

6

There's a small part of me, the part that believes in fairytales and happy endings that thinks maybe the box could be the answer. If it works to take all the humans back to New York, then the king's objective will be met and we won't need fairy dust to do it. I wouldn't have to marry the king and maybe he'll go easy on me.

That dream dies as I watch a dark square object slowly sink to the ocean floor beneath me.

I dogpaddle upward, the reflection of the moonlight showing me the way. Fairies aren't great swimmers, in part because of the way our wings interfere with the water, and I gasp and choke for air when my face breaks the surface.

I can't see the goon, but the yacht and the shore are impossibly far away.

"Help!" My voice is small and gets lost in the roar of the sea. I flail and flap my arms. The current jerks me down and I spin, my wings pulling painfully at my back. My face breaks the surface again, and I gulp air.

Fairies live for a long time, but we're not immortal. And I'm about to drown. The salt of my tears mix with the sea. I won't have a chance to say goodbye.

I close my eyes and except my fate. I feel a tug on my shoulder and I expect to be pulled down one final time. Except that I'm pulled up instead. I open my eyes to see Jangle's face straining as she flaps her wings, dragging my soggy body out of the water and toward the beach.

We both drop onto the wet sand with a thud, breathing hard and heavy.

Tears stream down my temples and into my ears. "We lost the box," I whimper.

"At least we didn't lose you, Tink."

I reach for Jangle and squeeze her hand. "You saved my life. Thank you."

"You're welcome."

The horizon grows a dewy purple. "We should find Peter," I say.

"No, we should go home. We have an appointment with the seamstress this morning."

Just then we hear men's voices. I scurry to my feet and Jangle helps me to hide behind a log.

Hook's growly voice echoes through the lagoon. "It was a decoy!"

I search for any sign of Peter being captured and breathe with relief when it's only pirates returning to the yacht.

Hook cusses when he sees that the goon is missing. We don't wait around to find out what he's going to do when he discovers the box is gone.

~

My wings ache and I bite my lip to stifle a groan as Jangle applies a honeysuckle salve.

"This stuff is amazing," Jangle says. "You'll be good as new in the morning."

This time I groan loudly. "It's already morning."

I get dressed when she's done, wondering how I'm going to get through this day of fittings and wedding planning with no sleep. Plus, I'm worried about Peter. At least I know Hook didn't capture him, and in two days I'll be in possession of more queen's fairy dust, my own, to send him back to New York where I know he longs to be.

"We have to tell him we failed," I say.

"We can't do it now. The king has a full day scheduled for you."

My maiden and guard barely disguise their disapproval when we exit Jangle's hut. They expected me to be sleeping in my bed when they awoke. They flank us as I link my arm with Jangle's and we walk through the village to the seamstress's hut. The village is busier than usual, but a hush follows our wake. Then the activity resumes and I realize with a start that it's being decorated and prepared for my wedding.

My wedding.

Streamers and lights are being strung, flowers are being arranged. I smell sweetness coming from the bakery—cupcakes and decedent treats being baked and prepared.

We arrive at the seamstress's business hut. A dozen fairies are bustling about, measuring, cutting, sewing things, and, as is becoming normal when fairies see me, a hush descends. Faces are expressionless, lacking the admiration or joy you'd expect from meeting and waiting on the future queen. They don't like me. In their minds, I'm an unworthy candidate, and I agree. They don't understand why the king has chosen me and I can't explain.

Fiona, the head seamstress, crosses the room to greet us. She has pink hair piled high on her head and wears a mid-length tunic. Her mouth curls up in a forced smile. "Welcome. It is our pleasure to serve you today."

"Thank you for helping me on short notice," I say. Not like she has a choice. Everyone in the fairy kingdom is compelled to do their part when the king makes a decree.

Jangle takes on a less formal, more normal tone. "Hello, Fiona. What've you got for us?"

"We have terrific fabrics, woven by our own artesian weavers. We'd been expecting that the king would eventually take a bride..." She pauses and purses her lips. "The fabric has been on standby for many months."

She takes us to her collection of fabric spools. Fiona hadn't exaggerated. They are exquisite in detail and quality.

"These are stunning," Jangle says, running her fingers over the shiniest one. "So soft."

I turn to Jangle, "What color do you want your dress to be?"

She shrugs. "I don't know. What do you think?"

Fiona arrives with a sample, a shimmering silvery satin that reflects every color of the rainbow. Jangle gasps and Fiona chuckles. "Now you don't have to choose just one color. You can have them all."

We sort through patterns and since Jangle is obviously enjoying this more than I am, I let her decide. It takes her so long, I almost fall asleep on my feet. "Just pick one," I mutter. She finally settles on a design. It has a fitted bodice with a square-cut neckline and thin off-the-shoulder straps. It spreads out like a dome from the waist to the floor, with a poufy crinoline underskirt. Her chosen fabric is detailed with white gems and pearls.

The silvery rainbow maid-of-honor dress is similar, but shorter, falling just below the knees.

The next stop is cake and then flowers. Three tiers of chocolate with white marzipan icing and a small sculpture of a fairy prince and princess on top. The bouquets are a colorful mix of tropical flowers, with strings of white gems and pearls (Jangle says they compliment the dress), strung from the stem.

I'm relieved when it's settled.

"I think I need a nap," I say.

Jangle tugs on my arm. "No time for sleeping." I'm annoyed that she doesn't even look tired. She continues. "The king is waiting on us for tea."

My guard and maiden take their positions and we walk to the castle. I know I should be thinking about the king and the wedding, but my mind is continually pulled to Peter. I'll have to tell him we lost the box. I hope he won't do anything rash and get into another mess with Hook.

We're escorted back to the courtyard, and I'm feeling a sense of déjà vu. Another repeat performance of the tea we had the day before. Is it possible I'm already bored?

The king joins us and kisses our cheeks in greeting. I dislike the scratch of his beard against my face, but Jangle giggles with a blush. It's obvious she's in her element.

"How are the preparations going?" the king asks me.

"Well, your majesty," I say, wondering what exactly I'm

to call him once we're married. "The dresses, flowers and cake have all been decided upon."

"It's going to be a very beautiful wedding," Jangle says. She impulsively reaches out to brush the king's arm and giggles. *A move I'd seen her do many times with Dylan.* "You will be pleased."

The king's gaze moves from the spot on his sleeve touched by Jangle to her face. I'm worried he'll reprimand her for her forwardness, but instead he smiles.

A flush of fury spreads across my chest. I can't believe her! She's flirting with my fiancé!

I sip my tea and burn my tongue. Gah.

In the last two days I've traveled inter-dimensionally, escaped the clutches of Hook and his men, got engaged, almost drowned, prepared for a wedding, and all with very little sleep. My eyelids droop as I try to follow the conversation. I know I should be grateful Jangle is talkative and friendly, but instead, bubbles of irritation brew in my belly.

"Your bride-to-be looks very tired," Jangle says.

The king eyes me and I smile apologetically. "I'm sorry. I didn't sleep well last night."

"Then you should go home and get some rest. Tomorrow is a big day."

Jangle and I say our farewells and follow a castle keeper, who shows us out. Once we are on our way, I find I have renewed vigor, spurred on by anger directed at Jangle.

"Okay, what's going on, Tink?" she says, picking up her pace to keep up.

I get right to the point. "You were flirting with my future husband."

She huffs. "I was not."

We reach my front door and stop. “Yes, you were.”

“Fine, maybe I was. But you were ignoring him. Besides, I think he’s a nice guy.”

“He’s not a *nice guy*. *Blink*, Jangle. He’s the king!”

“Whatever. Doesn’t mean you have to act like a wet noodle whenever you’re with him.”

I speak through tight lips. “You don’t get it.”

“I get plenty.” She parks her hands on her hips and taps her toe. “I know marrying him is supposed to be a punishment for you, but I can’t help but wonder what *he’s* being punished for.”

7

Everyone in the fairy kingdom is working day and night to pull off my wedding in record time. The least I can do is get enough rest so I don't fall asleep at the altar. I go through the motions of readying myself for bed for the sake of the maiden and guard. Despite my exhaustion, anxiety keeps me from sleeping. If I'm going to tell Peter what happened to the box, I have to do it tonight. He probably thinks we have it. Or, he's figured out by our silence that there was a problem and thinks Hook has it. I don't put it past Hook to mislead Peter into a trap.

I slip out of bed and redress quietly. My maiden snores softly as I tip-toe by. The guard grunts as I inch open the door.

I yelp as a shadow moves in front of me. It's another guard. "I'm afraid I can't allow you passage."

"I just need a little fresh air," I say. "Is there a problem?"

"The king requested extra protection for you on this important night."

My guard must've told the king of my previous late night disappearances. I swallow. "Of course. Good night."

Inside, I lean against the door, arms tight over the ache in my chest.

~

My maiden shakes me, and I'm pulled out of a deep tunnel of sleep. I'd been dreaming about New York City. Peter and I were holding hands as we walked through Central Park. It felt so real—the flesh of his palm warm against mine, red and yellow leaves falling to the ground, people lined up at hotdog stands and drinking steaming cups of hot coffee.

"It's a very special day for you," my maiden sings.

I put on a happy face. "So I'm told."

The dresses have been delivered and they hang on my bedroom door.

"Is Jangle here?"

"She has not yet arrived. I'll send a guard to fetch her."

I nod and wonder if my maid-of-honor is even talking to me. Breakfast waits for me in the kitchen: fresh biscuits with butter and jam, hot tea, and a basket of fruit. A fairy could get used to all this attention and being waited on hand and foot. I'm starved and I eat plenty. This is the last morning I'll ever wake up and have breakfast by myself in my little hut. I push away at the melancholy.

Jangle arrives and we dress with the help of my maiden.

"I'm sorry for last night," I say.

Jangle shrugs. "You're nervous. I understand."

I hope my new status as queen won't harm our friendship. I reach over and squeeze her hand.

"Did you see, you know who?" she whispers.

I shake my head. "I was on lockdown."

The maiden does up the buttons that run up our spines. Jangle helps me with my veil. "You look beautiful." Her mouth smiles but I see a flash of sadness in her eyes.

THE VILLAGE SQUARE is heavily decorated with flowers and streamers. A path is roped off down the middle, and ends at the gold-plated elevated alter overlooking the ocean. Pipers line the way, and when they see me and Jangle waiting there, they begin to play. The king arrives in his royal chariot guided by two ponies decorated with golden bridles and reins. Trumpeters standing on the castle balconies sound their horns. Cheers rise from the crowd as the king leaves the chariot and takes his place on the altar.

The music stops and everyone is quiet.

I look at Jangle and she winks at me. The flutes start again, and we walk down the path together. The king watches us but I avert my eyes. The pageantry and the fuss, it's all a fraud. We don't love each other. This is my *punishment*. I might as well be shackled and flogged.

Jangle hands me over to the king and stands to my left. The king takes my hand and I tremble. This is it.

The music stops again as the master of ceremonies joins us. He faces the crowd and clears his throat. "Welcome, friends. We have gathered here today..."

The master of ceremonies is interrupted by a thunderous "*STOP!*"

In one synchronized motion all heads swivel toward the back.

Peter.

8

Peter's blue eyes scan my white gown and veil, and settle on my face. "Don't do this, Belle."

The king's expression hardens. "Who is this human boy, and how did he pass into the fairy kingdom?"

It's a rhetorical question. There is only one way. The king knows I showed it to Peter. Another rule broken.

I look back at Peter. I know I'm the only one he sees and, in this place, the only one he hears.

"He's the lost boy I sent back to New York."

A round of murmurs erupts in the crowd. The king raises a hand and everyone is silenced.

"Did you use your fairy dust to open his eyes to our village?"

He's making me admit it aloud. I lower my eyes, flushing with shame. "Yes."

Peter steps closer and the fairies nearby have to scramble out of his way. "Belle?"

"Peter, you can't be here. Please leave."

"You don't have to do this. We'll find another way."

The pressure in my chest builds like a tsunami. I look at Jangle with desperation. She blinks back, unable to help me. Her eyes rest on the king and fill with sympathy.

I have an idea.

"Your majesty," I say, turning back to the king. "Is it possible that you are about to marry the wrong girl?" My eyes dart to Jangle and back to the king. His eyes flutter as he considers what I'm suggesting, and then they return to Jangle.

"I have nothing to compel her," he says.

I step closer. "She likes you. And not just because you're the king."

"She does? How do you know?"

"Because I've known Jangle my whole life, and I know her."

The king stares over my shoulder at her. "She is alluring, I admit. Strong, intelligent. Beautiful."

"And loyal," I add. Which is more than I can say for myself, and the king knows it, too.

I step back and wave Jangle over. Peter stands with his arms hanging loosely. I raise a palm to indicate that he should wait.

The king approaches Jangle and speaks softly. "Tinker-bell has suggested that perhaps you would like to be my wife. Please, if she is out of line, step away and nothing further about this matter will be spoken."

Jangle's eyebrows arch high. I whisper in her ear. "He's a nice guy."

Her mouth drops open and then closes again. She addresses the king, "Are you asking me to marry you?"

"I am."

"Tinkerbell?"

"It's okay with me, if you want this."

Jangle's lips turn up into a wide smile and she bursts out laughing. "I do. I do want this."

"Awesome!" I shout to Peter. "Jangle's going to marry the king!"

The crowd goes wild. Fairies love unexpected drama.

Jangle and I switch places. I snap my fingers and her dress turns into the bridal gown and mine becomes the bridesmaid dress. The master of ceremonies struggles to keep the shock off his face.

The king takes Jangle's hands and says, "Let's begin."

I turn to Peter and give him a thumbs up. He returns the gesture and grins.

9

I run to Peter and he lifts me like a doll and twirls me around.

"You're not married?"

"No. Jangle is."

He frowns and lowers me down. "What happened?"

"It's okay. She's happy."

"That sucks for Dylan, but I'm glad you're coming back with me. Nice dress, by the way. Much nicer than that white one you had on."

I laugh. "Thanks."

He grins and stares at me hopefully. "So, where's the box? If I fiddle with it enough, I should be able to get it working. All it took to get us here was to bang it on the floor."

My wings droop with the dread I feel. I walk quickly until we're far away from the village and stop under a large, silkwood leaf, wanting to hide.

Peter bends down and pushes the leaf aside. "What's wrong? Did something happen to the box?"

I swallow and my lip trembles. "Not all the guys left the ship. One stayed to guard things and he managed to grab Jangle. She threw me the box, but the goon slammed into me before I could catch it. I fell overboard. Along with the box."

"It's...in the sea?"

I nod. "I'm sorry, Peter."

I turn away, ashamed that I failed the mission. A tear escapes my eye and rolls down my face. Peter turns my chin and catches it with his finger.

"I'm the one who's sorry. I shouldn't have asked you and Jangle to do something so dangerous. I'm just glad you're okay."

We sit together at the edge of the silk forest overlooking the ocean. Peter's T-shirt smells like ocean water and his jeans have been hacked off at the knees like he did it with a knife. His sword is in a sheath hanging on his back.

I'm in Jangle's silvery rainbow dress with her little cap and veil on my head, much more formally dressed than I normally am.

We're startled by a gruff voice from behind. "This day just keeps getting better and better." It's Hook. We spring to our feet. "My two favorite people in one place."

Peter shouts, "Leave us alone."

"There's nothing more I'd rather do," Hook says with a scowl. "Just give me the box."

My eyes flicker to Peter. Hook doesn't know about the box. His goon either couldn't swim or he was too afraid to tell the truth.

Peter stiffens, "I don't have it."

"I don't believe you." Hook draws his sword. "Give me the box and we'll call a truce."

"Even if I had it, I wouldn't give it to you," Peter says, drawing his.

"Brave words." Hook's beady eyes narrow to slits. "Let's see if your actions can match them."

"No, stop!" My wings flutter and I fly above their heads. Hook swings at me and I dodge the blade.

"Belle, stay out of it!" Peter commands. "I've got this."

I land in a branch of a tree. "Peter?"

"I need to do this myself, Belle."

I think I understand. No I don't. But if Peter doesn't want me to help, I'll honor his wishes. I just don't know if I can watch.

They each take a front en guard stance and their blades crash together. I cup a hand over my eyes.

I hear the dragging of feet and clanging of steel, and I can't stand it. I fan my fingers apart and watch.

Hook thrusts and Peter parries left, his sword stopping Hook's from reaching him. He counters with his own thrust.

Hook parries and defends himself. "You've been practicing."

Peter thrusts again. "You can say I've developed an interest in the sport since my last time here."

They shuffle back and forth, thrusting and blocking, stirring up dust, disturbing wildlife. Birds squawk as they fly away from their nests. Furry creatures scurry up trees or into underground burrows.

The clinking sounds of their colliding swords fill the forest. Peter is limber and strong, but Hook is stronger with more experience. Perspiration forms on Peter's face, his dark hair falls into his eyes. I want to fly over and brush them clear, but Peter wants me to stay out of it.

Hook's head is shiny wet and sweat drips down his nose. Peter stands his ground and I'm proud of him. If the situation weren't so dangerous, I'd be swooning at his bravado and stern-faced determination.

I wonder how long they can go on back and forth, stabbing, blocking, parrying. Finally, Peter backs up and catches his heel on a root. I gasp as he loses his balance and falls to his back.

"Peter!" My wings flutter and I'm tempted to help, but I wait.

Hook lunges, but Peter rolls to the side just in time, swinging his leg, tripping Hook. Peter springs to his feet as Hook hits the ground. Hook loses grip of his sword and it slides. He reaches for it but his fingers just miss. Peter puts his foot on Hook's back and digs the tip of his sword into his neck.

"Say uncle," he says. Hook ignores him and Peter puts pressure on his sword.

Hook flinches. "Uncle!"

I fly down to Peter. "What are you going to do now?"

He grunts. "I don't know."

I use a little fairy dust to instruct a piece of vine to break off and tie Hook's wrists behind his back. When he starts swearing, I snap my fingers and a vine ties around his mouth.

"Nice work," Peter says.

We look at each other at a loss. Do we take him to the tree fort? Back to the ship? Hike back up to the caves? And then what do we do?

"Tinkerbell..."

I spin toward the sound of Jangle's voice. "Jangle?"

Jangle appears dressed in a long shimmering pink gown. "That's your majesty to you."

I gawk and she laughs. "Just kidding. The town's gone crazy with the bride switch—such drama!—and now the preparations for the big party are on. I'm supposed to be getting ready and so I only have a few minutes."

"To do what?"

"Send you all back to New York. That's what you want, right?"

I catch Peter's eyes and he nods adamantly.

"As you know, it's the king's wishes that all the humans go. I see you've got Hook's cooperation."

"I'll collect the boys," I say to Peter, "if you can ensure all the pirates are on board the ship."

"The boys won't want to come."

I wiggle my fingers. "They're not going to have a choice."

"Great," Jangle says. "I have to get back, but I'll sneak away again in half an hour."

Before I can thank her, she's gone.

Peter pokes Hook with his sword, then grabs his arm. "Get up."

I fly to the cave and I'm pooped out when I arrive. The boys are sleeping even though it's mid day.

"Wake up, sleepyheads," I sing. "You have a boat to catch."

We're all on the ship: Hook and his men, Peter and the Lost Boys, and me.

Waiting.

Where is *her majesty?*

Oh, my gosh. Jangle's the blinking queen! It's more than I can wrap my head around in the moment. The men and boys groan and grumble but I've used my fairy dust to muzzle and bind them. It won't last forever.

Finally, she appears. I race to the dock to greet her.

"You can do it? You have the dust?"

"I'm the queen. Unless there's a time period it takes to kick in."

My heart skips a beat. What if her fairy dust doesn't' work? Hook's not easy to contain and I don't know if we can make it another day.

"It has to work, Jangle."

"I know. And in case it does..."

I grab her hands. "I'll miss you." A lump forms in my throat and a tear escapes. "You are my very best friend."

Jangle's face scrunches up like she's holding back tears. "And you are mine. We've shared an amazing adventure." She hands me a small satchel. I open it up to find a number of gems, currency for me in New York.

"Thank you," I say, wiping a tear.

Jangle wipes away one of her own. "And if you ever want to come back..." She smiles. "Just wish upon a star."

"Oh, Jangle." I squeeze her hard. "You're going to be the best fairy queen ever."

"I hope so. Now get on the ship. You don't want to miss your ride."

I pull myself away from her and fly back to the boat. I relish the use of my wings and how my body floats like a bird's through the air. This is one of the many lovely things I'm giving up by leaving Neverland.

I land on the bow and grip the rail with both hands. Peter stands beside me.

"We're ready," he shouts out. "And thank-you!"

Jangle walks the dock until she's just a few feet away. "Pleasant journey, friends." She snaps the fingers of both hands and blows her dust our way. It grows dark like a sudden storm approaching.

Next thing I know, the boat tips sharply onto its side and we all fall, tumbling out onto dry earth.

10

I knock my head and everything's a blur. Peter shimmies over to my side. "Belle?"

I catch sight of my hand as I reach for the bump on the back of my head. I take in my body. Everything is bigger, including my silvery party dress.

"Are you okay?" Peter's gaze scans me from head to toe. His eyes blink, like it's a shock to see me in my human form.

"Yeah, I'm fine."

I'm aware of the yelling and commotion going on around us. Peter helps me to my feet. People point and shout about the large boat that appeared in the park out of nowhere. Hook and One Eye shout at each other. The other men sprint away. The power of my fairy dust thinned enough for them to escape the vine tie-ups. The Lost Boys stare at me and Peter and then at each other, gasping and grabbing at their chests. They've all aged more than two years in an instant. They're taller, broader in the shoulders and have scruff on their faces.

"Man!" Curly says, jumping at the sound of his own voice, now much lower.

One Eye and Hook circle around us.

"Get 'em!" Hook says. Peter grabs my hand and we run. One Eye bumps into a lamppost leaving Hook on our heels. We dodge pedestrians and street performers. Hook gets caught in the legs of a clown on stilts, who collapses, trapping Hook in wooden posts. His wig falls on Hook's bald head and I almost laugh.

Police whistles blow in the distance and I see a couple riding speedily on their bicycles toward us. We jump off the path, out of the way, and don't slow down until we're certain Hook is off our tail.

"Let's go to your place," Peter says. "Hook doesn't know where you live."

I mumble something, completely aware that Peter hasn't let go of my hand. I don't let go either.

I'm shivering before we get there. New York is colder than Neverland. Peter wraps his arm around me and I'm suddenly much warmer. We arrive at my apartment and I wave at Mrs. Weeks as we enter.

"You should tell me when you go on vacation," she says loudly. "I thought you skipped town. I almost rented it out to someone else."

"I'm paid up to the end of the month," I say halfway up the stairs. Then I remember, I don't have a key.

I call down. "Mrs. Weeks, I've seem to have lost my key. Can you let me in?"

She grumbles as she fumbles with a master and hobbles up to meet me and Peter by my door. "It's going to cost you for a replacement."

It's strange coming back to my apartment on 7th without Jangle. Everything is as we left it. Neat and tidy except for the two dirty tea cups in the sink. A thin layer of dust coats the furniture and the floor.

"Are you going to be okay?" Peter asks.

A strangling noise escapes my throat. I'm not ready to be alone. I nod my head, but Peter can read my expression. He takes a long stride to my side and pulls me into an embrace, and I tremble.

"I can stay for a while," he whispers in my ear. I want to tell him to go, that I'll be fine, but I can't.

"I'll make tea," I say instead. I busy myself while the kettle boils, wiping the table, sweeping the floor.

"Can't you just snap your fingers to do that?" Peter asks. He smiles crookedly, his dimples showing, making my pulse leap. I'm sure I look amusing. Fancy party dress, ballet slippers, mussed up hair, and a broom.

"I can, but that's a frivolous use of my fairy dust." I'm not sure if I'll run out like I did before, plus physical activity helps to release some of my anxiety. The whistle blows and I stop house cleaning to make the tea. There are packaged cookies in the cupboard and I bring them out. It's been a while since either of us have eaten.

"What's going to happen now?" I ask.

Peter dips a cookie in his tea. "I don't know. I'm assuming the police have the boys and are asking questions they can't answer. Even if they tell the truth, they won't be believed. It could get messy."

We finish up and I clear the table.

Peter stands. "I should go. I need to let my mom know I'm okay."

I nod. "Of course."

I wring my hands, feeling the anxiety in my stomach spin and swirl. Peter eyes me carefully.

"I can wait a little while longer."

I'm washed with relief that Peter won't leave me yet. "Are you sure?"

He steps to the couch and sits down. "Yeah. I'm tired. Let's just rest for a bit before tackling the next giant."

He pats the spot beside him and joy springs in my being. I sit and he wraps an arm around my shoulders, pulling me close.

"Everything's going to be okay, my Tinkerbell," he says.

In that moment, I believe him. I sigh contentedly and close my eyes. Peter's breathing steadies into a regular rhythm. I focus on that and soon I'm sleeping, too.

I'm too exhausted to dream. When I wake up, Peter is gone.

11

I spend my first night back lying on the couch, pretending Peter is still with me. My room is too eerie in the dark with all the strange apartment noises. The streetlight shines into the living room, brightening the darkness, and the sound of people talking and moving about outside is kind of comforting. It's dawn before I fall asleep again.

When I awake, I'm starving. I wash up, dress in jeans and a sweater, marveling again at my human body, and then head for the café on the corner. I order two croissants with butter and jam and eat them both in record time. I sit at the window people watching, hoping for a glimpse of Peter. Will he come back for me?

I think about the Lost Boys and where Hook might be. Time crawls and I itch to get out. I walk down 7th toward Central Park. It's cold and I wrap my arms tightly around my winter jacket. I head to where we landed with the yacht the day before. There's a tow truck with guys winching it behind. People stand around and stare. I hear snippets of conversation, everyone curious as to what really happened.

I wander around the park until I grow tired and then head home. I pass an electronics store. TV monitors face the street in the window displays and a news program is on. I go inside to listen.

The faces of the Lost Boys flash across the screen. Reporters speculate on what happened to them. Hook's face suddenly appears and I take an involuntary step backward. He's been arrested for the kidnapping of the boys.

"Wild, huh?"

I swivel around to the voice of the clerk standing behind the counter. He pushes glasses up on his narrow nose. "I'm supposed to believe a yacht appeared in Central Park outta thin air? People say the craziest things."

I smile and leave quickly.

Remembering my empty kitchen cupboards, I stop at a grocery store to pick up a few things. My mind is numb as I take in the huge store. Rows and rows of cans and boxed goods, frozen foods and fresh fruit and vegetables. I'm overwhelmed by the choices. I leave with nothing.

I imagine Peter waiting on the steps of my apartment building and I break into a jog. When I turn the corner, the steps are empty and I stop, feeling deflated.

I dread the thought of another night alone, and not for the first time I wonder if maybe I made a huge mistake in coming back. Peter has a life. Plus, he's a human boy.

I'm a fairy from Neverland. I don't belong here.

That night, I stare out the window, looking for the star. If I could see it, I'd make my wish, but it's cloudy and dark, not a star in the sky. Instead there's snow. I see the flakes like a gigantic puffball, lit up under the streetlamp. We don't have snow in Neverland. I bundle up in my winter clothes adding a scarf and hat, and head outside.

I reach out my hand and watch the flakes land. They're cold but so pretty. I hold my palm close to my face so I can examine them. Sparkly, like jewels. My hot breath melts the flakes and they pool into small drops.

People walk up and down the sidewalks—mothers and fathers with their children, couples holding on arm and arm, groups of friends hanging out.

My loneliness is magnified as I watch them. I swallow the lump that has formed in my throat and head back inside. I take off my damp outer things and let them drop to the floor. I sit on the couch in the dark. My invisible wings weigh heavy down my back like they're soaking wet.

I stare blankly at the floor. It takes me a moment to realize someone's knocking at the door.

I want it to be Peter.

It is.

He stands with a bouquet of poppies in one hand and a picnic basket in the other. "I hope you haven't eaten yet."

I shake my head and feel my mouth tug up in a big smile.

Peter walks in through the darkness of the room and puts the basket on the table. "Saving on electricity? Good thing I brought help." He removes a thick, red candle from the basket and lights it. He motions to the flowers. "These will wilt without water."

I snap out of my stupor. Peter brought a picnic. Peter brought a candle. Peter brought flowers! I find an empty jar, fill it with water and bring it to the table.

"I thought we'd do a do-over," he begins, "of our picnic in

the poppy field. Since it's snowing we have to bring it indoors. I hope you don't mind." The candlelight reflects in his eyes, and his dimples jump from his cheeks. And my heart melts.

I finally find my tongue. "I don't mind." At all.

Peter sets out paper plates and napkins. "If I remember correctly, we had crackers and goat's cheese and cherry tomatoes."

I giggle.

"I added ham sandwiches and chocolate brownies. I hope you don't mind."

Peter could've brought a stuffed giraffe and I wouldn't have cared. "Sounds awesome."

He passes the food around and even though I'm starving, my stomach is swirling so much with his nearness, I find it hard to eat.

"How is your mom?"

"She's okay. She was pretty crazy with me disappearing for a second time, but I managed to calm her down. That's why it took me so long to come back. Dad's fine, too. I told him the box was destroyed and he said good riddance."

I nibble on the cheese and crackers while he finishes his sandwich. He takes the large slice of brownie, sets it between us and hands me a fork.

"You mind sharing?"

I grin and accept the fork, taking the first bite. The candlelight warms up the room and gives off a pleasant cinnamon scent. Sharing the brownie is romantic. My wings sizzle and perk up straight. I see them in the reflection in the jar. Peter sees it too and laughs. "Cool!"

Then he takes something from his pocket. It's a piece of

art paper, folded in half and half again. He unfolds it and flattens it on the table. There's enough candlelight to make out what's on it. Four sketches. My heart flutters.

"This is my story," Peter begins. The first square has a boy on a picnic in a poppy field with a little fairy. The second square is a view of them from behind on a hill overlooking a village. The third square is an older boy watching a human girl across the hall. The girl has a ponytail and hoop earrings. In the fourth one...they're kissing.

It's signed, *Love, Peter*.

I'm undone!

He points to the first picture. "Wasn't there something you wanted to say to me?"

I nibble my lip, holding onto an embarrassed smile. I glance up and his blue eyes hold onto me. "I like you, Peter."

He leans over and his lips meet mine. He speaks through his kisses, "I like you, too, Tinkerbell."

The End

WHAT TO READ NEXT!

A teen swim athlete discovers a merfolk world that threatens to keep her out of the ocean forever.

Dori Seward can't wait to get out of Eastcove, a sleepy fishing village on the border of New Brunswick and Maine. She bides her time by hanging out with friends, attending swim club, and holding her biggest competition, Colby-who wants more than just friendship, at arm's length.

Then Tor Riley comes to town and he has everything Dori dreams of in a boyfriend-looks, athleticism and mystery.

But Tor also has a tantalizing secret and Dori is determined to find out what it is. The truth is crazier than her wildest imaginations and more dangerous, too.

Dori has new fantastical enemies , and they will do anything to get to her.

Her life, her dreams and her love for Tor are all weighing in the balance. Will Dori risk it all in order to have it all?

Read on for the first Chapter of SEAWEED!

***

Check out The Clockwise Collection!

SEAWEED - CHAPTER ONE

HE STOOD at the bonfire with his head high, shoulders back, radiating a military type of confidence. With one hand he swept his dark hair across his forehead and even through the flickering orange hue I could tell he had amazing eyes.

Something drew his gaze to mine. Fate? Providence? My heart stopped beating. He smiled shyly then glanced away, his focus returning to the erratic dancing of the flames.

I'd never seen him before which, in Eastcove New Brunswick, was an unusual occurrence.

My best friends, Samara and Becca, stood beside me, each with a can of Coke in their hands.

"Who is that?" Samara shouted over the noise of the music blaring from a truck that was backed up close to the pit. Four teens sat squeezed together on the tailgate laughing at someone's joke.

Becca shouted back, "I think it's a *new* guy."

Samara fiddled with her long black braid. "Since when does anyone new move to Eastcove?"

Good question.

"He's cute!" Becca said.

"I saw him first." I gave him a little finger wave and started to make my way to the other side of the fire. I meant to clearly establish my intentions to claim this new boy.

I was intercepted by Colby Johnston.

"Hey, Seaweed." He moved in a little too close for comfort. I took a subtle step sideways.

"Hi."

I couldn't stop twisting my neck, watching the mysterious new guy. Another girl was chatting him up and a tickle of irritation curled up in my gut.

"What're you looking at?" Colby's gaze followed mine. "Ah, him."

I couldn't believe I hadn't heard about *him* already. Eastcove was a dying fishing village, the kind of town people *left*. A new family would've definitely made the gossip hotline.

"So, about us?" Colby said, like he'd said it a thousand times. Which he had.

I took a sip from my water bottle and tried to pretend I didn't hear him.

"Dori. We need to talk about this."

I let out a frustrated sigh. "Okay, talk."

He swigged back his drink, then spoke into my ear, "I know you already know this, but I guess I always thought we'd get together sometime. Sometime soon."

I did know this. I think everybody knew this. We were swim team champions. We were good friends. Even Samara and Becca thought we'd make the perfect couple.

Colby's dark eyes reflected the jumping flames, and I

resisted the urge to reach over and rub his buzz cut, wanting to make everything okay.

Instead, I shook my head softly. "I'm sorry." I hated hurting him. I couldn't help that I didn't feel the same way.

His head fell forward. "I know, Seaweed. Forget I said anything." He slipped away, losing himself in the crowd. I blew out a heavy sigh.

The flames of the bonfire licked high toward the murky, open sky. The burning wood snapped and popped at its base. Smoke meshed with the salty essence of the sea and I breathed it in slowly. Peering through the sparks I kept my focus on the mystery guy. He caught me looking at him and this time he didn't look away. We gradually moved toward each other, until finally we were side by side.

"Hey."

"I'm Dori Seward," I said, loudly.

"Dori?"

"Yeah, like the fish in the movie." Did I really just say that? "It's a nickname because I like to swim. A lot." Okay, so much for smooth. Just kill me now.

He motioned for us to move away from the music toward the waves slapping the shore.

"It's a little quieter over here," he said. Then he shook my hand. "I'm Tor Riley." It was warm and strong.

"Where did you move from?" I asked, tucking my hands back into my pockets.

"Maine."

"So, you're not that far from home."

"I guess. I still have the Bay of Fundy."

He sipped his soda and I relieved my dry throat with my water.

"What do you think of Eastcove so far?"

He shrugged. "It's okay."

"What brought your parents here?" I knew there wasn't much left for work.

Tor fussed at the sand with his shoe. "Uh, I'm not here with them. They, uh, travel a lot. I'm living with my uncle."

I got the impression it was a touchy subject.

"What about you?" he said, turning the tables. "Tell me about you."

We headed back toward the warmth of the bonfire as I gave him the rundown of my average family—a mom, a dad, two brothers. I was about to broach the less than exciting topic of pets when I was interrupted by shouting and loud laughter on the other side of the fire pit. Sawyer shook his can and let the contents fly. Mike got him back with his drink, and before long everyone was in on it.

I looked at Tor and he smirked. That was when I did the stupidest thing ever. I opened my water bottle and swung it at Tor, splashing him right in the face.

I thought it would be funny. It was all in the name of fun and games. But instead of laughing and throwing his soda back at me, he looked at me with wide, horror-filled eyes.

Next thing I knew, Tor was sprinting down the beach into the darkness.

"Tor!" I yelled. With all the shouting, the blaring music, and the roar of waves crashing to shore, no one heard me.

"Tor!" I took off after him, and in the mayhem, no one noticed. "I'm sorry. Please, come back."

I could make out his outline in the moonlit darkness when I followed him around the bend. My heart raced and I wanted to tackle him to the ground until he told me what was going on.

I didn't have a chance. I got to a cropping of rocks just in time to see him dive into the frigid ocean.

ABOUT THE AUTHOR

Lee Strauss is a USA TODAY bestselling author of several cozy historical mystery series and young adult books including; The Clockwise Collection (YA time travel romance); The Perception series (young adult dystopian); Seaweed; and Love, Tink; with over a million books read. She has titles published in German, Spanish and Korean, and a growing audio library.

When Lee's not writing or reading she likes to cycle, hike, and stare at the ocean.

leestraussbooks.com

MORE FROM LEE STRAUSS

On AMAZON

THE CLOCKWISE COLLECTION (YA time travel romance)

Casey Donovan has issues: hair, height and uncontrollable trips to the 19th century! And now this ~ she's accidentally taken Nate Mackenzie, the cutest boy in the school, back in time. Awkward.

Clockwise

Clockwiser

Like Clockwork

Counter Clockwise

Clockwork Crazy

Clocked (companion novella)

Standalones

Seaweed

Love, Tink

GINGER GOLD MYSTERY SERIES (cozy 1920s historical)

Cozy. Charming. Filled with Bright Young Things. This Jazz Age murder mystery will entertain and delight you with its 1920s flair and pizzazz!

Murder on the SS Rosa

Murder at Hartigan House

Murder at Bray Manor

Murder at Feathers & Flair

Murder at the Mortuary

Murder at Kensington Gardens

Murder at St. George's Church

Murder Aboard the Flying Scotsman

Murder at the Boat Club

Murder on Eaton Square

Murder on Fleet Street

LADY GOLD INVESTIGATES (Ginger Gold companion short stories)

Volume 1

Volume 2

Volume 3

HIGGINS & HAWKE MYSTERY SERIES (cozy 1930s historical)

The 1930s meets Rizzoli & Isles in this friendship depression era cozy mystery series.

Death at the Tavern

Death on the Tower

Death on Hanover

A NURSERY RHYME MYSTERY SERIES(mystery/sci fi)

Marlow finds himself teamed up with intelligent and savvy Sage Farrell, a girl so far out of his league he feels blinded in her presence - literally - damned glasses! Together they work to find the identity of @gingerbreadman. Can they stop the killer before he strikes again?

Gingerbread Man

Life Is but a Dream

Hickory Dickory Dock

Twinkle Little Star

THE PERCEPTION TRILOGY (YA dystopian mystery)

Zoe Vanderveen is a GAP—a genetically altered person. She lives in the security of a walled city on prime water-front property along side other equally beautiful people with extended life spans. Her brother Liam is missing. Noah Brody, a boy on the outside, is the only one who can help ~ but can she trust him?

Perception

Volition

Contrition

LIGHT & LOVE (sweet romance)

Set in the dazzling charm of Europe, follow Katja, Gabriella, Eva,

Anna and Belle as they find strength, hope and love.

Sing me a Love Song

Your Love is Sweet

In Light of Us

Lying in Starlight

PLAYING WITH MATCHES (WW2 history/romance)

A sobering but hopeful journey about how one young Germany boy copes with the war and propaganda. Based on true events.

A Piece of Blue String (companion short story)

Made in United States
North Haven, CT
31 October 2021